TWO DOWN IN TAHOE

A CROSSWORD PUZZLE COZY MYSTERY

LOUISE FOSTER

This is a work of fiction. Names, characters, places, and incidents are either the product of the author's imagination or are used fictitiously. Any resemblance to actual person, living or dead, business establishments, events or locales is entirely coincidental.

Two Down in Tahoe; A Crossword Puzzle Cozy Mystery

Copyright 2020 by Louise Foster
ISBN 978-1-955458-03-0
ALL RIGHTS RESERVED

No part of this book may be reproduced in any form or by any electronic or mechanical means, including information storage and retrieval systems, without written permission from the author, except for the use of brief quotations in a book review.

❀ Created with Vellum

This book is dedicated to John A Walker, Jr.
You were a kindred spirit, a member of the family, and so much more to all of us.
Though you're gone now, you'll always be with us.

WHAT COULD POSSIBLY GO WRONG?

Come to Tahoe. Help a buddy. No problems. No pressure.

How could I refuse?

Twelve hours later, my PI friend is missing. His client is dead. And I'm at the murder scene.

With the police eyeing me as a suspect, what can I do but find the killer?

And, better yet, complete my crossword puzzle.

1

9 Down; 4 Letters;
Clue: To discover by chance
Answer: Find

"We need an electric drill." Marcus Belden, my eleven-year-old foster son, stared at the yellow, plastic box on the kitchen table with a laser-like intensity. His eyes narrowed in determination as he flipped a pancake onto the serving dish.

His golden-hued skin and straight, silky black hair marked his Korean ancestry, but the mischievous gleam in his dark eyes was all him. He's my ray of sunshine. Even though he eats me out of house and home, and even if he is the reason I was in the Emergency Room of Langsdale, Nevada, until midnight last night.

Which is where I got the mysterious box.

The box looked like a small self-contained toolbox, about

the size of a paperback. Hard molded plastic, five-by-seven inches, two-inches deep. The latch was a simple tab. It should have opened with the flip of a thumb.

It didn't. Someone had glued it shut.

Relishing the smell of bacon hanging in the air, I sipped my hazelnut-flavored coffee. A rush of affection overwhelmed me at the sight of the boy-child who had stolen my heart and turned my life upside down several years ago. In the next heartbeat, a dose of reality brought me back to the moment.

"We don't have a drill." I frowned at Marcus's head, which had inserted itself into my line of vision. Putting my finger on his forehead, I gently pushed him back. "You need to stop focusing on that box."

"We have to get it open."

"No, we don't." A lack of caffeine after a late night had dampened both my curiosity and my trepidation. "Whatever is in here will keep. It obviously wasn't meant to be opened easily."

The unsettling thought sent a shiver up my spine. Questions and possibilities pulled at me, but I squashed them. I did not need trouble.

"What if Rickson needs help?" Marcus asked. "The guy who chased him through the ER had a gun."

"Rickson knows where to find me," I said. "Which is more than I can say about him. Besides, the cops arrested the other guy."

Welcome to my life. Tracy Rae Belden. Thirty-five-years-old. Five-nine. Spiky brown hair that goes in and out of style. Slim.

Moderately slim. Okay, not as slim as I used to be, but who steps on the scale more than once every three years?

"Cook or eat." I pointed to the stove then a chair. "I'm done discussing this box."

Marcus shot me a frown. "This isn't over."

"I didn't think it was." I gave him a mock glare. As expected, my stern words did no apparent damage to his psyche. After being abandoned at a young age, he'd lived on the streets for a while. He was tough. At least on the outside.

I met him three years ago when he tried to steal my wallet. Instead, he stole my heart. We bonded over books in the local library. Including, yes, the Trixie Belden Young Adult mysteries from decades ago, my supposed "cousin".

Yes, I'm shameless. It's best to know that up front.

I needed an "in" to gain the boy's trust and get him off the streets. It worked. He's been living with me ever since as a ward of the state. I'm trying to make the arrangement permanent, but a tsunami of bureaucratic regulations has the matter tied up in a thousand knots.

Unlike my foster son, I don't look for trouble. I don't have to, it finds me. Like yesterday. At nine o'clock in the morning, a pipe burst in my bathroom. At ten last night, Marcus cut his hand on a broken car window. In between, B & T Inc., the fledgling handyman business my best friend and I recently started, lost two jobs.

Big jobs, with paychecks that would have paid the rent for months. Now my only guaranteed income was my part-time gig as a private detective. That's the one that pays the bills.

Well, most of the bills. Most of the time.

That's also the one that gets me in trouble with my boy-child. My goal as a PI is to cash the paycheck. Period. His goal is to live up to our family heritage and solve the case, whether we get paid or not.

That's just crazy talk.

The job I enjoy the most, pays the least. It's a work-for-hire gig creating crossword puzzles. The money barely keeps me in flavored coffee, but puzzles are my addiction. Once I start one, I have to solve it to the very last square or it haunts me. Besides, creating clues and answers that I have total control over keeps me on the right side of sane.

I picked up my cup of coffee. The aroma alone woke up the blood vessels in my brain, ambrosia with a touch of hazelnut. "If Rickson doesn't get in touch this morning, I'll contact Crawford and see what's going on."

"Bossman left for his Canada fishing trip yesterday." Marcus, who wanted nothing more than to be a PI, made it sound like we both worked for Crawford Investigations.

"Oh, I forgot." Typical male. Never around when you need him. I pulled my rattled thoughts together. "That area doesn't have cell service."

Marcus punched me lightly in the shoulder. "Until he returns, you're in charge."

Unlike my crossword puzzles, I couldn't solve this puzzle by switching out the clues and answers. The yellow box sat there taunting me. What could it contain?

My first guess? A seven-letter word for agitate or harass.

Answer: trouble.

"We have to investigate." My son waved the box in front of my face.

I refused to take the bait. Keeping food on the table fed the body. Creating crossword puzzles fed the soul. Being in charge brought only trouble.

"Getting up to speed on Rickson's case is your duty." An overly somber note deepened Marcus's tone, in contrast to his slim, undersized frame. "This is a piece of a puzzle."

The boy knew my weakness.

"Rickson is your co-worker. Your friend. Your buddy." His tone rose as my bored expression remained unchanged. "How can you leave him out in the cold?"

Drama never takes a day off in this house.

"Langsdale is three hours north of Las Vegas. It's rarely

cold here." I can state the obvious, too. It's also best to take every chance I can to ground the boy in reality, rather than feed his flights of fantasy.

"I was speaking metaphorically." Marcus scrunched up his nose, evidently looking for another argument. "You won't be able to live with yourself if you do nothing."

"Sure, I will," I assured him. "I'm good at doing nothing. Besides, Rickson hasn't asked for my help and I doubt he needs it."

"He hunted you down in the ER." Marcus pointed the pancake flipper at me. "He passed you the box while staring down the barrel of a police gun."

Good grief. "I was there. Remember? The cops never drew their guns."

Marcus threw his hands up in the air. "Rickson was chased by a vicious assailant. Did you miss that?"

"Rickson is six-foot-nine in his stocking feet. He's over three-hundred pounds of solid muscle. David Ferguson, the skinny, redheaded guy who chased him and claimed Rickson stole that box, was maybe five-seven."

My son drew his undersized frame up to full height. "Vicious can come in small packages."

I had no comeback. Fighting a smile, I raised my coffee in salute and took a long sip. Ferguson's claim had started me wondering what Rickson had gotten himself into with his latest case. Unfortunately, Crawford, my boss of seven years, my friend for fifteen, wasn't around to ask.

Though Rickson and I both worked for Crawford Investigations, the big guy is a retired homicide detective, twenty-five years on the force. I'm a newbie with less than a year under my belt as a solo investigator in the field.

Langsdale has a population of twenty-two thousand, but the city has transformed itself from a once thriving town of wealthy silver mines into a high-end resort. The pricey boutiques, eclectic gourmet eateries, and high-priced galleries offering exclusive auctions, attract both national and international tourists. All awash with disposable income. A specialist was even brought in to design a world-class golf course. The constant flow of tourists, residents, and cash keep Crawford Investigations plenty busy.

Unfortunately, my income barely makes it from one month to the next. My second-floor apartment sits in a so-so neighborhood in a faded, three-story building. My main floor is a large, open room. A kitchenette in the front corner overlooks the street. My bedroom is in the back corner. Marcus's bedroom is up a small flight of stairs on the second level.

"Oh, come on, T.R." The boy dropped his actor's mask, replacing it with a thirty-year-old attitude in an eleven-year-old body. "I won't survive not knowing what's inside or who sent it."

"Frustration is good for the soul." I didn't even flinch at hearing my grandmother's words coming out of my mouth. "It builds character."

"I have enough character." He assured me with aplomb. "What I need, after my tortured, deprived childhood, is instant gratification."

"If you're done cooking, turn off the burners." I pushed myself to my feet. "I'll put this somewhere safe and we'll deal with it later."

When a stubborn gleam shown in his eyes, I braced myself for battle. Instead, he heaved a sigh. "Don't do anything with it behind my back."

"Don't worry," I assured him as I headed into the other room. "I have no intention of messing with this thing."

I stepped out of his line of sight. Feeling like a child

playing hide-and-seek, I checked over my shoulder before hiding the package.

As I returned to the kitchen, Marcus flipped the last pancake from the grill to the platter. "What if we x-ray the box?"

Same song, second verse. Luckily, a drumbeat on the door saved me. "Come in."

Kevin Tanner, twenty-eight-years-old, longtime friend, current business partner, and recently minted boyfriend opened the door. He strode across the large, open living room like a man on a mission.

My heart did a little skip at the sight of him. I couldn't stop the smile that touched my lips. I've known him for ten years. He was eighteen when we met, so our instant chemistry settled into the best-friends category. As the years flew by, he started to push for more, but I resisted.

My luck with love makes my shaky bank account look good. I hated the thought of risking our friendship. However, having fought against my attraction and affection for several years, all the walls I'd built crumbled a few weeks ago.

Maybe because one of my last investigations brought me up close and personal with my ex. At some point during that case, I realized how much I'd grown up since I'd made the mistake of marrying an arrogant, self-absorbed man-child.

I knew I would never have cause to doubt Kevin's character, loyalty, or love.

My call to action came when Marcus told me about the blind date Kevin's work buddies had set him up on. Hurt and fury erupted in me like a volcano. I was ready to find him and the unknown woman and do... I don't know what.

That's when my son shrugged and said, "Why do you care? It's not like you and Kevin are dating."

I should have smelled a Marcus-sized setup that instant, but I had boiling lava in my veins. When I calmed down, I realized that due to my reluctance to commit, I might lose Kevin entirely. The very thought opened a void in my heart.

Still, I hesitated. Though I trust him with my heart and my son, part of me wondered if, after the newness wore off, he'd wake up one day and change his mind. But I screwed up my courage to the sticking point and decided to move forward. Two days later I ambushed Kevin and asked him out on an official date. I later learned that the alleged blind date had been a work party.

Since our "getting to know you" stage has been the longest one in history, we leaped into the relationship with both feet. Though finding time alone isn't easy, thanks to my inquisitive son, I love the feeling of being in love.

The memories and conversations flashed through my mind as my boyfriend walked across the room. The fact that his T-shirt didn't have a wrinkle on it and his khaki pants were perfectly pleated didn't surprise me. I just don't know how he manages it. My clothes don't leave the store looking that good.

Kevin stands six-foot-two and has a body hardened by years of working construction. Add to that the fact that he's been graced with wavy black hair and blue eyes to die for and it's hard to make him look bad.

"Little early to be spacing out, Belden." He pulled out a chair and shot me a distracted look that seemed at odds with his teasing words. Leaning over, he brushed a kiss across my lips.

I blamed my woolgathering on last night's ER adventure and a dangerously low caffeine level. Okay, blame it on love. Ignoring the uncertainty coiling in my gut, I went on the offense. "You look worried. Does Juan want the Great White Beast back?"

Kevin froze in the act of grabbing a mug off the shelf and shot me a look of recrimination. "Don't even joke about that."

He's currently making payments to his mechanic on a 1967 pearly white Cadillac, otherwise known as the Great White Beast.

I smiled. "Someday the rightful owners will find out where their Caddy is and you'll be out the money you've spent."

When he didn't leap to the defense of his beloved vehicle, I knew something had him worried.

"What's up?" I asked, all too willing to forget my own troubles.

Marcus leaned over the table. "What's the prob, man? Spit it out."

Kevin's smile didn't quite reach his eyes. He raked a hand through his hair. "I'm not sure where to begin."

The scent of fresh warm pancakes hit me. "A full stomach always helps me think."

Kevin's expression lightened and he sniffed. "Smells good."

"Thank you," I said with pride of ownership.

Hesitation, or perhaps fear, flashed in his eyes. "You made the pancakes?"

"I could have." None of my past attempts had ever looked this good, but I *could* have.

Marcus set the platter of hotcakes on the table next to a plate of bacon. His expression never wavered. Cooking isn't his only talent. He's a great little con artist.

Kevin studied the stove. "No smoke. No scorched grill. I'm betting on the kid."

So, I'm not Betty Crocker. "It's not my fault the batter got in the burners. The stove top moved when I wasn't looking."

Kevin speared a couple of hotcakes. "Happens to a lot of people."

"I helped." I pointed at the plastic bottle of syrup. "I nuked it with my own little hands. See? The label reads Hot."

"I'm impressed," Kevin assured me.

For the next minutes, we occupied ourselves with smearing butter and pouring syrup until I broke the silence. "Tell me what's got you worried."

Kevin took a bite. "Godert has been named as Murph's replacement."

"Your old boss?" I don't know why I asked. I mean, how many Murphs could a guy know? I blame Rickson's package for my confusion. "You were happy when Murph retired. I was there when we waved him and his wife off for their RV tour of America."

"What's bad is that Godert has it in for me." Kevin bit off the words. "I've had run-ins with him in the past. Now, he's changed my schedule and I'm on the list for reduced hours."

I grimaced in sympathy. "That's not going to pay the rent."

"Let's get back to the box," Marcus said.

I sighed. That's my boy – never say die. I set my mug down and met his gaze. "Kevin and I are talking."

"You and I were talking about the box before he came." Marcus's innocent stare was amazingly believable.

"Forget the box," I said, wishing I could.

Kevin didn't even ask. He mopped up his syrup with a bite of pancakes and bacon and lifted his gaze to Marcus. "What happened to your hand?"

Marcus wiggled his fingers to show the bandage to better advantage. "Cut it on Mr. Rheault's broken windshield last night at ten o'clock. We were in the ER until after midnight."

Kevin shifted his gaze to me as I picked up my mug. "What was he doing in the street at that time of night?"

"Do you know, you're the first person who asked me that?" Gratified someone else showed an interest in my son's welfare, I never dreamt of taking offense. During the years

Marcus has been in my life, Kevin has spent as much time raising the boy as I have.

"After Mrs. Colchester woke us up for the street fight, I saved the kitten from the fire." Having given his version, Marcus, took a bite of pancake.

Kevin favored me with a raised brow.

"It sounds so much worse in the light of day." I took a breath then decided we didn't have time for the gory details. "A few facts are missing, but the players are there."

"Uh-huh." Kevin sipped his coffee. He knew Mrs. C, my seventy-plus landlady, well enough not to be surprised at her role in the latest Belden crisis. "And in gratitude for his rescue, the kitten gave you this mysterious box we're going to drill open?"

Marcus laughed. "Rickson slipped the box to T.R. after a gunfight in the Emergency Room."

Kevin froze, then looked at me for a reality check. A rattling windowpane filled the silence.

Marcus's explanation sounded like a TV blurb for an adventure show. I raised my mug to my lips. "I hate to admit it, but that's pretty much what happened."

Kevin cocked his head. "Hear that?"

The window rattled louder this time. It sounded like it was coming from upstairs.

"It's in the bathroom." Marcus bolted out of his chair.

I caught him on the fly without spilling a drop of coffee.

It's taken some time, but I'm definitely getting the hang of this parenting biz. I put aside my cup. "Stay here."

Turning toward the stairs, I grabbed the wooden bat leaning against the railing. I may not be an Iron Chef, but a tomboy past has left me with a swing that can clear the bases. It's come in handy during some of my stints for Crawford. I told myself the noise was nothing but the wind or perhaps an errant squirrel dropping by for breakfast.

Halfway up the steps, I felt, more than saw, Kevin behind me.

"Hey, sport," Kevin spoke over his shoulder to my son. "How about you lock the door so nobody sneaks up behind us?"

Marcus nodded and ran toward the door.

Kevin has a knack with the boy.

I favored my buddy with a raised brow. "You know something I don't?"

"I've learned to cover all exits when I'm with you." He came even with me and reached for the bat as we walked into Marcus's bedroom. "I'll go first."

I pulled the bat out of his reach. I was in the mood to bash somebody. "You might be too nice."

Kevin wisely didn't comment.

I stepped over an electronic robot then did a two-step to avoid a remote-control truck.

"Maybe we should let them come in and take their chances with the obstacle course," Kevin whispered.

I swallowed a nervous laugh.

A tapping sounded from behind the bathroom door. I stepped to one side, gripping the bat firmly.

Kevin twisted the knob and flung the door open.

I jumped into the room, bat poised for a home run. The room and the lone window were empty. Some of the tension drained away. "Nobody's here."

As my shoulders relaxed, a dark-haired form popped up outside the window. The man's shoulders were wide enough for an elephant, and the face would have looked at home in a police line-up.

My heart leaped into my throat. The bat was already in motion. I swung for the outfield with the guy's head as the ball. Then my brain recognized the face. "Rickson!"

I almost pulled a muscle trying not to break my bathroom

window. Catching my balance, I watched Kevin flip the lock and open the pane.

Anxious to vent my pent-up nerves, I fixed Rickson with a glare. "You're a detective. You can't find the front door?"

Minutes later, Rickson finished squirming through the window and stretched to his full height. In these close quarters, he made Kevin look like a child.

"When did you start double locking the window?" Rickson asked in an aggrieved tone.

"Since people started using it as a separate entrance."

"Hey, Kev." Rickson's smile brought to life a puckered scar that ran across his right cheek. "How you doing?"

Kevin leaned against the bathroom door, twirling the bat. "Not bad. You?"

Rickson shrugged. "Can't complain."

"If you two are done with the social niceties, how about we get some breathing space?" I gestured toward the door.

Kevin spun around, hoisted the bat on his shoulder, and led the way through Marcus's bedroom.

The boy-child peered at us from the top stair. His face lit with a smile. "Hey, Chichi."

"Rickshaw boy, you got the goods?" Rickson asked.

Rickson's Chinese mother endowed him with his golden-hued skin, his nickname, and the right to make Asian jokes. His English father accounted for his size, his police career, and a love of soccer, all of which had contributed to his bashed-in face and assorted scars. "Do I smell the Korean pancake special?"

Moments later the three of us watched Rickson plow through the remainder of the pancakes and bacon.

"You do the best flapjacks I ever ate, kid."

What was it with men and food? I'd waited long enough for an explanation, time for the thumbscrews. "Today, you crawl in my window. Last night, you hunted me down and passed me a box full of incriminating evidence. What gives?"

Rickson's face lost all expression. Eyes wide, face pale, he grabbed my shoulders with a tight grip. "What evidence? Not the box? Tell me you didn't open it."

I stared at him, stunned by the raw fear that roughened his tone.

2

14 Across; 8 Letters;
Clue: Visit places of interest
Answer: Sightsee

Rickson's meaty paws slowly lifted me out of my chair. As he drew me closer, I could see the sweat beading on his upper lip. Dread seemed to have etched new lines on his scarred face.

With my heart beating a tattoo in my chest, I managed to shake my head. The action helped loosen my frozen tongue. "We didn't open the box. I hid it."

Syrupy scented air whooshed out of his lungs. He released his grip as if an unseen puppeteer had cut the strings holding him upright. He collapsed in his chair. His eyes looked heavenward. "Thank, God."

"What is going on?" Puzzlement and a hint of impatience rang through Kevin's tone.

I hope he didn't expect me to answer. As my butt smacked my chair, I fought to recover my balance.

A fist pounded on the door, sending my already stressed heart into my throat.

Rickson pulled his gun from his shoulder holster. Two strides took him halfway to the door.

"Everyone all right, ducks?" The casual tone marked by a British accent was so at odds with the circumstances I had to giggle.

"We're fine." Kevin cast me a sideways glance then motioned Rickson to lower his gun. "It's Mrs. Colchester. I'll let her in. Marcus locked the door when we heard you upstairs."

"She's our maid," Marcus said proudly.

"I thought she was your landlady." Rickson frowned as he slipped his weapon into his holster. "Isn't she kind of old to be a maid?"

"Over seventy," I told him. "It's a strictly voluntary position."

Rickson cast a confused look at the door. "She wasn't British last time I was here."

"The accent and her job as my maid are recent developments. They're about eight, ten weeks old." I pulled my mug closer. "I've been digging into her motives behind the changes, but I haven't turned up anything."

"Crawford won't check Interpol," Marcus told Rickson.

"And he calls himself a friend," I muttered.

At that moment Mrs. C shuffled into the kitchen behind Kevin. Her five-foot-six-inch frame had a comfortable amount of padding with white hair that had all but eclipsed her once blond curls. Her fuzzy bunny slippers, a birthday gift from Marcus, flapped against the tile floor. "I caught sight of an unexpected visitor on the security camera. Glad to see it's a friend."

Marcus shot me a smug grin. "And you said we didn't need a camera on the roof."

I gave Rickson a hard stare.

"I was staying off the radar." Was the big man's excuse. "We got trouble."

"A case." Marcus pumped a fist in the air. "I knew it."

"What's this *we* business?" Far more cautious than my son, I've learned not to blindly follow Rickson's lead. I pushed myself to my feet. The man's a homing pigeon for problems. "I got my own troubles."

Rickson stared at me with sad puppy eyes that were a mix of gray and brown. After a moment, his furrowed brow cleared as if lightning had struck. "You owe me. I covered for you with the kid's social worker last month. Remember?"

I froze like a mouse who'd just bit into the cheese. I heard the trap click, but I couldn't see a way out. Breath escaped my lips in a slow exhale. My brain realized what my gut feared from the first sight of Rickson. I was caught.

Darned loyalty. It's okay when it works in my favor, but that payback thing is annoying. I heaved a sigh. I wouldn't walk away from a friend in trouble. "What would this involve?"

Rickson stared at me for a long moment. Then his expression lit up as a grin spread across his face. "I got a plan."

A sinking feeling filled my stomach. This was getting worse. The big guy didn't get many ideas and the ones he did have, rarely worked out well. Before snack bars and fast food, he had trouble planning breakfast.

As the trap snapped shut, I found myself eyeing a crumpled business card Rickson dug out of his shirt pocket. His thick, sausage-like fingers all but engulfed the tiny slip of paper. I held back a groan.

"I need a distraction. You're good at that. You annoy

people." Having delivered this backhanded compliment, Rickson's massive shoulders shrugged, reminding me of twin boulders. He shook the torn business card at me while he retreated toward the door. "Just one quick meeting with the clients and you're done. I'll split the fee."

I perked up, watching the bait swing on the hook.

"Come to Lake Tahoe. Sightsee. Go home." The big guy sounded like a tourist ad gone bad. "It's easy money."

Kevin snorted. "There is no such thing."

My gut agreed with Kevin, but the siren song of ready cash short-circuited my brain. The bathroom pipe wasn't going to fix itself. Besides, if I was going anyway, I might as well get a paycheck. "Fine, but I'll need to arrange for someone to stay with Marcus."

My son shot to his feet, already pointing an accusing finger at me. "You're not leaving me behind."

Kevin gave me a pitying look. "I love that you try to play the mom card but get real. You know we're all going to go in the end."

Rickson looked toward the door like a trapped animal. He covered the distance between us with a single stride and slapped the card in my hand. "I wouldn't put the kid in danger."

I met his mixed gray eyes and reluctantly conceded the point. That didn't guarantee danger wouldn't find the boy, not to mention me.

"And so, it begins, the next case of the Belden Detective Agency." Marcus's whisper came like the voice-over in a documentary.

Rickson turned toward the door. "I have to get to Tahoe to tie off some stray ends."

"Don't you move." I shot to my feet, matching Rickson step for step. "What about last night? You came all this way to dump off a plastic box?"

The big man smacked his forehead.

"Is that one of your stray pieces?" I shifted direction. "I'll get it."

"I can't take that." He backed away as if I'd threatened him with a rattler. "It's trouble."

"So, you gave it to me?" My curiosity surged even as a sense of impending doom crept up my spine. "The guy in the ER said you stole it from him."

"The box belongs to the client." Rickson made a dismissive swipe with his meaty paw. "David Ferguson, the guy in the ER, stole it first. I found the box at his place. So, I grabbed it. He must have seen me."

Did that excuse Rickson's theft? "What's in the box? Evidence for that adultery case you're on? If I'm involved, you have to give me the facts."

"It's adultery, but it's not. Go to the meeting, then get out. You'll be fine."

His words knocked the air out of my lungs. The somber tone of the former police detective sent sharp talons crawling up my spine. But it did nothing to clear up my confusion. Rickson is a great investigator, but logic and organization aren't his strongest suits.

"Oh, de-yar." Mrs. C breathed the words in a soft tone as she poured herself a cup of coffee and snagged some toast and a few pieces of bacon. Settling in a chair, she had the attitude of a moviegoer watching the opening credits. "This sounds rather intriguing."

Rickson's wide mouth tightened to a flat line. A buzzing sound brought him to life. He pulled out his cell phone and checked the screen. His jaw clenched. "Gotta go."

"You're not leaving until you fill in some blanks." I wasn't about to let him off the hook. As I opened my mouth with the first of many questions, the big man continued.

"I'll call you on the road with details." He spoke over his

shoulder as he strode toward the door. "I have to get to Tahoe to set up for tonight. Stay at Pine Trail Inn, on the card."

"Wait." I followed, trying to read the card at the same time, but it was like walking and chewing gum. I couldn't do both. I stopped and lowered my eyes to the card. "Tell me more."

Silence was my answer. I looked up.

The doorway was empty.

"I'll be in touch." Rickson's voice floated up the stairs.

I clenched my fists. "Get back here."

A door slammed shut downstairs.

"Mrs. C, you'll have to find someone to watch the building while we're in Tahoe." Marcus didn't miss a beat.

Fingering the hotel's business card, I turned and eyed Marcus. "Someone to watch the building?"

"We can't leave our maid behind," Marcus said.

As if Mrs. C did anything except let herself into my apartment, eat my food, and help with the odd crossword puzzle. Okay, she did laundry, but only because she liked to.

"I'm sure Mrs. C doesn't want to run off toward God knows what kind of trouble." Even as I said the words, I knew I was wasting my time. Why did I bother?

"Lake Tahoe is lovely in late October." The older woman waved away my comment with a cheery smile. "I'll ask me friends to watch the place while I'm gone. They can keep an eye on your apartment as well. I can't let you scoot off with no one to watch your rear."

Just my speed, a bodyguard from the geriatric generation.

Like a queen off to welcome her guests, Mrs. C turned toward the door. She stopped after a step. "We *will* leave this morning, won't we? I have to tell me friends."

I hesitated. Part of me was looking for a way out of this loyalty trap. But with my curiosity engaged, logic and caution never had a chance. "We'll take off as soon as we get organized."

Marcus smacked his forehead. "We have to be home by Friday for Halloween. Steve and I have our route mapped out. It's a five-mile loop that heads past the best homes."

"We'll be home for Halloween," I promised. "But we are not walking five miles. No one needs that much candy."

Kevin put his arm over my shoulder. "We need to be on the lookout for a Plan B. This case sounds anything but straightforward."

"If it goes long, Marcus is out of school until Wednesday. There's a teacher's conference Monday and Tuesday." I think the school board arranged random days off for the teacher's mental health. God knows, they need an occasional break. "Too bad I can't get a day off from getting pulled into crazy cases."

"You sound a little short-tempered, Belden." Kevin's teasing tone, coupled with his smile, added extra heat to the surge of warmth flooding my veins. "Anyone would think you're not used to chaos."

"I prefer controlled chaos." I pulled my gaze away from his eyes and ordered my beating heart to calm down. Time to focus on business, not my newly freed love.

Kevin planted a kiss on my cheek. My guy's handsome face held a thoughtful expression. "We may need extra ammunition."

The ominous note that underlaid his usually carefree tone fed the fear in my belly. I stared in puzzlement since neither Kevin nor I owned a gun.

He met my gaze with a smile. "I'm sure Rabi could use a weekend by the lake."

Rabi, retired from Special Ops, used to pick up packages for my now former full-time job. He was a tall black man with ashen skin stretched over a skeletal frame. His coal black, shoulder-length hair fell in perfect waves that gleamed in the sun. Marcus adopted him as a surrogate uncle within days after the boy moved in with me.

"You're going to hijack Rabi and drag him into this mess? I thought you liked him." Privately, I admitted the logic of bringing the other man along. Though I hated to involve Rabi in trouble not of his making, his stalwart presence would be reassuring.

"The Belden Agency can't start a case without all its members." Marcus was instantly onboard. "Besides, Rabi would be hurt if we left without him. I'm riding shotgun with Kevin."

I toyed with the idea of insisting Marcus pack his own bag, but his help would double the time it would take me to get organized. "Fine, you two go see if you can con Rabi into wasting his weekend on this mad excursion."

Not that I doubted the outcome. Raised as a con artist from birth, Kevin could sell sand in the desert. Besides, Rabi would sacrifice a limb before he'd take a chance that anything might happen to Marcus.

As I watched my two guys walk out the door, promising a quick return, I remembered Crawford telling me that it was better to have backup and not need it, than to need it and not have it.

Instead of being reassured, an ominous cloud seemed to crowd out the daylight. Why was I suddenly sure that Rabi's help would be needed? And why did I have the feeling I'd need it sooner rather than later?

3

32 Down; 9 Letters;
Clue: Not identified; No known name
Answer: Anonymous

"You must be Ms. Belden." The chirpy desk clerk's enthusiastic greeting matched a smile that could have lit half the strip.

So much for anonymity. After a three-hour drive from Langsdale to Tahoe, I hadn't taken ten steps into the Pine Trail Inn when my name echoed through the airy two-story atrium. What had Rickson done -- post my picture on the internet?

"Yes, we're the Belden party." Mrs. C's British accent leaped into the void my stunned silence left open. "I'm glad to see you're expecting us."

"Mr. Schmidt has been waiting to speak with you. He should be here any minute." The pearly whites focused on

Mrs. C. "Your rooms are ready, a double suite with a connecting door."

I couldn't afford a suite, especially not here. I'd expected a small motel. However, the sweeping drive, lined with manicured hedges, had led to a sprawling Georgian style hotel artfully secluded by huge pines. Between the doorman and the marble floor, the place reeked of money.

Fortunately, since Rickson had arranged this stint, payment was his problem. All I had to do was play my part and not get shot.

"Two adjoining suites will be adequate," Mrs. C's casually snobbish tone brought me back to reality.

A man stepped through a doorway behind the counter in a tailored dark gray suit.

"Mr. Schmidt," The receptionist turned her smile on him. "The Belden party has arrived."

Walking up to the desk, he looked my way without meeting my eyes, then, focused his gaze over my left shoulder. "I hope you had a nice trip. If you're hungry, we have two restaurants on property and a full room service menu available. Your meeting regarding the construction project is set for seven o'clock this evening."

What construction project? How could I meet with the clients when I didn't have a clue what the case involved? How did this guy know more than me?

Despite his promise to call me, Rickson had been out of touch since he'd bolted from my apartment this morning. In addition to the drive to Lake Tahoe, it had taken two hours to get everyone organized. In all that time, my repeated texts and calls had gone unanswered.

I should have listened to Kevin; there is no such thing as easy money. A pique of annoyance brought me to life. "Was an information packet left for us?"

Hopefully, Rickson had left something. Without him here, I'd need a roster to keep the players straight.

"Of course." The man pulled a large manila envelope from beneath the counter. "It arrived this afternoon."

The envelope was the size of the family Bible I'd used to crack walnuts. I wondered if this package would do me even that much good. Who had pulled this material together in the hours since I'd spoken to Rickson? What was going on?

"I'll take that, Ms. Belden." Rabi's polite murmur sounded in my ear as he took the package from the manager.

Evidently, I got to be top dog. Having played a hooker, an addict, and a mental patient in previous operations, being a businesswoman was a step up. Though I realized in the next heartbeat that also meant I'd be the main target if anything went wrong.

What else was new?

"There are two door cards to each suite. If you need more, let the front desk know." The manager gestured to the small envelope on the counter. "The limousine will arrive at six-thirty to pick you up."

Kevin stepped into the picture. "We'll drive ourselves."

Mr. Schmidt aimed a glance over Kevin's head, then, straightening his cuffs, did a one-eighty toward the office. "The front desk personnel will take care of any details. Don't hesitate to contact me if you need anything further."

The final words floated to us from around the corner. The perky desk clerk, evidently used to her boss's behavior, turned toward us with a smile in place. Then her gaze landed on Kevin.

Her frozen gaze didn't waver from his baby blues when Mrs. C and Marcus walked to the elevator with Rabi.

I knew from experience I couldn't compete with his Adonis-like looks, but it helps to speak slowly. "We'll need the address and a map of the area."

I could use my phone's GPS for directions, but I like to see the layout of an area. Kevin could find the place from the address alone. His built-in compass makes it impossible for him to get lost. I'd once gotten turned around going to the grocery store in my hometown.

"Could you send the map to our suite?" Kevin asked.

Nancy's gaze never wavered. "I'll bring it myself."

"Thanks." He gave her a blinding smile.

We turned to the elevator. Marcus and Rabi had gone ahead. Thankfully, Mrs. C had waited. I hadn't heard the room number and I didn't have a key.

By the time we got to the suites, all the bedroom doors stood open. Marcus's undersized frame was settled on the sofa. He had his feet on the coffee table and a room service menu in his lap.

A delicately modeled bronze dancer graced a side table. French doors opened onto a balcony overlooking a gorgeous view of the mountains. The delicate scent from a bouquet of creamy orchids and dark purple blossoms teased my nostrils. "What a way to live."

Most of the people who came here had nothing better to do than hit the slopes or appreciate the scenery. Lucky us, we were heading into heaven only knew what kind of trouble.

A kitchenette, complete with microwave and fridge, graced the corner to the right. The posh living room, decorated in tan, mint-green, and rust, took my breath away. Instead of two beds, there were two separate bedrooms along one wall. Two suites were overkill. "The five of us could live here with room to spare."

"You're with the guys, Kevin." Marcus jerked his head behind him where Rabi, still wearing his jacket, leaned next to the connecting door. "This is the girls' suite. Each one has two bedrooms. I'm sleeping on the foldout couch."

He smiled as if the gunshots in ER, Rickson running off

couldn't affect him. Didn't he realize how much trouble we could be facing?

Then it struck me that during his years on the street Marcus had lived through worse. At least now he had a family that would stand by him, an offbeat family, but family nonetheless.

I glanced at the crew he'd dubbed The Belden Agency. If I had to run from one mess to another, this was the group I'd want at my side. "You want the front bedroom, Mrs. C?"

"If you don't mind, ducks," she said, already heading for it.

"What's on the menu?" As long as someone else paid I intended to eat well.

"They have steak, lobster, all kinds of stuff. I'm taking orders." Marcus tapped his lip with the pen in his hand as he studied the menu. A pad lay on the sofa cushion. "Who's paying for this?"

"Not us," I said with a careless shrug. "Maybe whoever needs saving. Crawford can deal with the bills when he returns. That's what he gets for leaving me in charge."

"Awesome." Having been delivered from our usual penny-pinching, Marcus settled into the plan. "Rabi's having a sixteen-ounce T-bone with grilled onions, medium."

"Sign me up for one of those." Kevin's voice sounded from the depths of the other suite. "Rare."

"Ditto," I called distractedly. "Eight ounces. Medium, with mushrooms."

Mrs. C came trundling out of the front bedroom with her bunny slippers flopping merrily. She carried a menu in her hands. "Oooh, Beef Wellington."

"Is that what you want?" Marcus had his pen at the ready.

"Absolutely. They have Yorkshire pudding." Mrs. C sounded as if she might go into spasms of delight, then she gave a sorrowful sigh. "Probably not homemade."

"So, you don't want the pudding," Marcus persisted.

"Oh, luv, I have to try it." Mrs. C sat in the other chair and opened the knitting bag looped around her wrist.

"They have ice-cream sundaes." Marcus cast me a sideways glance as he wrote down the latest order.

I sat and flipped open a menu lying on the table. "It'll melt by the time you're done eating."

Marcus smiled. "Not if I eat it first."

I considered for a moment. Miss Manners would be appalled, but after seeing my weekend derailed, I felt rebellious. "Go for it."

"You're the best, T.R." Marcus's grin widened. Chewing on his lip, he studied the possibilities with a knit brow.

Give a kid an ice-cream sundae and life is good. I, however, had to face the manila packet on the table.

"Mint chocolate chip with hot fudge sauce." Marcus's voice held a note of finality. He scribbled on his pad. "What about you, T.R.?"

Leaning forward, I opened the envelope and considered having a sundae as a reward for reading the files. Then I shook my head. "I better be good."

Mrs. C's knitting needles clicked with steady regularity. The colorful yarn now reached to the floor. I wondered how big this woven wonder would end up being.

"Mrs. C?" Marcus asked. "Dessert?"

The older woman shook her head. "I have to watch me girlish figure."

Marcus's brows rose, but thankfully he kept his mouth shut. He looked over his shoulder. "You better have one, Rabi. You're getting pale. You need more chocolate in your blood."

I grimaced, but Marcus was too busy chuckling at his childish joke to pay attention.

Rabi's mouth turned up.

Marcus bent over his pad again. "Chocolate ice-cream with chocolate sauce. Kevin, what about you?"

Marcus's yell carried into the next room and probably into the hall. However, Kevin had returned and was standing behind him.

"Nothing," Kevin answered in a matching yell then settled on the end of the couch by my chair.

I really wanted to cuddle next to him but keeping my distance was best when we were on the job.

My gaze lingered on him, taking in the wink he shot my son. What would I do without him? A warmth curled in my gut at his nearness.

As if sensing my attention, his sapphire eyes met my plain gray ones. I caught my lower lip in my teeth. Amazing that it took the death of my ex-hubby's second wife and a twenty-year-old murder to push me into this romance. Now, instead of telling myself that Kevin's and my eight-year age difference made me too old, I felt like I was sixteen again.

I smiled, grateful for his solid presence as I up-ended the packet. A bound report hit the table with a thud, followed by loose papers that looked to be either blueprints or maps. The crest on the top page showed an ornate blue curlicue edged in silver and guarded on either side by a roaring lion.

"You have to get a sundae," Marcus whispered to Kevin behind his pad. "Or she'll eat mine."

I reached for the top letter. "I heard that."

Kevin shrugged agreement.

Marcus bent to his pad. "Kevin wants butter-brickle with hot caramel sauce and pecans."

"Hot caramel sauce?" The image of the rich concoction diverted my attention. That kid knows me too well.

"I'll call in the order." Marcus raced for the phone. A rhythmic tattoo on the door sidetracked him. "I'll get it."

I didn't see Rabi move. He simply appeared between Marcus and the door.

"Order the food," Rabi said. "I got the door."

Marcus rolled his eyes at the obvious diversion but he headed for the phone.

Rabi slipped a hand inside his jacket, where a shoulder holster would sit. He peered through the peep-hole before moving to the side. "Who is it?"

"Delivery from the front desk." The desk clerk's voice carried into the suite.

Rabi opened the door six inches and peered out.

I raised my brows. All this for Little Miss Sunshine?

Apparently reassured, he opened the door and moved aside.

The perky blonde took no notice of him. Her eyes zeroed in on Kevin. Her smile widened. "I brought the map."

She held the paper out to Kevin who quickly closed the distance between them. Her grip shifted to reveal a corner of an envelope peeking out between the folds of the map. "This should be everything you need."

Kevin didn't miss a beat. "Thanks again."

With a lingering gaze at Kevin's baby blues, she sailed through the door Rabi held open.

"Half-an-hour." Marcus hung up the phone, his gaze riveted to the packet in Kevin's hand.

"B & T, Inc." Kevin read from the envelope then looked at me. "When did we bid for a Tahoe job?"

"I have no idea." And I handle the business side of our fledgling company. "How could this fit in with Rickson investigating a possibly cheating spouse?"

"You have top billing, B." He tossed it to me with a satisfied smirk then sat on the couch. "You read it."

"I knew there was a downside to fame." I turned it over. The neat script on the envelope didn't look familiar. I ripped it open. Cramped scribbling covered the two sheets of lined notebook paper. "This is Rickson's writing."

Kevin groaned as he unfolded the map. "We'll be lucky if we can figure out half of it."

Rickson had been incommunicado for hours. Now, what looked like his case notes were in my hands. Who had sent them? Where was he? I hid my concern behind a calm mask and concentrated on the jumbled letters and crowded words. Rickson's penmanship was questionable at best. "If this man hand-wrote his arrest reports, I'm surprised he got anyone convicted."

Marcus sat on the sofa, crowding Kevin to catch a view of the notes. "What does it say?"

Squinting didn't make the words more legible. I went with my best guess. "'House tense. Job not straightforward.'"

Mrs. C stopped weaving to untie a knot. "So, Mr. Rickson is warning you it's not a simple case."

"These are his case notes to himself," I said. "*He* doesn't think this is a straight job."

I bent my mind to the note. Rickson's scrawl, combined with his questionable use of the English language, demanded my entire concentration.

"'Not straightforward,'" I repeated. "'Be sure to cover the basics. My grandson always. Loyalty betrayed.'"

"And we're off... to a bad start," Kevin muttered. The map lay forgotten across his lap.

I nodded then returned my attention to the squiggles on the paper. "'Father – family first; Mother – very proper; Todd – knows more; Sheila – jockeying for power; Quinlan – position of trust; Linda – outside looking in; Verdeen – weakest link, wants out?'"

"That can't be all," Kevin exclaimed impatiently when I paused.

"Just trying to make sense of it." Rubbing my forehead, I

struggled to decipher Rickson's scribbles. "'Pu… Pae… shonk – -'"

"Prushark." Kevin tapped the map. "The Prushark estate is where we're going tonight. According to the map, it's the size of a small village."

"Wonderful." Size meant money and money meant power. I studied the note. "It could be Prushark. 'Prusharks ballroom renovation.' Why would he note these details? What logic connects a construction job with a cheating spouse?"

"Maybe there's a body." Marcus stared at me from the middle of the couch, hanging on every word.

"Why aren't you glued to a computer game like most kids your age?" I asked.

Marcus made a face. "Murder is way better."

I looked to Kevin for support. All I got was a shrug.

"Most parents would be happy to have their child interested in their career," Kevin said.

"That's it." Marcus's eyes lit up, seizing on any excuse to explain his fascination with murder and mayhem. "I'm interested in your life."

I shot Kevin a mock glare. "You're supposed to be on my side."

"Give it up, Belden." Kevin picked up the map again. "Electronics can't compete with flying bullets."

I narrowed my gaze, but the two of them just sat there. I sighed in defeat. "Where was I?"

"You were at the ballroom renovation," Marcus said.

I found my spot. "'Good' - - no, that's not it. Guard? I think it says 'Guard -- dog died at animal hospital Saturday. No dogs allowed.'"

"Odd comment," Kevin muttered.

"As opposed to the rest of this?" My frustration bled through my tone as I looked for logic in a Rickson's notes.

I stared at the words again. Puzzles are a hobby of mine,

jigsaw, crossword, Sudoku. I like figuring out the clues. Once I start, seeing the completed result is basically a compulsion. Rickson's pages weren't coherent enough to give me a beginning.

"Which of these rambling clues are we supposed to follow?" Kevin, as usual, focused on the facts.

I searched for a solid lead, only to come up empty-handed. "We must have received the wrong sealed envelope. These pages were clearly meant for someone else."

Marcus exchanged skeptical looks with Kevin then shook his head in mock sorrow.

"Nobody appreciates my brilliant wit." With a groan, I plunged into the seemingly aimless notes. "'Inside job. Checked offices. Deets to C, COC.'"

"Details to Crawford?" Marcus suggested with a puzzled frown. "What does COC stand for?"

"I think you're right on the first part." Kevin patted the boy's shoulder. "Rickson would have reported to Crawford about the complications. I got nothing on COC."

Neither did I, so I took up reading where I'd left off. "His scribbling gets worse. This is dated -- Saturday. Today?"

Hearing the shock in my voice, Kevin leaned in. "If he hot-footed it here while we got organized, he'd have made it hours ago."

I stared at the crowded words, determined to get through this incredibly unhelpful message. "'Saturday – box safe. B gang coming.'"

"That's us." Marcus smacked his chest. "We're a gang."

Mrs. C's hands lay idle in her lap. She eyed me with a confused expression. "Would Mr. Rickson have confided a more complete record to anyone else? The authorities, perhaps?"

I shared her frustration, but I could only shrug. "If you

mean the cops, no. He was never with the Tahoe police force."

"Crawford was and Rickson knew their names." Marcus practically yelled the words. "That's what COC stands for, Rickson used to call the Tahoe cops: Crawford's Old Crew."

"Why would he drag them into a case about adultery?" The answer was – he wouldn't. Whatever went wrong with this case had thrown the investigation completely off-track. "There's not much else. 'Estate. Intruder.'"

The ink trailed away in a squiggle. Uh-oh.

4

11 Down; 4 Letters;
Clue: Facts provided
Answer: Info

Rickson's note ended in a streak of ink.

Mrs. C raised a brow. "Who was the intruder?"

The others eyed me expectantly.

I checked the back of the page, but it was blank. I held out the piece of paper. "That's all it says."

Kevin snagged the note from my hand. Always cool-headed, he studied the paper with a calm expression. "No name."

Marcus crowded close, reading over his shoulder. "No clue. Nothin'."

I tried to ignore the knot in my stomach. "Good thing Rickson's too big to bring down."

My words didn't sound very confident. But then, I didn't feel confident.

Kevin slipped the envelope off my lap and tapped the neat penmanship. "Rickson didn't address this. Whoever sent these notes knows we're involved in the Prushark investigation."

"The desk clerk had them." Suzy Sunshine, alias Nancy at the front desk, didn't seem to have a stake in the case, but as the last link in the chain she was the logical place to begin.

"I'll talk to her." I retrieved the pages and envelope from Kevin. "You'll only distract her."

Rabi pushed away from the wall.

I motioned him back. "She'll be more likely to talk if I go alone."

Rabi and Kevin exchanged glances. Kevin's jaw clenched, but he finally nodded. "Ten minutes. Then we're coming down."

"I promise not to disappear in broad daylight," I said. "Besides, I'm wiry. I can take her."

Alone in the elevator, Rickson's words haunted me. 'I wouldn't put the kid in danger.' How could I believe him when he was now among the missing?

I looked at the mirrored walls. A harried-looking woman stared at me. Sticking the papers in my pocket, I ran my fingers through my hair and smoothed my polo shirt. It didn't make me a supermodel, but nothing would.

When the elevator opened, I pasted on a polite smile and headed for the check-in desk. A mother-daughter pair wearing Gucci and Armani respectively finished their business and walked away. Their stilettos tapped a steady rhythm out the main entrance.

A twentyish, African-American man with a square jaw and a neat mustache had joined Nancy behind the desk. Since the girl had delivered the envelope ala James Bond, mentioning it in front of a witness didn't seem my wisest course. I widened my smile and jump-started my brain for an opening line. Nothing came to mind so I decided to wing it.

"Ms. Belden, it's nice to see you again. May I help you?" Nancy's big-brown-eyes begged for a problem to solve.

Fortunately, I specialize in off-the-cuff half-truths. I confided in her with a conspiratorial air. "My partner and I are going to the Prushark estate regarding a job and I'm kind of nervous."

"You're going to refurbish the ballroom for the Winter Fest." The young man, Josh, according to his nametag, offered this tidbit.

I hid my surprise. Evidently, everyone knew the cover story of the week. "What is Winter Fest?"

"An annual mega-party disguised as a charity event. The Prusharks sponsor it." Nancy practically quivered with excitement. "Todd Prushark, the oldest son, is expanding it big time. He plans to put his mark on it since he's in charge now."

Josh aimed a congratulatory smile at me. "He's picky, but he pays top dollar."

"That's good." I didn't have to feign enthusiasm. Part of me yearned to find a way to do the job and pocket the paycheck. "When is Winter Fest?"

It was late October now. The party couldn't be for a few weeks.

"Last week of January," the two answered in chorus.

"Time enough then." I knew zilch about fancy parties, but thanks to Kevin, I knew about prepping and painting a large room.

"I'm surprised they don't use a local firm." There had to be plenty of contractors in Tahoe who would love to be on Prushark's payroll. "Or their own construction division."

Nancy pursed her perfect, pink mouth. "Hiring your firm is a publicity stunt. This year's Winter Fest is dedicated to promoting female-owned businesses. I don't know how you were picked but your firm was announced in a press release yesterday."

"Pete and Matt Monroe, the father and son of Monroe & Son Construction, are onboard. They're a division of the Prushark company. They might be at tonight's meeting, but you better sign the contract quick." Josh cast me a meaningful glance. "There might not be a Winter Fest."

This sounded intriguing. I hid my excitement behind a concerned expression. "Why not?"

Josh's gaze shifted toward the office.

"Mr. Schmidt left for dinner ten minutes ago," Nancy answered his unspoken question.

I waited with every outward sign of patience. Inside, my nails did a tap dance up my spine. Feeling like a character in a Bogart movie, I checked out the lobby. Empty. I turned to Josh and raised a brow.

Nancy shot a glance my way. "His uncle works on the estate, but he refuses to get me the inside scoop."

Josh retreated from her ire. "Uncle Steve said no one was talking, until now."

The young woman's delicate fist pounded the varnished counter. "What have you heard? Spit it out."

I shared her impatience, as well as her curiosity.

Josh eyed the narrowed eyes of his co-worker, not to mention her clenched fists. "We're not supposed to gossip."

"Oh, come on." Nancy leaned closer to him. "It's bound to come out soon, so, it's not like it's a secret."

Of course not, that's why we were all whispering.

Josh scanned the lobby one more time, then we all moved closer. "Mr. Prushark is taking back the reins of power."

Nancy gasped. "How could he? They said he wouldn't recover."

Josh smiled, pleased at his coup. "I heard it yesterday. He shocked everyone with his recent progress."

I hadn't even known the man was sick. I hid my rampant curiosity behind a, hopefully, casual air. "What happened?"

Nancy's eyes shown with excitement. "A major stroke twenty months ago. That's when Todd, the oldest son, and Sheila, the daughter, took control."

"They were both under the old man's thumb before," Josh said. "Word is old man Prushark isn't happy with their changes."

I wanted to ask for details, but the mention of a stroke had me curious as to the couple's ages, which the packet had failed to include. "How old are Henry and Diana Prushark?"

"She's in her mid-sixties. He's early eighties." Nancy glanced at Josh who confirmed her estimate with a nod. Then, the young woman continued. "She played professional tennis in her twenties. She was Diana Pearson then. She opened a sports equipment chain. When she married Henry Prushark, he added her stores to his business and she retired to a life of luxury."

Interesting switch for Mrs. Diana Prushark - one day a professional athlete and entrepreneur, the next day a stay-at-home wife.

"He's old school. His companies have the fewest women managers in the state," Josh added, eager to show off his knowledge of the local celebrities. "Sheila has the best head for business of the three children. When the younger son died three years ago, people assumed Mr. Prushark would give her equal authority with her oldest brother."

My interest meter rose. I sensed a definite motive for trouble. "Did he?"

"He never gave her credit." Nancy's tone sharpened. "She remained a mid-level manager."

"Sheila oversees half the companies now. She's expanded their market and income," Josh said.

The Prusharks evidently had more than their share of family quarrels. Unfortunately, I wasn't sure how this news fit in with the case.

An alarm beeped. Nancy looked at Josh. "Your turn."

Josh shrugged and walked away.

Not sure how long he'd be gone I leaned in. "Who gave you the letter you brought to the room?"

"Victoria Quinlan brought it this afternoon." Nancy kept her voice low.

"When?" At least I'd know what time Rickson ran off.

"Two-thirty," Nancy said. "She told me not to let it out of my sight until I handed it to you or Mr. Tanner. She said you'd need it tonight. If you have questions, she'd be the one to ask."

I had a bushel full of questions. "Who's Ms. Quinlan?"

Nancy's brow furrow. "You don't know her?"

Realizing my error, I waved a careless hand. "I've spoken to her, but I've never been sure of her exact title."

"She's Mrs. Prushark's business manager," Nancy said. "She started as a secretary years ago."

"You talking about Quinlan?" Josh sailed in. "With Mr. Prushark taking over, she's on shaky ground."

Nancy frowned. "He would never have promoted a woman to such an important job."

She directed the final sentence at me. So, I leaped into the conversation. "Sounds like she might be fired."

Nancy shrugged. "Mrs. Prushark won't like to let her go."

Josh leaned close to me. "When the old man takes over, she's out."

"He could cause plenty of trouble." Nancy sounded excited at the prospect. "I wonder how Todd and Sheila will take losing power now that they've had a taste."

I'd been wondering that very thing. I couldn't make any of these family dynamics tie to possible adultery. Quinlan evidently had a motive for causing trouble, but she was our contact.

At the moment, I didn't even know for sure what problem we'd been hired to solve. Unfortunately, neither Crawford nor Rickson were around to fill in the blanks. I'd left a message at Crawford's office, but Roxie, his administrator, hadn't returned my call.

My gossip buddies seemed to have run out of news from the Prushark camp. I decided to cover all the bases on the off chance I might get lucky. "Has Mr. Rickson checked in yet? Big guy, six-nine, scar on his right cheek."

Josh started shaking his head halfway through my description. Nancy's eyes grew wide at Rickson's size, but no recognition shown in her gaze. It had been a gamble. A moment later, when guests cut short our gabfest, I headed to the room.

The delicious aroma of grilled steaks hit me when I opened the door. My stomach growled, and a wave of weariness came over me. After last night in the ER and today's tension, I was beat. With no thought but food, I shut the door and made a bee-line for the dining table.

Marcus looked up from his hot roast beef sandwich. An empty ice-cream dish sat at his elbow.

The tightness around Kevin's eyes eased.

Rabi studied me silently while Mrs. C concentrated on her Yorkshire pudding.

Ignoring the questioning looks, I slipped into the chair next to Kevin and facing Marcus. I unrolled the napkin and grabbed a spoon. "Oooh, hot caramel sauce in a separate dish. No melty ice-cream. These are my people."

Marcus pinned me with a piercing gaze. "What did you find out?"

I spooned a bite of Kevin's sundae into my mouth with one hand while taking the lid off a covered plate with the other. "I found out I'm starving."

Marcus frowned. "T.R.--"

"Little Miss Sunshine got the letter from Ms. Quinlan at two-thirty today." My gaze shifted to my steak. With an effort, I held back from attacking it. "Neither she nor Josh, the other clerk, have heard of Rickson. They didn't blink at his description."

Kevin's brow furrowed. "Why would he send us here?"

I reached for my knife. "Rickson didn't pick this place out of his hat."

"Maybe someone involved is staying here," Marcus suggested.

I stabbed a piece the tender meat. "You may be right."

The kid was a natural at this detective stuff. Way better than me.

I claim no skill. Being too stubborn to quit is my only qualification. I keep slogging away until all the clues in the puzzle are answered.

"I looked over the specs on the job while you were out," Kevin chewed thoughtfully. "Victoria Quinlan is the business manager."

I cut a bite of my steak, then gave a quick update on what I'd learned.

Kevin raised a brow. "Sounds like no one is happy at the prospect of the old man getting better."

With my mouth full, I nodded.

"If Quinlan had something to hide, she wouldn't leave us the notes." Marcus spoke around a huge bite of his sandwich.

I pointed my fork in his direction. "Don't talk with your mouth full."

He chewed then swallowed. "It was only half-full."

Never give a kid wiggle room. I narrowed my gaze, trying

to look tough. "Don't talk while you have food in your mouth. But you're right. Quinlan giving us Rickson's message does knock her down a few pegs on the list."

"Suspect everyone." Kevin sounded like the villain in a melodrama then he sobered. "Remember Rickson's first line; this isn't a normal case."

"Then, we better check out Monroe & Sons." My growing irritation was mixed with a healthy amount of worry at Rickson's continued silence. "They're the construction division of the Prushark Corporation."

Kevin's fingers drummed a rhythm on the table. "Why wouldn't they do this smalltime job?"

I relayed the publicity stunt aspect. Suddenly weary, I focused on eating. My mind, however, gravitated toward the allure of the puzzle. So many empty boxes waiting to be filled. I love the symmetry of a crossword puzzle. However, Rickson had given me nothing helpful in Langsdale and his notes were jumbled to the point of being useless.

"What else was in the manila envelope?" I asked Kevin.

"Layout and history of the estate." His casual tone indicated no great revelations.

Figures.

He continued. "Blueprints for the tennis court, the patio, stables, fishponds, swimming pools--"

"Pools? Plural?" I'd have been happy with one. "I had no idea the Prusharks were so wealthy."

Kevin smiled. "They have riding trails, too. But don't worry, the stables are far enough away from the heliport so the horses don't get spooked."

I stared at him. "You're making this up."

He cast me a heart-stopping look. "We could set up housekeeping in one wing of the house. No one would notice."

"I'm hoping they'll adopt me." Marcus chimed in.

"Ingrate." I glared at Marcus in mock anger. Then, I shifted to Kevin's sundae and decided to save it from oblivion. Relishing the mix of warm caramel and cold ice-cream on my tongue, I tried to wrap my mind around the idea of that much wealth. "I was impressed with a suite."

When the phone rang, we all turned.

Hope rose. If I knew Rickson was safe, I could focus my energy on being annoyed at him.

Mrs. C patted her mouth with a napkin, giving her an air of genteel elegance. "I'll get it."

I tried to downplay the call. "Probably the estate, confirming our arrival."

"Belden and Tanner Suite." Her British accent made us sound almost legitimate.

"Oh, it's you." Mrs. C's voice lost the polite edge reserved for strangers.

"Not the estate," Kevin said in an undertone.

It could still be Rickson. I didn't say the words aloud. Despite Marcus's brave front, I knew he was worried. However, instead of calling Kevin or me to the phone, the older woman listened intently.

"This afternoon, you say? I'm sure she wasn't expecting anything of the kind." She turned and met my gaze. "It's me friends. Your car is gone."

I jolted upright. Whatever I'd expected, having someone steal my fifteen-year-old Buick wasn't it. "What?"

"It's been impounded by the bobbies." Mrs. C sounded as if she were announcing the time.

A shockwave sped through my veins. "Why?"

She listened for a moment. "Improper licensure."

"That's a lie." My car's a rambling wreck with bald tires, but it's *legal*. I felt like I'd been accused of cheating when, for once, I knew the answer. I looked around in frustration. "What am I going to do about my car?"

No one offered a solution.

I looked at Mrs. C. "Can they get it out?"

She relayed the question. After a moment, she looked at me. "Not on a Saturday night, luv. The towing fee is over one hundred dollars plus a bit each day. They'll try first thing Monday."

I groaned. What could I do? "I'll fight city hall when I get home. Tell them to keep a close eye on the apartment."

Mrs. C turned to the phone.

Rabi, silent so far, glanced at me. "You can go to small claims court. If your car's legal, you'll get a refund."

Though the option provided no answer, the thought buoyed my spirits.

Mrs. C hung up and shuffled her bunny slippers to the table.

I spooned up a bite of ice-cream. Things have to be much worse than this to throw me off my food. "Why is nothing easy with Rickson? He was given a simple job, a cheating spouse. Now, he's pulled me in while he goes off on one of his crazy schemes."

Marcus sat, a thoughtful look on his face.

A pang of conscience hit me. "Don't worry. Rickson will call in with an update. He's got things under control."

"I'm not worried." The boy dismissed my concern with a shrug. "I was wondering why contractors are being targeted if this is about adultery."

I licked the final bite of ice-cream off my spoon. "What do you mean?"

"Monroe & Sons were squeezed out of an easy job." Marcus pointed his fork at me. "Now, our car has been towed. This could be connected to Rickson's problems."

"It's suspicious," Kevin said. "But why would someone target Tracy?"

I had no answer, but I don't like coincidences. The sweet

taste on my tongue melted away. I forced a swallow. "I'm not a contractor."

"Your and Kevin's names have been released to the press." Marcus counted out the points on his fingers. "Everyone in Tahoe thinks B & T, Inc. is the new Prushark contractor. That puts you on the hit list."

Just what I needed; a bulls-eye on my back.

5

1 Down; 7 Letters;
Clue: Not in its expected place
Answer: Missing

Building contractors having troubles? The unexpected connection hit me squarely between the eyeballs. I'd forgotten about the press release, but I refused to admit defeat. "That's pretty thin logic."

"I like it." Marcus punctuated his statement with a decisive nod.

I smiled. "That's because you thought of it."

Kevin polished off his steak and pushed away his plate. He rewarded Marcus with an admiring gaze. "It's the best theory we've got so far."

"See?" My boy-child stabbed a bite of roast beef then eyed me with a smug expression. "It makes more sense than anything else."

"I'll give you that." I toyed with my creamed corn as my

mind played with the possibility. Filling in puzzles, whether crossword or jigsaw, intrigue me. I itch to find a pattern. Could this be it?

Kevin jerked a thumb toward the letters and maps on the coffee table. "If you or I are being targeted because of the supposed Prushark job, it's possible whoever is behind this could have found your address and called the cops about your car."

"The timing could work." I may be stubborn, but I'm not stupid. "Whoever Rickson has on the inside got us hired, at least on paper, so we could be at tonight's meeting."

"Has to be Quinlan." Marcus knelt on his chair and leaned halfway across the table. "As the business manager, she could make you guys look good."

Mrs. C speared a single green bean from her plate and nibbled at it. "Strange that anyone would plan or agree to a business meeting so late on a Saturday night. Based on Mr. Rickson's agitation this morning, the gathering may be crucial to his investigation."

I mulled over the possibility. "None of this explains why Rickson would be involved in a construction project or why Prushark contractors would be targeted."

"We'll have to watch our backs." Kevin's grifting background made him a diehard skeptic. He also had a point.

The fact that Rickson evidently underestimated the situation weighed on my mind. After all, the big guy had disappeared. Anybody who could take him down had to be dangerous and the more we dug, the dodgier it would get. "I'm going to get answers tonight if I have to nail somebody to the wall."

"I'll bring the hammer." Kevin winked, and the tension in the room eased. "Speaking of the meeting, it's getting late."

"I could go and snoop around while you guys are talking." Marcus's eyes lit up at the possibility.

"Absolutely not." I may have dragged him into this fiasco, but he was staying on the sidelines.

I try not to waste time on guilt. It's a useless emotion. Decide. Do it. Move on. But that logic didn't help this time.

If Marcus's social worker found out about this episode, I'd have a hard time defending myself. For that matter, if Marcus or Mrs. C got hurt, I'd have a hard time facing myself.

"You, Mrs. C, and Rabi are going to stay put," I ordered.

Rabi at least had the firepower and skills to keep the other two safe.

"T.R., we're a team." Marcus groused.

"The team needs information." I pointed to his tablet. "You're the internet whiz. Find out what you can about Monroe & Sons."

Kevin tapped him on the arm. "Look up the announcement of B & T, Inc. working for the Prusharks. When did it hit the presses? What details were included?"

Marcus's face took on a serious expression. He sat up straighter. "I'll have the dirt by the time you return. Get it? Contractors? Dirt?"

I rolled my eyes at the cheap pun.

"Crawford must have a file on this case." Kevin stood as he spoke. "Mrs. C, you remember Roxie from the Christmas party?"

"I never forget someone who dances on a table." The older woman sighed. "You don't see that much anymore."

"No, you really don't." I wanted to ask when it had ever been common for wild-eyed redheads to tap dance across six tables then conga on the bar, but, having been in the conga line, I kept my mouth shut.

Kevin didn't miss a beat. "Roust Roxie and get the goods on this job."

I pushed my chair away and stood. "Mrs. C, you also have a connection with the cops in Langsdale, right?"

"Oh, absolutely," she said. "A dear little man --"

"See if you can get in touch with him." I interrupted her reminiscences without regret. She tells great stories, but now was not the time. "Find out if the police have any details on why my car was impounded and who called in the complaint."

"Of course," she said.

"What about the shootout in ER?" Marcus asked. "Ferguson, the guy who chased Rickson, was arrested. We could get the lowdown on him, too."

"Good idea." My admiration was not feigned. "I forgot about him."

"I'll run a search on his arrest record," Marcus said.

Having a plan made me feel better.

Kevin tapped his watch. "Time for battle, General."

I didn't know if it was his cavalier attitude or his mere presence, but my load of fear lessened. I resisted the urge to pull him close and not let go.

Evidently having a romantic relationship has destroyed my focus.

Marcus fixed Kevin and me with a stern look. "You two be careful."

"We'll be fine." I filled my tone with all the confidence I could muster.

"Check in." Marcus parroted the words I always told him when he left to visit his friends.

"You got it," I said.

"Every half-hour." Marcus prompted.

He must really be worried. "I'll call when we hit the gates and before and after our conference."

The tension on my son's face eased slightly. "Maybe Rabi should go with you."

"Rabi stays here." My blood pressure spiked at the very thought. Leaving Mrs. C in charge of Marcus would be like letting the fox guard the chickens.

When Marcus's brow furrowed, I decided to be proactive before he could think of a rebuttal.

"Rabi wasn't invited," I said. "He stays."

Marcus wasn't one to give in without testing the limits, but on this point, I wouldn't budge.

Ten minutes later, Kevin's luxurious Caddy swept along the hotel's curving drive. Though I may mock the Great White Beast, that car is the most comfortable vehicle I've ever ridden in.

Don't tell Kevin or Marcus I admitted that.

Dressed in my usual meeting-with-clients outfit of a basic black dress with a matching jacket, I could pass for an up-and-coming businesswoman. Kevin would have looked good in frayed jeans and a dirty T-shirt. Instead, he set my heart tapping in a button-up shirt and a casual jacket. If Nancy had seen him, she'd have melted on the spot.

Kevin had worked up a rough calculation based on the dimensions of the ballroom. I'd studied the information enough to fake my way through a meeting. Now we had to get to the estate and meet these mysterious clients.

"I wish I'd let Marcus drill that box open when we had the chance," I admitted.

"I'm going to tell him you said so," Kevin warned.

Hiding a smile, I stirred restlessly in the seat. "Quinlan better fill in some of the blanks since she evidently wants us involved."

"I want to know how she got Rickson's notes." Kevin's tone turned serious. No matter what Crawford had signed on for, Kevin's priority would be on family and friends before solving the case.

In the following silence, my thoughts turned to more

mundane facts of life. "You think there's any way we'll wrap this up tomorrow?"

Kevin's baby blues slid in my direction. "Depends on how many more gunfights we get into this weekend."

"Don't say that." The very thought made me twitchy. I still expected Rickson to pop-up from somewhere as suddenly as he'd appeared at my apartment.

Kevin touched my arm with a reassuring warmth. "This is Rickson's case, not yours. We'll fake our way through the meeting and keep all eyes on us while Rickson finishes his game. He'll be in touch."

I tried to put my fears to rest. Talking about the meeting brought me back to the ballroom renovation. If only it were real. I sighed for the paycheck I wouldn't see.

With my full-time job gone, I needed to find a way to pay the rent. Heaven knows I'll never get rich by schmoozing people. Charm takes too much effort. "We need to put some serious effort into promoting our company when we get home."

"You must have ESP." Kevin shot me a serious look. "Godert caused trouble for me before. Now that he's ruling the roost, it'll get worse."

Before I had a chance to pursue that angle, the car slowed.

We'd reached the hills around Tahoe a short time ago. A stone wall, glowing pink in the fading sunlight, bordered the right side of the highway.

I realized we'd been driving beside it for a good distance. "Why are we slowing?"

Kevin glanced at me. "This is the estate."

A quick right turn brought us face-to-face with a pair of white metal gates, complete with ornate scrolls and an intricate family crest.

I craned my neck for one last glimpse of the highway. The wall, glowing pink in the setting sun, extended as far as the eye could see. "I've seen ranches in Kentucky smaller than this."

Kevin smiled at my stunned reaction. "I told you it was the size of a village."

He rolled down the window and spoke our names into a speaker embedded in a stone post. Security cameras mounted on the gate and perched atop the wall watched our every move. A moment later, the gates opened with majestic slowness.

Heading into this fortress reminded me of my promise to call Marcus. I hit the speed dial for my son. After Kevin rolled up the window, I gestured toward the cameras. "Somebody doesn't like unexpected company."

"I noticed."

Leaning back, I mentally urged Marcus to answer his phone As the gates closed behind us a sense of trepidation washed over me. I felt a childish yearning to be at the hotel.

Years of working with Crawford have taught me that the only thing harder than getting into a secure area… is getting out of it.

6

3 Across; 8 Letters;
Clue: Old, unsolved investigation
Answer: Cold case

The iron gates of the Prushark estate clanged shut behind the Caddy like a death knell. Uncharacteristic worry skittered up my spine as a third ring to Marcus's phone went unanswered. When his voice mail kicked in, I hung up and dialed Rabi.

"Trapped." Kevin drove along a wide, curved lane. His melodramatic tone contrasted with the amusement glittering in his gaze. "Too late to turn back. Our heroes were never seen again."

Annoyed he could read my mood so clearly, I sought for my usual bravado. By the time I had a comeback ready, the Caddy had rounded a corner and I was, for once, speechless.

To the left, a mammoth fountain adorned what seemed like an endless carpet of green. Manicured pines flanked the lawn and sculpted hedges framed the scene as perfectly as a painting. A stone turret peeked out over the evergreens.

The place could be the setting for a fairytale. Instead of a troop of elves to greet us, a man in khaki pants and a burgundy jacket drove a golf cart toward us at breakneck speed. When he drew close, he held up a hand, palm out.

Kevin raised a brow. "A rent-a-cop in a go-cart."

"Don't laugh," I warned through gritted teeth. "The man has a gun."

Not to mention an eagle eye. Concentrating on our approaching visitor, I was annoyed to hear Rabi's voicemail message. Why was no one answering?

"Where are you guys?" Irritation bled through my tone. "We're on the estate. Call me when you get this."

The security guard's assessing gaze studied us through the windshield. Deep lines in his craggy face almost concealed a network of scars on his right cheek and chin. He turned the golf cart around and pulled up next to the driver's door.

He fixed each of us with a measuring look that reminded me of Rabi. "Tanner? Belden?"

Good guess since we'd said as much at the front gate. I held in the comment and nodded.

"That's right." Kevin kept his voice business-like.

"Follow me." Without another word, the golf-cart man sped away.

"We goin' to the big house." Kevin kept the car a few lengths behind. "Good thing they sent an escort. These straightaways confuse me."

Since the drive had no turnoffs, even I couldn't have gotten lost. "I wonder if they're expecting trouble or if they're always this paranoid."

"The guy checked us out like an ex-cop," Kevin said.

"Ex-military." It shot out before I thought.

He glanced sideways. "What makes you so sure?"

"His bearing reminds me of my career-military cousins." Or maybe the buzz cut gave him away. Either way, it fit.

"There's the pool house and tennis courts." Kevin pointed toward a gravel path in the distance. "How could Rickson get close enough to track anybody in here for adultery?"

"I doubt they committed the deed on the estate."

Kevin's brow furrowed. "Did I hear you leave a message?"

My jaw tensed. "No answer from Marcus or Rabi."

His frown deepened. "Marcus should have jumped on the phone."

I rubbed my forehead. "Maybe something's interfering with the signal on the other end. I'll call the front desk and have them connect me to the room."

Just then the drive curved around to reveal a stone mansion, complete with leaded windows. The façade gleamed with a rosy hue in the fading sun. A cobblestone drive led to a set of dazzling white steps.

Kevin whistled softly. "That tower is five stories high."

I tried to keep my jaw from dropping but it wasn't easy. "I've seen museums smaller than this place."

Kevin stopped the Caddy in front of the steps.

A valet in the same burgundy/khaki combo as our escort opened my door before I could touch it. "Welcome, Ms. Belden."

With a firm grip on my briefcase, I stepped out of the car. Contacting Rabi would have to wait.

A third man appeared at the driver's door. "I'll park your vehicle, sir."

Kevin double-clutched the car keys before he slowly deposited the key-ring in the other man's palm.

As the valet got in the Caddy, I caught a well-concealed grimace in my buddy's eyes. I hid a smile. The sacrifices we make.

"Sir, Ma'am, if you'd come this way?" My escort, the only man left, gestured to the door at the top of the stairs.

A moment later, we walked into the main foyer. A polished marble floor reflected the gleaming lights of a crystal chandelier.

A dusky-skinned woman, dark hair drawn up, glided toward us with an air of majesty. Her eyes, a mesmerizing mix of brown mixed with gold, filled her narrow face. As she held out her hand, childish laughter and the quick patter of running feet froze her in mid-gesture.

A small boy ran toward the front door like a rocket clad in blue jeans and a red shirt. His solid build carried the promise of a broad frame as he grew. The way he lit up the hall with light and motion reminded me of Marcus, full of boyish enthusiasm.

"Benjamin Jonathan Prushark, stop right now." The softer sound of running feet brought an out-of-breath, thirty-something woman into view. When the boy skidded to a stop before a couple of smiling staff standing shoulder-to-shoulder, she slowed to a walk.

The child's dark sandy hair was as straight and thick as wheat stalks growing in a summer field. His green eyes met hers with a pleading look. "Outside, Mommy."

After a nod of thanks to the staff who'd blocked his escape, the young mother bent to his level. Her triangular shaped face and silver blond curls leveled off next to his square jaw. Her stern expression softened to a smile. "After you finish lunch and pick up your toys, we can go outside. Not before."

She held out her hand. After a glance at the door, he linked his chubby fingers with hers. She shot a look of apology our way as the two disappeared into the hall.

The woman who'd greeted us, shrugged in apology as well. Dismissing our escort, her gaze shifted to Kevin and me. "Sorry for the interruption. I'm Victoria Quinlan. Thank you so much for coming."

I grasped the slender hand she held out. "Tracy Belden. This is my partner, Kevin Tanner."

Kevin's expression was a polite mask. "Ms. Quinlan."

After shaking his hand, she stepped back. "I hope your accommodations at the hotel are adequate."

Concern sounded in her voice as if our happiness was all that mattered. Where would she move us if we were unhappy? The Taj Mahal?

"They're beautiful. Thank you." Already impatient for answers, I felt my poker face slip.

Quinlan, evidently reading my mood, gestured toward a hall. "Why don't we go to my office? We have time before we meet the others."

When she turned to lead the way, Kevin leaned close to me. "She could seduce a monk."

I gave a quick nod. If this case involved adultery, she could be the source of the trouble.

Before Quinlan reached the mouth of the corridor, footsteps sounded behind us. Heavy, strong steps that seemed to ring with an air of determination.

"Victoria, a moment." A commanding voice filled the two-story atrium. "Matt and I finished speaking with Todd. I'd like to go to the office. What about this late meeting? Is it happening?"

Quinlan turned with an easy grace.

Kevin and I faced the newcomer as well.

Two men strode forward, stopping within arm's reach of us. The older man, with gray overtaking mud brown hair, had the pugnacious look and lined face of the horse ranchers and farmers of my Kentucky-bred youth. Self-made men who'd grasped their chances with both hands and made their own success.

The other man was a generation younger and slightly taller. The same determined expression was mellowed by the benefit of being the second generation. His build was much like his father's, square and solid, but not yet running to fat.

This had to be Monroe and son.

"Pete and Matt Monroe." Quinlan gestured toward the two men then waved her hand toward Kevin and me. "Let me introduce our guests for this evening's meeting: Tracy Belden and Kevin Tanner."

The older man's scowl didn't change. His gaze shifted past me. He locked onto Kevin, then squared off to confront my guy.

Unwilling to be ignored, I thrust first myself, then my hand forward. "Tracy Belden. My partner and I are looking forward to working with you."

Pete, the older man, hesitated for a blink of an eye before grasping my hand in a tight, no-nonsense grip. The bone-grinding pressure was there and gone by the time my brain registered the pain. "You being here is a waste of time. I could have finished the renovation by now."

During Pete's unyielding judgment of the publicity stunt, Kevin, Matt, and I exchanged handshakes and greetings.

Pete's scowl deepened. "Victoria, call the others. Let's do this now. I gave up my office time tonight to be here. I should be there working. Call the others."

"Todd and Sheila appreciate you sacrificing your routine for this late meeting." Quinlan's sympathetic tone made no obvious impact on the man's frown. "This was the one time that worked for everyone."

Admiration infused Kevin's expression. "You work late every evening?"

"Every day but Sunday. Everyone else is gone. I got the place to myself." The self-made man pointed a finger at my guy. "List the projects. Find the materials. Organize and execute."

"That's the way my grandmother built our family business." Kevin's admiring tone gave no hint that their family's enterprise was million-dollar con games.

Just like that I knew where Rickson was and why we had to be at this late meeting. I mentally congratulated Kevin on picking up on the older Monroe's habits. What I didn't know was why the big guy couldn't have found thirty seconds to text me.

Matt clapped his father on the shoulder. "Dad's determination built the company. His never-die attitude keeps us going."

So why was the Prushark company a partial owner of Monroe & Sons Construction if Pete stayed on top of the jobs so diligently? The proud man didn't seem like the type to let go of his creation. Perhaps Marcus's research would answer that question.

"Zach?" Quinlan's summons prompted one of the young men to step forward. "Would you escort Pete and Matt to the second-floor conference room? There are drinks and appetizers set out. Mrs. Prushark should be there shortly."

Pete did not go quietly, but eventually, he did go.

Quinlan began our aborted departure a third time. This time we made it to the far end of the corridor where she glided through a doorway. By the time we entered, she was seated behind a deceptively simple cherrywood desk. "Please, sit."

Outside the double windows that framed her, daylight began to fade to twilight shadows. The tops of the mountains gleamed dazzling white in the dying sunlight.

I tossed my briefcase on one of the leather chairs. I was done with polite. "Where's Rickson?"

The perfect mask creased. "I hoped you knew."

I schooled my expression to give nothing away. I was flying blind. How much had Rickson told her of his plan?

"When did you see him last?" Kevin's gaze remained on the Business Manager as he walked by an antique globe on a three-foot-tall pedestal. With a quick touch, he sent the globe spinning on its axis. "How did you get his notes?"

Her expression tightened. Smoothing her perfectly coiffed hair, Quinlan took a second to regain her composure.

"He was in the gatehouse at one-thirty this afternoon. He said Tracy and you would attend the meeting tonight. The man was scribbling and talking. It was rather jumbled." She put a hand to her forehead as if trying to make sense of Rickson's scheme gave her a headache.

I knew the feeling. When Rickson gets caught up in his strategies, he tends to leave out every third word-- kind of like his notes.

"We had just finished discussing tonight's meeting when we heard gunshots from the direction of the greenhouse." Quinlan gestured to her left. "I told him to let the guards handle it. Then Rickson remembered seeing Ben in that area. He ran off before I could stop him. I haven't seen him since."

My gaze strayed to the mountains. Slate gray shadows inched across the snow-tipped peaks. The disappearance of the light seemed to match this case as it descended into a morass. "Ben was obviously unhurt."

"Thank, God. He's four-years-old. The Prushark's only grandson." Quinlan gestured toward the foyer. "His mother, Linda, was married to their youngest son."

A child in danger and Rickson takes off without thinking. That was the big guy all over. With the boy's cheeky grin and infectious laughter dancing in my memory, I could hardly blame him.

Kevin's gaze narrowed. "Was anyone hurt?"

"No, the guards fired at an intruder." Quinlan delivered her answers in a quick, concise manner. "He got away."

I cringed at yet another shooting. She seemed to take the gunfire in stride. "Do you have intruders on the estate often?"

"Never." Quinlan clipped off the word, seemingly oblivious to the dichotomy between her claim and the facts. "Girard, our security chief who escorted you up the drive, is investigating how he got on the grounds."

Translation: they have no idea.

"Did anyone see where Rickson went?" I asked, hoping for some illumination.

"The man's hard to miss." Her lips quirked up in a brief smile. "The guards observed him chasing the intruder. They didn't catch either of them. It makes me wonder why we pay them such exorbitant salaries."

"Don't blame them too much," I said. "I've tried to nail him down for two days, and he slips away every time."

"Any idea of the intruder's identity?" Kevin's fingers walked along the globe's equator. "Or the motive for the break-in?"

A haunted look gleamed in Quinlan's eyes before she lowered her gaze. She straightened an already neat pile of folders. When she looked up, her regal mask was firmly in place. "From the description, it was David Ferguson."

The redheaded man from last night. "Fiftyish. Wiry build. Red hair."

"That's him." The other woman's eyes widened. "Where did you see him?"

"He chased Rickson through the ER last night at gunpoint." The daylight outside had given way to night as inevitably as fall gives way to winter. Nineteen hours ago, I only had Marcus's cut hand to worry about, now questions and chaos surrounded me.

Kevin glanced at the door. "When are the others expecting us?"

"Seven-thirty," Quinlan said. "Rickson chose the time, which worked out for the best. Mrs. Prushark had appointments off the estate earlier today. I had you come early so I could explain."

"So, explain." I was past my patience quota for the day.

Between the disappearing daylight and Kevin's fingers walking from Asia to Africa, the omens against this case were building.

"Tell me why an out-of-towner like Crawford was hired." Kevin's business-like tone was far from threatening, but the hint of steel made it clear he wouldn't be put off. He spread his hand on the antique world, stopping all motion.

I stepped within arm's reach of the woman in case she bolted. I'd been this close to Rickson twice in two days and all I had for my trouble was a basket full of questions.

"Crawford was hired *because* he's an out-of-towner. The family couldn't risk details leaking out." A haunted look gleamed in Quinlan's eyes only to be quickly hidden. "Mr. Prushark knew of Crawford's discretion from cases he worked on the Lake Tahoe police force, years ago. Once I confirmed Crawford reputation, I contacted him about our… issue."

"Scandal among the rich and famous," Kevin uttered the words as if reading a headline. His fingers tapped along the Nile River. "Juicy gossip even in Tahoe."

"What was Crawford hired to investigate?" A terse note sounded in my voice. Insight was all well and good, but I wanted answers.

"Adultery." Quinlan spat out the word with none of the hesitation people usually reserve for it. "Several weeks ago, Mrs. Prushark received a letter that stated Linda had an affair. It claimed Ben isn't her husband's child."

So, Rickson was hired to check out a cheating spouse. Was Linda in love with Matt Monroe perhaps? "Does her husband know?"

Quinlan tensed for a heartbeat. "He died two years ago."

"Of course, he did." I took the news without flinching. What could I say at hearing one more outlandish twist?

Kevin's raised brow was the only sign the bizarre announcement had broken through his con man training.

"The Prusharks had three children." Quinlan spoke in an unruffled tone. "Todd, the oldest, is forty-four. He married last year but he and his wife have no children so far. Sheila, the daughter, is thirty-eight. She was married once in her twenties, but the union was childless. Since then, she's dedicated herself to her career. Paul, the youngest, and his wife, Linda, had Ben a few years before Paul died in a car accident."

"The only heir so far." The size of the fortune that had built and maintained this estate staggered even my wild imagination. Four-year-old Ben, the poor little rich boy, faced the future burdened with inheriting it. Hopefully, he'd have siblings or cousins someday. For now, the urgency to investigate a long-ago affair didn't make sense.

"At least, he won't have to share." Kevin's words brought me to the present.

"You see why we had to keep this hush-hush." Quinlan broke into the frivolous aside.

"Wait a minute." I held up my hand to forestall further info dumps. "This whole affai-- problem boils down to whether Ben is actually his father's son."

Quinlan gave a short nod.

"Have you people heard of DNA testing?" My impatience was about to boil over. The solution was obvious and incredibly simple. "It should be easy to confirm whether he's a Prushark."

"The thing is... " Quinlan's lips kept moving but the sound had stopped, like a lip sync where the recording fails in mid-song. Then she pressed her lips together and a look of compassion filled her eyes. For once, she looked like a real person. "Mr. and Mrs. Prushark don't want to know. Mr. Prushark never wanted to pursue the issue. He only suggested Crawford when his wife insisted."

Quinlan's announcement took me by surprise. Marcus's face popped into my mind. I realized that, despite the money-filled chasm that separated us, the Prushark's situation was similar to mine. It didn't matter to me that Marcus and I had not one blood cell in common or that he looked nothing like my ancestors or me. I couldn't love him more.

In a kind of reverse snobbery, part of me had counted their wealth against the Prusharks. I'd cast them as heartless villains.

Sometimes it's nice to be wrong.

Quinlan smiled softly. "Ben is the child of their dreams. He is their grandson. No matter what."

Kevin sauntered past the globe. His fingers trailed against the spines of the books lined on the shelf. "Then why hire someone to prove adultery?"

"They don't want to prove it. The goal is to protect Ben and the family from any hint of scandal without conceding to the threats." Quinlan put her hands out as if to stop Kevin and me from running off in a mad dash and doing that very thing. "Mrs. Prushark has gone to great lengths over the years to keep the family name out of the tabloids. Crawford was hired to find any evidence of adultery and destroy it."

Here was a new twist on an old story. Almost against my will, determination filled me to help the people who'd gone to such lengths to protect the smiling little boy in the hall.

Kevin also had no gibes.

Quinlan continued. "The letter threatened to publish

evidence of the affair, presumably incriminating pictures, unless Mrs. Prushark used her money and influence to get a specific candidate elected to the state legislature. The candidate is opposed to everything the family supports. It said further instructions would arrive. A second message followed three weeks later. It instructed Mrs. Prushark to prove herself by arranging a fundraising dinner for the middle of November."

"A politically motivated blackmailer?" Kevin thrummed his fingers of the globe. "That's a change from the usual greed."

"I'd have asked for a cool five million to be wired to a secret account in the Cayman Islands." But that's just me.

Quinlan aligned two pens laying on her desk. The woman either had a neatness compulsion or her nerves were feeling the strain. "Rickson was introduced as a security expert, hired to complete an outside audit of our construction division, Monroe & Son Construction."

Another contractor connection. "Why would that be necessary?"

"There were some losses last year," Quinlan admitted, shifting her eyes to one side. "It's been handled, but it was a convenient cover."

I seized the opening, slim though it was, to find out about the Monroe connection. "How did the Prushark company come to be majority owners of Monroe & Son Construction?"

Quinlan's expression closed in on itself. She straightened the folders on her desk without looking at them. After several seconds, she heaved a sigh. "A month prior to his stroke, Mr. Prushark gained majority control of the Monroe company due to a technicality in a loan contract. There was ill-feeling on the part of the Monroes. Todd has been negotiating with Pete and Matt to allow repayment and return majority control to the Monroes."

Kevin touched the globe and stopped it instantly. "Why would a businessman return a valuable property if he didn't have to?"

"Perhaps because he grew up with Matt Monroe." Quinlan's expression softened. "Todd didn't agree with his father's shady maneuver. Nor did his wife, Jordan Monroe, Pete's only daughter"

Kevin shot me a sideways glance. "A determined woman is a strong motivator."

I hid a smile at his comment. My interest meter shot straight to the red zone. "What did Mr. Prushark think of his son's decision?"

Quinlan's neutral mask descended with the finality of a play's final curtain. "Let's return the case. We've gotten off-track."

I wasn't sure we were off-track, but I had the answer I needed. The old man would never let the majority interest revert if he had his way.

Quinlan folded her hands on her desk. "Sheila and Todd discussed using the ballroom renovation to publicize the charity aspect of the Winter Fest; female-owned businesses. When Rickson told me that you worked for Crawford and that he needed you here tonight, I sent out a press release stating you had been hired."

Which most likely got my car towed.

"The letters are extortion. Rickson would have suggested bringing in the police, which, I'm assuming, was rejected." When Quinlan nodded, I paced the short distance between the two leather chairs. That would explain Rickson's note about Crawford's old crew.

Kevin walked to the window, glancing out as if distracted. "Where does Ferguson fit in?"

A look of surprise skittered across Quinlan's face, before her mask slipped into place again.

I smiled to myself. She wasn't the first person to underestimate him because of his good looks and youthful appearance. Since I did a lot of the talking, his insightful questions surprise people all the more.

When Quinlan hesitated, I figured she needed a prompt. "Ben doesn't have red hair. So, I know that's not the problem."

"Of course not." An angry flush flooded her neck. "Though he has his mother's blond hair, rather than black like his father, Ben's square face and green eyes are classic Prushark traits."

If she thought her imperial manner would intimidate me, she was mistaken. "Then how is Ferguson involved?"

Her lips pursed together in a thin line. "He worked for Monroe & Sons. He did several jobs on the estate five years ago when the affair allegedly took place. A few months ago, when thefts in the construction accounts led to Ferguson, Sheila fired him."

I exchanged a puzzled glance with Kevin. "When was he charged? Was he convicted?"

Quinlan met my gaze with a cool look. "The Prusharks preferred to keep the matter quiet. No outside inquiry was involved."

"You let a thief walk away?" I fisted my hands in frustration. "Is the evidence not strong enough? Investigating crimes is what the police do. They're good at it."

The other woman faced me directly. "The evidence is rock solid, though he swore he was framed."

I waited for more. I didn't get it. She sat with her hands on the desktop. I wasn't about to move on when I couldn't fill in the blanks for my mental crossword puzzle. The Prusharks had no reason to keep the thefts a secret.

"He did something the company could be held accountable for. That's why you don't want publicity, to limit your liability." Kevin, who'd been pacing like a trapped panther, spun on his heel. "He swapped expensive material and equipment for cheap substitutes. He either sold the equipment or pocketed the money. It's particularly dangerous with wiring and load-bearing materials."

Quinlan's eyes widened in surprise.

I felt a rush of satisfaction that my guy had scored a direct hit.

The other woman held up a hand. "The fraudulent material has been traced. Repairs have been made. Forget the construction angle. Ferguson's role is related to timing. We received the first threatening letter three weeks after he was let go. Since then, he's repeatedly attempted to sneak onto the estate."

I mulled over the latest revelation. The puzzle was taking form but the pieces didn't fit. "Why would he throw away his chance for a big score on a political candidate? And why is he trying to sneak onto the estate?"

For the yellow box? Rickson said Ferguson stole it first. Then Ferguson realized Rickson took it and trailed him to Langsdale.

Kevin sauntered by the globe without a glance. His fingers snapped a quick beat at this side. A sign his brain was busy as well. "Ferguson came sniffing around after the first letter?"

"He has to be behind these threats." Quinlan's face flushed an angry – and unattractive - purple. "No one outside of myself and Mr. and Mrs. Prushark knows about this issue."

Kevin snorted. "If I had a dime for every time I've heard that, I wouldn't have to work."

"Mrs. Prushark counts on me to safeguard the family's privacy. It was my duty to keep this quiet." The words rushed out in a hard tone. She aimed a laser-like glare at me. "This has to end. You have to resolve this issue."

Her strident attitude put my back and roused my curiosity. "Who is pushing for a quick fix?"

She pressed her lips together, but when the silence lengthened, she caved. "Mr. Prushark never wanted to hire a PI. When his wife refused to back down, he insisted on Crawford. At the last meeting with Rickson, Mr. Prushark demanded Crawford's agency be dismissed. He swore Ben was his grandson and no one would ever prove otherwise. He wants to face down the blackmailer."

Despite what the hotel staff had said of the old man's chauvinist attitude, part of me admired his devotion to the little boy. However, the only way to help the family would be to solve the case. "How do you receive the threats?"

"In the mail. Manila envelopes with a printed address label. Addressed to Mrs. Prushark." The woman straightened her shoulders.

"What is Ben's blood type?" I asked. That alone might eliminate Paul Prushark as the boy's natural father.

"The same as his mother and father -- O positive," Quinlan answered in a distracted manner. "It's the most common type."

"That doesn't help." The only way to know for sure would be the more detailed test. I blinked in surprise as the implications hit me.

"What are you thinking, Belden?" Kevin stopped in the center of the room. "I know that look. All your gears and switches are flipping inside that fast-thinking brain."

Lost in thought, I didn't respond immediately. "Ben was conceived and born while Paul was alive. If Ben has his mother's blood type, there's no way anyone can know who his father is without full DNA testing."

A dawning awareness lit Kevin's expression. "What inspired the threats? Why now?"

"This is getting us nowhere." Quinlan slapped her hands on the desk. "Rickson knows the answers. He said a solution was at hand. You need to contact him, discover who's behind these letters, and put an end to the threats."

"Is that all? I'll get right on it." I smoothed down my blazer and swallowed my impatience. My gaze wandered to the blackness outside the window. High on the peak, a handful of lights were strung out in a jagged line that seemed random as this case. "Do you know what Rickson found? What leads he followed?"

"He visited Monroe & Sons." Quinlan's gaze flicked to mine then away as if deciding whether to continue. "He insisted on a list of building contracts for the past five years. He questioned the staff extensively. He seemed to pursue several odd tangents in his interviews."

Odd described a lot of Rickson's methods, but the man had rarely left open cases, either as a police detective or a private investigator. "When did he give his last report?"

"Wednesday morning." Quinlan's gaze shifted to the right and down, a sign of searching for a memory, before focusing on me. "Rickson and Mrs. Prushark met alone. Mr. Prushark was in therapy and I had a delivery crisis."

"Did you read his notes?" I asked.

"I glanced at them." The other woman's hesitation smacked of guilt. "They don't make a lot of sense."

My suspicious meter dropped out of the red zone. I couldn't argue with Quinlan's assessment. "What's with the guard and the injured dog? No dogs allowed?"

"I don't know where he got the information or why he cared." Quinlan pinned me with an accusatory look as if blaming me for Rickson's unorthodox methods. "He reported that one of the Monroe managers took his dog to the animal hospital. Rickson obviously misunderstood."

"I'm confused." Not for the first time. "Why do you believe he misunderstood?"

The other woman gave me a pointed look. "Mr. Prushark is severely allergic to dogs. Anyone who is regularly on the estate—which includes the Monroe managers—is aware of this, and they are forbidden to own a dog. So, Rickson was wrong."

About what he heard? About how to read a suspect? After a thirty-year history of investigating?

I don't think so.

Before I could say anything, the door was flung open. Caught off guard, Quinlan and I jumped at the same time.

"Sheila." The woman's professional mask fell into place, covering her thoughts like ivy on a stone wall. "I thought we'd join you in the conference room."

Pasting on a business-like expression, I turned to face the sole Prushark daughter.

She was shorter than me by several inches. Five-four, without the three-inch stilettos. She had a curvy, medium build. Square face. Green eyes. A long black braid draped over one shoulder. The classic Prushark looks sat well on her. Her gray, tailored skirt and jacket were offset by a deep red top. Every inch the executive.

She strode into the room, accompanied by the aura of a tightly coiled dynamo. Her gaze skimmed over Kevin then me with a quick assessing measure. Her red lips softened ever so slightly. "I was under the impression you were to bring our construction consultants directly to the conference room. Did I miss a memo?"

Ohhhh, Prushark scores on a quick jab to the ribs.

Quinlan stood. With heels, she was close to my height. She topped Sheila by half-a-head but she was clearly outmatched. "I was filling them in on the timeline for the renovation."

I was careful not to so much as glance at Kevin after Quinlan's comment. Sheila might not be clued in on our true mission, but not much would get past her.

Sheila stopped at a point where she could keep the three of us in view. "The renovation is our agenda for the meeting."

I stifled a groan. I thought I'd left agendas behind when I parted company with the corporate world, which was when I met Kevin. Clearing him of murder cost me my job and gained me the man I love. I've never looked back.

Was Sheila the one in charge of the construction division? Taking the bull by the horns, I stepped forward, hand outstretched. "I'm Tracy Belden of B & T, Inc. This is my partner, Kevin Tanner. We're thrilled at the opportunity to work on this project."

Sheila would expect an up-and-coming construction firm to butter her up. Her handshake was firm and business-like.

Kevin stepped forward. Turning up his charm, he zeroed in on Sheila like he was a moth and she was the only light in the room. "It's a pleasure to meet you, Ms. Prushark. I'm eager to work on this project."

The business woman's expression softened. Her gaze lingered on Kevin for a brief but telling heartbeat. With a final shake, she released his hand. "I'm happy to meet you both. I'll be interested to hear your presentation."

The polite tone held an inarguable dismissal.

Sheila turned to Quinlan, whose posture reminded me of a private facing a drill sergeant. "Victoria and I have a few things to discuss. Do excuse us."

Quinlan smoothed her jacket. Any hint of her previous uncertainty vanished. "I'll return for you shortly."

As the two women walked toward the door, Sheila glanced over her shoulder. "I hope the presentation lives up to your recommendation. My mother took it upon herself to announce you had been hired. My vetting would have been much more thorough."

She slid the jab in adroitly, making no attempt to hide her irritation at being outmaneuvered. Then, turning on her heel, she glided out of the room.

As the door shut behind them, Kevin's shoulders tensed. "Companies always use the same hotel for visitors. Anyone who knows the Prusharks would know to watch the Pine Trail Inn for our arrival."

A cement block took up residence in my gut. "Whoever's behind this could have been waiting for us to leave."

My unanswered phone calls to Marcus and Rabi suddenly vaulted from worrisome to ominous.

7

4 Down; 9 Letters;
Clue: Unknowns; Not acquainted
Answer: Strangers

"Don't panic." My attempt at comfort was more for me than Kevin. I fished my phone out of my purse with shaking hands. "We could be blowing this connection all out of proportion."

His gaze zeroed in on my phone. "What makes you think Marcus will answer now?"

"I'm calling the front desk."

"You know the number?" Despite the circumstances and our long relationship, his voice held the same disbelief mine did when he navigated through a new city.

I shrugged. Numbers came as naturally to me as directions do to him. My heart thudded in my chest almost drowning out the phone ringing in my ear. How could I have been so complacent? So naive? So–

"Pine Trail Inn, how may I help you?" Nancy's greeting interrupted my self-recriminations.

"This is Tracy Belden," I said. "Would you connect me to my suite?"

"Of course. Please hold."

A moment later the suite phone started ringing in my ear. With each shrill buzzing, my fear escalated.

Kevin never took his gaze off my face. Evidently seeing the worry in my expression, he crossed to me in a single stride. His arm settled around my shoulders, pulling me close. I rested against him, feeling his heartbeat. When I put the phone on speaker, his breath fanned my cheek.

His nearness brought on a flashback to the early months of getting to know Marcus. Kevin had played an integral part in earning the boy's trust. The three of us had been through so much in the months and years since then. Step-by-step, we'd walked the journey together.

Nancy's voice broke in after the fourth ring, interrupting my rambling thoughts.

"There's no answer." However, Nancy didn't pause. "They may have gone out with your other workers."

I felt the blood drain from my face. A lump of ice settled in my chest as I met Kevin's stunned gaze.

"Ms. Belden?" Nancy asked. "Did you hear me?"

Her voice jump-started my brain. "You mentioned the other workers arrived."

"You and Mr. Tanner only missed them by minutes." Nancy's lilting voice prattled on, evidently without a care in the world. "They stopped at the front desk to get the suite numbers."

She sounded like I'd failed in not keeping them fully informed. But how could I, since I hadn't known other workers existed?

"They were on the elevator before I thought to tell them

the rest of your party was in the suite." Her voice picked up speed. "I called your assistant to remind her that the late arrivals could still order from the restaurants. Mr. Schmidt is very clear we should offer late guests full service."

Kevin raised both fists in the air before pulling me close. The tension in his face eased.

"Thank God for full service." Breath whooshed into my lungs. They'd been warned. My thoughts centered on the words like a prisoner focused on the governor's pardon.

Between Rabi's Special Ops, Marcus's street smarts, and Mrs. C's-- all right, I didn't have a clue about her background: British spy, Cold War mole, whatever. She would have held up her end of an escape.

God save the Queen. They'd been warned.

I collected myself enough to remember Nancy. "Do you know if anyone called for room service?"

"No." A disappointed tone sounded in her voice. "As soon as I told Mrs. Colchester the crew was on the way, she hung up. I didn't see any of them leave, but since no one is answering, perhaps they went out together."

Let's hope not.

"Do you want to leave a message?" she asked.

"Sure." The answer came automatically as I fought to hold onto my new mantra. They'd gotten away. They had to have gotten away. "Have them call me."

"Certainly." Nancy's perkiness increased at being given a task. "Will there be anything else?"

When I shook my head, Kevin nudged my arm. He gestured to his face, staring at me with an intense gaze. "Nancy, this is Mr. Tanner. Did all six of the workers come? We need to pay them for their travel."

I gave him a thumb's up. Good thing one of us was thinking clearly.

"Two men came to the desk," Nancy said. "I can ask the doorman if anyone waited in the car."

"That would be a help," Kevin said.

Instrumental music sounded from my phone. I rubbed a hand over my forehead. "How long have we been gone?"

"An hour." His words were clipped. Nervous energy built around him like a racehorse waiting to bolt out of the starting gate. "We're leaving."

The music stopped abruptly, so I just nodded.

"Mr. Tanner?" Nancy's voice piped into Quinlan's office. "Only two men arrived. Also, their car is gone."

I had a sudden need to end this conversation. I wanted to be at the hotel. I wanted to see Marcus and the others safe and sound.

"Could you do one thing for me?" I asked hurriedly. "Would you write a description of the two who came? So, there's no confusion when I contact the others."

"Su-ure." The young woman drew out the word, the ingrained habit of "the-customer-is-always-right" evidently warring with "what is this woman thinking"? "I'll do it now. It's slow anyway."

"Thank you so much." I clicked off.

Kevin shoved my briefcase and purse at me. "Forget the meeting."

I grabbed my stuff and hurried to the door. As I reached for the knob the door swung in, barely missing me.

A thirty-something security guard filled the doorway. He rocked on his heels at my unexpected nearness. After a heartbeat, he broke the silence. "Ms. Quinlan regrets there's been a delay. She asked you to wait here."

My jaw tightened at his words.

Kevin stepped forward until he stood toe-to-toe with the guard. "We're leaving."

The man's expression could have been carved from stone. "You can't."

Kevin's hands clenched into fists. "Got out of my way."

Rarely heard anger filled his voice.

The guard stood like a block of concrete.

I thrust myself between them.

"My son is in trouble. He isn't answering his phone." I didn't have to fake the desperate note in my voice. "I'll call Ms. Quinlan as soon as I can, but my partner and I can't stay for the meeting."

The man didn't budge. "He's ignoring you or he's in a dead zone. You're not leaving."

I gathered myself to step aside and let Kevin have him.

"Mr. Henry Prushark is dead." The guard uttered the statement in a solemn tone. "The police are on their way."

"Dead?" Shock coursed through me. I opened my mouth for a get-out-of-jail-free comeback, but my mind had gone blank.

Kevin was still balanced on the balls of his feet. Ready for the bell to start the boxing match. Fists clenched, he eyed the other man.

The guard set his feet. They looked ready to slug it out despite knowing it would serve no purpose. Maybe just to pass the time so they wouldn't waste a good buildup. With men, who knew?

The possibility of a fight brought me to my senses. With the patriarch dead, the family could hardly allow two strangers to waltz off into the night. Even if they did, the cops would come after us with sirens blazing.

My shoulders slumped. My gut felt like lead. In my heart, I knew that whatever happened with Marcus, Rabi, and Mrs. C was past the stage where Kevin and I could ride to the rescue. I put a hand on Kevin's arm. His muscles were tight beneath my touch.

"We have to go." He spoke without interrupting his stare down.

I hated to admit defeat, but facts were facts. A dead body trumped an hour old crisis. With Marcus's face swimming in my mind, I forced out the words that would make a bad situation worse. "We're not going anywhere."

The guard gave a nod and took up a position with his back to the closed door.

Kevin's jaw hardened in a stubborn line. He wanted nothing more than to race to the rescue of the boy who'd captured both of our hearts. Instead, Kevin slowly unclenched his fists and allowed me to pull him away. "We can't sit here."

I shared the sentiment. With my hand clinging to Kevin's arm like a lifeline, I pulled him toward the window and lowered my voice. "Making a run for the car sounds good. Except, I have no idea where the Caddy is parked and we don't have the keys."

Kevin slowly released his pent-up breath through clenched teeth. "So much for Plan A."

"They were warned." I repeated the words I'd been focusing on since speaking with Nancy. "Rabi would've gotten them out."

Even if he had to cover their exit with whatever he had in his shoulder holster. I don't know who I was trying to reassure more, Kevin or myself, but my words brought forth a mental image of a gunfight in the hotel corridor with Marcus ducking bullets.

I froze in my tracks. "What am I doing bringing a child into a case without the slightest clue of what is involved? What if something happened to Marcus?"

"It's impossible to corral those three." Kevin put his arm around my shoulders, taking his turn at comfort. "I don't want to think about what Mrs. Colchester could contrive with a bit of yarn and thirty seconds of warning."

Despite the circumstances, his words prompted a rueful smile that quickly faded. I wished my worry would vanish as easily. "Could the men at the hotel and the timing of Prushark's death be a coincidence?"

We stopped in our tracks. Considering the family history of power struggles, the odds of the old man having a heart attack would be astronomical.

Kevin cast me a sideways glance. "You know what Crawford says about coincidences."

The security guard stood in front of the closed door with the precision of a marine. Girard evidently ran a tight ship. Yet the security chief had a dead body on his hands, and not just any dead body.

Curiosity reared its ever-inquisitive head. My brain considered the clues, questions, and connections. My mental crossword puzzle shifted A new one took shape. But my heart couldn't forget the image of Marcus in danger.

Perhaps I could work both angles to my advantage. Fueled by desperation, I let a few quick steps carry me to the door.

"I'm sorry about Mr. Prushark, but you have to know we had nothing to do with his death." I spoke in a measured tone. I'm no good at faking tears and my sorrowful expressions look like scowls, which pisses people off. Fortunately, Kevin and I make an excellent "good-cop-bad-cop" duo.

The guard stared at me like an elephant would eye a gnat.

"We've only been on the grounds for half-an-hour," I said. "Until ten minutes ago, we were with Quinlan and Sheila."

Kevin stepped closer, oozing sincerity. When he turned on the charm, he could convince angels not to fly. "Your security records will confirm our story. How could we be involved with the old man dying of a heart attack?"

The guard's brow furrowed. "He didn't have a heart attack."

"How do you know?" Kevin's tone flipped from sympathetic to antagonistic. "Are you a doctor in your spare time?"

The guard's jaw tightened. "Mr. Prushark was found at the bottom of the rear staircase."

"That proves my point," Kevin retorted. "He had a heart attack on the stairs. He fell and died."

"You don't know anything," the guard scoffed. "The old man was wheelchair bound since his stroke."

Stunned silence followed his comeback.

The guard's face went slack. Regret. Worry. Fear chased each other across the man's face. He'd said too much and realized the fact too late.

Kevin's eyes mirrored the same realization I'd had.

The old man's death resulted from neither illness nor accident. It was murder.

The guard's jaw tightened. "I'll be outside. Don't try anything."

As soon as he left Kevin and I walked toward the desk. I eyed the comfortable leather chairs, but I wouldn't be able to stay seated. "Prushark's murder raises the stakes by a few hundred million."

"At least, the cops should get here quick." Kevin strode to the window with its false promise of freedom. "Being rich and famous earns first-rate service."

"What happened to their elaborate security?" I asked.

Kevin cast me a sideways glance. "It's designed to protect the family from people *outside* the gates, not blood kin."

His words reminded me of the tangled family squabbles. I stared at the shadows outside, unable to erase the image of Marcus eluding armed men. Who had sent the men and why? I gripped Kevin's arm. "Only Quinlan knew we were staying at the hotel."

His hand covered mine. "Everyone on the estate would have known."

His attempt at comfort warmed me, until I realized he was probably anxious to loosen my nails, which were digging into his forearm.

Nonetheless, his thumb stroked my skin. "Quinlan knew our room numbers. Our visitors had to ask."

"You're right." The flame in my gut died. I pried my hand off his arm. I had to stop jumping to conclusions. Yet the question remained. "Who sent those guys?"

Kevin paced in front of the windows, reminding me of a caged jaguar. "They knew our names, but not the room numbers."

The air stilled. My heart did a funny flutter in my chest as I fought to focus. "If they were organized, they could have found a way to get the room numbers in advance. Hack the hotel computer, something."

Kevin nodded. "Hopefully they're amateurs who were aiming for the two of us and got there too late."

His almost cheerful tone took me aback. I gave him a flat stare. The idea of being a target didn't comfort me as much as it seemed to please him. "I don't want to seem self-centered but knowing people are gunning for me doesn't make me feel better."

Another angle popped into my head. "They might be after that blasted box. Maybe they waited for us to leave. No one knew we would bring other people."

Kevin snapped his fingers. "Good point."

I glanced at the windows. "Shouldn't we have heard the sirens by now?"

Kevin shook his head. "The highway is on the other side. Besides, the police have to tread carefully here."

I gave an unladylike snort. In my neighborhood, the cops have no need for subtlety. A muffled trilling caught my attention. "They did use sirens."

Kevin gave me a strange look and pointed to my purse.

Realization struck me. I lunged at the chair. The trilling sounded again. My hand grabbed the phone and answered the call in one move. "Hello?"

"Guess what?" Marcus's voice sounded in my ear. "Mrs. Colchester can hot-wire a car."

His words didn't immediately register, only his voice. Relief turned my bones to mush. I grabbed Kevin's arm. "Marcus."

Kevin's tense shoulders relaxed.

I put the phone on speaker rather than repeat Marcus's side of the conversation. "Why didn't you answer your phone earlier? Where are you?"

"It's kind of a long story," Marcus said, then plunged in. "We turned off our phones so the bad guys wouldn't hear us. Then we snuck down the stairs, borrowed a car, and took off."

"Borrowed," Kevin whispered. A grin split his face, easing the tense lines of his face.

I shook my head. Later would be time enough to worry about the felonies they'd committed.

Marcus continued with his story. "After we got away, we circled around and staked out their car."

"How did you know which car was theirs?" I asked.

"Mrs. Colchester called the desk," Marcus said. "She really sounded German. I was looking right at her."

American. British. German. The woman was a United Nations of accents. "So, what --?"

"When they drove off, we followed," Marcus said.

I made a mental note to lecture Marcus on the immorality of stealing and lying. For now, I couldn't afford such qualms. "Where did they go?"

"Monroe & Son Construction." A note of triumph laced through his excited voice.

My interest flared. "So, the Monroes are more disgruntled than Pete let on. He sent his people to scare us away."

"They parked half-a-block away and watched it for about fifteen minutes. The place was dark."

My smile froze. This wasn't shaping up the way I had hoped.

Kevin shook his head. "The Monroes wouldn't stake out their own place."

"Then one guy shoved a package through the mail slot. When he jumped in, the car peeled away. I figured we'd go after them, but Rabi said not to tempt fate." Marcus's update ended on a disappointed note.

"Rabi did the right thing." So far, their strategic retreat looked to be the highlight of my day. "Where are you guys now?"

"Rabi rented a car. We left the other one in a parking lot." Marcus continued as if he hadn't heard me. "We checked into the Liverpool Hotel. We passed it when we hit town."

"Kevin can find it." Mrs. C had commented on the name at the time. All that mattered was that they were safely tucked away. Which was more than I could say for us.

"You guys done with your meeting?" Marcus asked.

"We never got started." I glanced at the door, but it remained closed. "Henry Prushark is dead."

Marcus gasped. "Someone killed him?"

Of course, murder would be the boy's first guess. Too bad he was right on target. "They found him at the bottom of a flight of stairs. Kevin and I need to wait for the police. You guys stay put. We'll be in touch as soon as we can."

I signed off and smiled at Kevin. Before I got my first word out, the door swung open.

A portly gentleman in a three-piece navy suit filled the

doorway. The vest came complete with a watch pocket to hold the dangling gold chain that stretched across his stomach. A peach handkerchief in his breast pocket added a dash of color. With his hair slicked-back, he could have been from another era. But the gaze he raked me with was too cynical to belong to any century but this one.

His eyes drilled first me then Kevin. "Belden and Tanner."

As he walked toward Quinlan's desk with a heavy step, my stomach started a slow crawl toward my feet. Unlike the rest of the people we'd met in Tahoe, he knew which of us was which.

The way the rest of my day had gone, that had to be bad.

8

*13 Across; 5 Letters;
Clue: Unexpected event; a new_____
Answer: Twist*

"Vandercoy. Homicide. Lead Detective." The rotund man, sitting at Quinlan's desk as if it were a throne, threw out the introduction in an off-hand tone.

I blinked to make sure the vision was real. In all my years of friendship with Crawford, my boss, I had never seen a police detective so decked out.

A gold pinky ring flashed as Vandercoy pointed to the security guard. "You're relieved of duty. Belden and Tanner are now my concern. This officer will escort you to the location where you can give your statement."

The detective motioned to the uniformed cop who'd accompanied him. After the door closed behind the departing security guard and the officer, Vandercoy waved Kevin and me to the empty chairs.

The detective folded his hands over his stomach and studied us through half-closed lids. A casual observer might have thought he was on the verge of sleep, but his eyes possessed an alert gleam. Silence settled into every crevice of the room.

He had no reason to hurry. His guy was dead. I, however, had dreams of getting out of here sometime before dawn. "My name is Tracy Belden - -"

"I know." A flick of his wrist accented his abrupt tone.

Though my impatience spiked, knowing he could haul us to the station kept a lock on my mouth.

He pulled a large cigar out of his jacket and pointed it at my heart like a laser. "Crawford ever mention me?"

The connection shouldn't have surprised me. My boss had worked in Tahoe and Vegas before moving to Langsdale. But I didn't remember this guy's name. I shook my head.

The detective twirled the cigar between his fingers then stabbed it toward Kevin. "You?"

Unsure whether he was offering the cigar or asking if Kevin knew of him, I waited for one of Kevin's quips. But my buddy shook his head.

"Ungrateful bastard," Vandercoy muttered.

Despite the detective's offbeat manner, I appreciated his assessment. After all, if Crawford had been around -- or even *available* -- I wouldn't be in this mess.

"I can't believe he never mentioned I saved his life." Vandercoy clamped his teeth over the end of the cigar so hard his jowls shook. When his head moved the light reflected off his slicked hair.

A bulb went off in my brain. "Beau Brummell."

Now that I had the connection, Crawford's description of an oversized popinjay fit Vandercoy to a tee. Unfortunately, it struck me one second too late he might not be pleased with the nickname.

"That's it." Vandercoy's hard eyes swiveled to mine. He slapped the oak desk hard enough to make the pencils dance, then his face creased in a smile. "I'd forgotten what that chain-smoking, drunken old frog used to call me."

I breathed a sigh of relief.

An admiring expression came over Kevin's face. "You figure in Crawford's stories all the time."

Now, why couldn't I be that diplomatic? Actually, while Crawford could turn any story into a laugh riot, Beau Br -- Vandercoy's skill came through as well. Especially the time he'd pulled an unconscious Crawford out of a burning car after a drug bust gone bad.

"So, you two got stuck holding the bag while he's off fishing?" Vandercoy laughed. "The man always knew when to make an exit."

I was beginning to like this guy.

The detective twirled the still unlit cigar between his fingers. "What's the story?"

Kevin snorted. "If only we knew."

Vandercoy raised his brows then turned to me.

One good thing about working for a retired cop was Crawford's rules about coming clean with the authorities. The law is the law and Crawford worked inside it; most of the time. We do have an obligation to protect our client's confidentiality. However, Henry Prushark was pretty much beyond our protection.

I started with Rickson showing up in Langsdale and worked my way up to the present. I asked whether he'd heard of Rickson contacting Crawford's old crew, possibly regarding extortion from the anonymous letters, but he shook his head. I skirted around Rickson's notes mainly because they made no sense.

"That's not helpful." Vandercoy spoke in a dismissive tone, but his eyes narrowed in thought.

I remembered Crawford talking about suspects who got distracted by "Beau's clothes" and, to their peril, failed to notice the mind behind the façade.

Vandercoy stuck the tip of the unlit cigar between his teeth then spoke around it. "We'll talk to your friends about the car they followed to the Monroe building. Get a description. See if they got the plate."

I made a mental note to remind Marcus not to mention the "borrowed" car.

Vandercoy's gaze remained riveted on me.

Waiting for people to fill the silence is a common ploy with police. Even if I'd known more, I had no intention of obliging the man. I *can* keep my mouth when it's in my best interests.

With an abrupt move, he pulled a pad and pen out of his jacket pocket without moving his torso and scribbled energetically.

"Nancy. Josh. Doorman." The detective muttered a list of hotel employees.

The door opened without warning. A Slim Jim uniform cop hurried to the desk and whispered in Vandercoy's ear.

I leaned toward Kevin for a little muttering of my own. "How soon do you think he'll cut us loose?"

Kevin scratched his chin, masking his mouth as he did. "Half-an-hour if the cards fall our way."

I sat back with a sigh. "I wish you hadn't said that."

I drive a fifteen-year-old Buick. His Caddy is on rent-to-own payments. We both work two jobs.

The cards *never* fall our way.

"I'll be damned." Vandercoy grabbed the cigar as it fell out of his slack mouth. He looked intently at Slim Jim. Finally, his gaze shifted to Kevin then to me.

Icy fingers clawed their way up my spine.

"On the case less than an hour and I already have

answers." The detective's jaw tightened. "We know what your drive-by friends dropped off at Monroe's. And we found Rickson."

I sat on the edge of my chair. "Where is he?"

"In surgery at Memorial Hospital," Vandercoy said in a somber tone. "He was in the Monroe building when the bomb blew."

A jolt shot straight through my heart. I grabbed Kevin's sleeve.

He surged to his feet, pulling out of my grasp. His muscles strained beneath his suit coat. With no one to fight, he stilled, fists clenched. "How bad is he hurt?"

Like a giant merry-go-round, the situation whirled faster and faster. Unfortunately, real people were being injured. I swallowed hard. "How bad?"

The detective tapped the cigar on the desk. "The wall that collapsed on him shielded him from the blast. The doctors said a normal person would've been killed. Someone built like a rhino is harder to take down."

"At least they have the right man." Kevin's glib words had a strained quality, but I breathed easier.

Life wasn't all bad if Kevin could make jokes. At least, Rickson was alive. If anyone was too stubborn to die, it was him. I shifted my gaze to the detective. "Can we leave?"

Vandercoy rolled the chair away and shot to his feet. His dark eyes locked on the door. He pointed to the Slim Jim cop. "Sanders, call the hospital. Give Tanner and Belden as Rickson's next of kin."

Sanders acknowledged him.

As I stood, Kevin gripped my elbow.

I frowned in annoyance. I wasn't eighty. But he'd gone into protection mode, and I was the only one handy.

Vandercoy's heavy footfalls took him past me. "Leave the name and number of your hotel with the detective at the front door. Be at the station first thing tomorrow. We'll have your people work with sketch artists."

Kevin snorted. "Marcus will love that."

At least somebody would get something positive out of this weekend.

Sanders, the Slim Jim cop, had to step lively to keep up with Vandercoy. Kevin and I kept pace as well.

"Where are the principles?" Vandercoy threw the comment over his shoulder.

"Todd Prushark is with his mother. The doctor gave her a sedative," the young cop said.

Pulling open the door without breaking stride, Vandercoy digested the news with a calculating look.

"Quinlan is arranging for the staff to be interviewed," the cop continued.

"What about the daughter?" Vandercoy spun on his heel. "Sheila."

Sanders screeched to a halt.

I pulled up short, barely avoiding a collision.

Kevin barreled into me, grabbing my shoulders for balance.

"She's working in the office until she's needed," the younger cop said.

"Is she?" A gleam of interest sparked in the detective's gaze.

Quinlan and Sheila had left together. Had they separated before or after her father's fall?

Sanders nodded as Vandercoy headed along the corridor.

I followed, hoping they'd lead us to the main entrance.

"I'll talk to Quinlan," Vandercoy said. "Then Sheila and the son, in that order. Did someone say their attorney is on the way?"

"He's here," the cop said. "He was part of the seven-thirty meeting."

News to me. But then I seemed to be in the dark about a lot of things. Something I intended to change starting now. "Who was unaccounted for when Prushark died?"

This time I was ready. When the detective spun around, I stopped on a dime.

"That is what I'm going to find out." Vandercoy's eyes may have held a grudging admiration, but I wouldn't swear to it. Without another word, he turned again and strode away.

When I started after him, Kevin stopped me with a touch on my arm. "We need to head for the main entrance. We can check on Rickson, then hook up with the troops."

"I thought we *were* going to the front door." When he turned right at the next corridor, I followed blindly. I had no breadcrumbs to throw on the path. If I lost him, I'd never find my way out. After a few steps, my mind started poking at the puzzle. "How could an injured dog play into this mess?"

"A man is dead. A building was bombed. Rickson is in the hospital." Kevin slashed a hand through the air. "Forget the dog. We're finding our people."

While I appreciated his concern for family and friends, the nagging voice in my head kept pulling my attention to the incongruity of the mutt like a magnet to steel. I answered his abrupt tone with my own. "Rickson wouldn't have mentioned the dog unless it mattered."

As soon as I heard my raised voice bounce off the walls, I dialed it down. This wasn't the time or place for a debate. While the cops and the murder might have distracted the security team from their normal diligence, from what I'd seen of Girard, I doubted it.

Kevin's expression remained one of icy determination. "We need to check on Rickson."

"I agree." As I focused on the dog angle, I lost sight of Kevin at a T-junction. Fortunately, he was waiting by a four-foot vase filled with wild-flowers. I touched his shoulder, letting my hand linger in a caress. "Thanks."

My smile froze as I stepped around Kevin's wide-shouldered frame.

The man blocking the corridor didn't wear the Prushark looks nearly as well as his sister. The black hair was shot with strands of early gray. Crow's feet and worry lines were etched around his green eyes and on his forehead. Bullish determination showed in his gaze. Todd Prushark was closer to my height of five-foot-nine than Kevin's, but the man was half-again as wide as Kevin.

Evidently, this Prushark sibling preferred to avoid the police. I wondered if he had something to hide. "Detective Vandercoy is looking for you."

"I'll deal with him later. I need to speak with you and Mr. Tanner." Todd's pale green eyes shifted to the hall behind us. "Step in here."

Gesturing to a door the tall vase had partially hidden, he stepped away, effectively blocking the corridor.

With no choice and more questions than answers, I preceded both men into a small sitting room. A leather sofa, two high-backed chairs, a coffee table. I ran a hand along the soft leather of one of the chairs. When I faced Todd, I remained standing.

Where his sister had seemed like a coiled dynamo, this man gave the impression of a battering ram. Different styles, but equal measures of force. Family dinners with this high-octane family must be like fight night.

Todd shut the door with a soft click. He advanced a mere half-a-step from the exit.

Kevin, a master at body language, took a position between Todd and me before shifting to one side. His first response was usually non-confrontational. He liked to study people first.

My style is more the poke and prod until something gives method. I closed the distance to Todd. Remembering just in time to play the role of a hired contractor, I dialed back my aggressive stance. "I know you've suffered a loss. I... we never expected to be caught up in such a tragic accident."

Todd's eyes narrowed at my use of the word accident.

"You know by now what happened to my father was no accident." The planes of his face settled into hard lines. "He was getting ready to resume his place as head of the company."

An odd thing to say to a new hireling. A strange tone underlaid his comment. Was it regret or relief? His father's re-emergence would have pushed Todd into the shadows. The murder resolved that problem.

How convenient for Todd.

Why was he even talking with us? I doubted Sheila would have been so forthcoming, but, then, I'd met her before her father's death. Now, she was out of sight and Todd was left in the power vacuum. The question was - had he created the situation?

"Was your father in favor of amping up the Winter Fest?"

The tightness around Todd's eyes eased at Kevin's curious tone. "My father believed in watching the bottom line."

My interest perked. Todd could proceed with his own vision of the future unhindered.

"How will your father's death affect the job?" Kevin gave a sheepish shrug. He gestured toward me. "This is a good-sized contract. We could use the money."

The solid wall of a man raised his chin. Seeming to collect himself, his expression hardened. He made a slicing gesture with his hand. "What might have been no longer matters. You should never have been called in."

Even if I had been here solely for the contract, I would have taken umbrage at such a dismissal. If only the money and the contract were real, I wailed silently. "I realize this a bad time. We can wait and meet later."

"The decision is made." Todd clipped off the words. "I'll see you're reimbursed for your time and trouble."

I didn't have to fake my interest at the mention of money. "Are we talking a percentage of the contract or a flat amount? Is the option open for discussion?"

Kevin's expression remained a polite mask. Only our long acquaintance gave me the insight to glimpse his amusement at my nose for money.

Todd did a double take, evidently surprised at my quick turnabout from concern to money-grubbing. He didn't know me like Kevin did.

The Prushark son shook his head. "Get out. Stay away. For your own well-being."

He turned and left before I could react.

I stared at the door then met Kevin's gaze. "Warning? Threat?"

"Hard to say." Kevin's posture morphed before my eyes as he shed the deferential attitude he'd adopted to put Todd off guard. A chuckle escaped his lips. "A percentage or a flat amount? Only you would ask that, Belden."

"We put time and effort into this. I want to know." I walked toward the door. "He also didn't answer me."

When we reached the main foyer, I tried to relax. I hoped to make our exit without confronting any more Prusharks.

The polished marble and glittering chandelier in the entryway were a perfect backdrop for the stiff security guards stationed by the door. A man and a woman with detective badges clipped to their shirts compared notes by the main stairs.

The scene looked to be carved from stone. No air stirred. No voice sounded. No one moved.

Kevin hit the frozen tableau at full throttle. "I'll check in with the police."

Though the old guy died in another wing, I cast a nervous glance at the floor by the stairs. Between bullets and bombs, this case was making me jumpy.

Chiding myself for nerves, I headed for the door. Halfway there I did a double take. The security guard from Quinlan's office was on duty. Maybe he could provide inside information. I stopped in front of him. "I thought you'd like to know my son is fine. He turned off his phone."

"Told you." His voice held an annoying paternalistic tone.

I reminded myself I was schmoozing and let it slide. "I wonder if you could help me with something."

"What would that be?" he asked.

What's the harm in asking about a dog? "On our way here, an older couple hit a dog with their car. They said they were going to take it to an animal hospital close by. I'd like to know if it survived. Where might they have gone?"

The guard frowned. "Zenox Animal Hospital is next to the Riverboat Casino as you head to town."

Footsteps sounded behind me. Kevin appeared at my elbow. "Ready?"

"Sure." I nodded at the guard. "Thanks."

A moment later the front door clicked shut and cool evening air embraced us. The Caddy sat in pearly white splendor in the driveway.

Before I could blink, Kevin had the driver's door open and was looking up at me. "You plan to spend the night?"

A hard glare in his direction earned me a jaunty grin. I gathered my dignity and walked down the stairs.

A security guard detached himself from a nearby group and opened the passenger door. When I looked up, I realized it was our golf-cart guy, Girard. "Thank you."

Surprised at the gesture, I stumbled over the words.

Steely gray eyes stared at me. Not a hint of sorrow softened the chiseled angles of his face.

As soon as I got in the car, Kevin turned onto the drive. "What was that about?"

"I don't know." I tried to nail down the fleeting impression I'd gotten from the chief of security. "He didn't seem broken up about the death."

"What do you expect? He works here."

We drove past a dark wall of hedges. The lights illuminating the fountain cast eerie shadows on the lawn.

I didn't have an answer to the Girard enigma. But he'd earned a place on my crossword puzzle. "There's more to him than meets the eye. I wonder who hired him and how long ago?"

The estate's oppressive aura held until we turned onto the highway. Then I kicked off my shoes and pulled out my cell phone. "Time to check on Rickson. I want that lug awake so I can get my pound of flesh when we get there."

"Vandercoy put him under police protection." Kevin's profile turned serious. "Jumping from adultery to murder ups the ante big time."

I set aside the image of Marcus running from men with bombs and dialed the hospital. Several frustrating minutes later a live human being finally gave me the lowdown.

"You look relieved," Kevin said, acting as if he hadn't been hanging on my every word.

"Considering he got caught in a bomb blast, it's better than I'd hoped." I shifted to face Kevin. "He has a skull fracture and they've stopped the internal bleeding. He's stable. He'll be in surgery for another couple of hours."

"Coma?" Concern filled Kevin's tone.

I shook my head. "He managed to stumble outside after the bomb blew. Once he's out of surgery, he should wake up."

Kevin rubbed a hand over his forehead. "Good."

The lights of the city, glowing against the valley floor, formed no discernable pattern. Kind of like this case. Too many clues. Too many people. Prushark's death proved someone was playing for keeps, and not only did I not have answers, I wasn't even sure of the questions.

Could all of this truly boil down to a five-year-old adultery accusation? Linda would be the one in danger if the accusation proved to be true.

"Do you know where the hospital is?" I asked, mostly to stop the worrisome thoughts. Kevin never got lost.

"Yes." A hesitancy in Kevin's tone drew my attention.

I glanced over in time to catch him eyeing me. A spark born of long acquaintance heated up an idea in my brain.

Kevin pointed at me. "You thinking what I'm thinking?"

"That the cops and doctors at the hospital will do Rickson more good than you and I?"

"Uh-huh."

"The least we can do for the guy is try to find some answers."

Kevin hit the accelerator, and the car surged forward. "Liverpool Hotel here we come."

"I'll update Rabi." I hit his speed dial.

"The cops are probably there by now. Vandercoy's on top of things," Kevin said.

I got Rabi on the phone. "I didn't like giving them your name and location but I had no choice."

"Understood," Rabi said.

"Do you think they'll have a sketch artist?" Marcus's excited voice came through loud and clear.

"We're cool." Rabi's tone held a trace of amusement. It disappeared with his next question. "Rickson?"

I told him what had happened after they'd left Monroe & Sons and repeated the prognosis, including the police protection. "We're on our way to you. We should be there in twenty minutes."

Kevin shot me a disgusted look.

I glanced at the speedometer. The needle hovered at ninety. It felt like a Sunday drive in the park. "Make that ten minutes and listen for the sonic boom."

That earned a chuckle from Rabi.

Kevin took a sharp corner without slowing. No screech of tires marred the silence. When we cleared the turn, a neon sign for the Riverboat Casino popped into view. A strip mall rose behind it.

I caught my breath. "Animal hospital."

"What?" Rabi asked.

"We have to make a stop." I rushed the words. At this speed, we could be a mile past the exit before I made my case. "We're by the Riverboat. I'll check in later."

Kevin had already pulled onto the exit ramp.

The battle I'd geared up for disappeared, leaving me with a sense of disappointment. "How did you know?"

"I heard the guard." Kevin drove by the casino. "If we don't stop, I'll hear about this dog all weekend."

"I thought you'd be harder to convince."

Kevin craned his head to check the traffic, before tossing me a glance full of affection. "What you lack in navigation and cooking skills, you make up for in sheer bull-headedness."

I relaxed, happy with my victory.

"You realize this place might be closed?" Kevin asked, driving up a slight hill. "It's nine o'clock on a Saturday night."

"It's an animal *hospital*," I pointed out. "Someone should be on duty for emergencies. Besides the sign is still on."

The Zenox hospital sat at the far end of the strip mall. From the top of the rise, a four-door sedan approached us with its headlights off.

Kevin flashed his lights but the car sped by without responding.

I tapped Kevin on the arm, vaguely noting two figures in the other vehicle. "I told you the place would be open."

"Don't get--"

A flare of noise and light swallowed his words. Shards of glass and chunks of stone flew into the air. The sign for the Zenox Animal Hospital sizzled like a sparkler. Looking like a giant Roman candle, it burst into flames. In seconds, the sign tilted then spiraled slowly toward the ground. It smacked into the concrete with a crash of sound and fury.

9

26 Down; 9 Letters;
Clue: Destructive blaze
Answer: Firestorm

A tongue of flame split the night as a second explosion ripped through the animal hospital. Bricks from the building flew sideways, forming a burning halo in the darkness.

Like a flash from a camera, the burst of fire temporarily blinded me. Stunned, I braced a hand against the dashboard as the Caddy shot forward like a rocket on a short fuse.

Before I could get my heart out of my throat, the car screeched to a stop. Kevin jumped out and raced toward the disaster. Chunks of stone and pieces of roofing material rained on the parking lot. Car alarms added to the mix.

I grabbed my phone and ran into the chaos steps behind Kevin.

Three dark figures were silhouetted against the bright

fire. A slim blond teenager wearing a green smock staggered across the parking lot. Tears streamed down her face.

Kevin grabbed her shoulders. "You okay?"

The girl nodded blankly.

Kevin's gaze shifted to the other two figures. He rushed past her.

I managed to loosen my white-knuckled grip on my phone enough to call for help.

"9-1-1, what is your emergency?"

"There's been an explosion." The blonde woke from her stupor and threw herself at me. Shaking like a leaf, she clutched me as if she were drowning. I fought to keep my balance as I spoke to the dispatcher. "I'm at Zenox Animal Hospital off Highway 50 by the Riverboat Casino."

The other two teenagers, a boy and a dark-haired girl in matching smocks, stared at the burning building with dazed expressions.

Kevin grabbed them both by the arm. "Is anyone else inside?"

My heart stopped. I barely heard the operator inform me help was on the way. If Kevin ran into that inferno, he'd never get out alive. I couldn't lose him. Compassion warred with logic as I pushed at the girl clutching me.

I had to stop Kevin from doing something brave and stupid.

The boy's stunned expression didn't change as he shook his head. "No."

Kevin thrust himself into the boy's face. "Are you sure?"

The second girl agreed. "It was just the three of us."

A high-pitched scream rose from the depths of the flames. I cringed in sympathy.

"The animals." With a roar, the boy surged toward the fire.

The dark-haired girl shrieked what sounded like Lollipop and struggled against Kevin's hold.

Kevin kept a grip on both. "Nobody goes in."

"They're trapped."

I wasn't sure who yelled, but the dark-haired girl looked dangerously close to wiggling out of Kevin's grasp. Pushing the blonde away, I raced to the others.

Abandoning chivalry, Kevin pivoted and thrust the girl away. She stumbled over her feet then slammed into a parked car. Freed of her, Kevin grabbed the boy with both hands and shoved him after the girl.

As soon as the two teens got their feet under them, they surged forward again.

Three strides brought me equal to the three combatants. The heat of the blaze warmed my skin. I positioned myself between the teens and the roaring fire.

Kevin blocked their path. "No further."

The blonde rushed in from the side. "The animals are fine. They left."

The set expressions of the boy and the brown-haired girl didn't change as they charged toward the flames.

Standing side-by-side with my guy, I caught a handful of the green smock. Like four tag team wrestlers, we struggled for several seconds. Then, a crash sounded from the building and the teens wilted.

The blonde stepped in once more. She flapped her arms like a windmill. "The animals were picked up earlier."

The other two teens perked up. Hope sparked in their gazes.

The boy shook his head. "No, the Frenchie and her puppies were still in the back."

"So was the poodle." The brunette stomped her foot. Her lip quivered.

For a moment the heat of the flames firing the night

faded. The numbers weren't adding up. I stared at the girl. "You only had two dogs in there?"

The blonde gritted her teeth. Attitude bloomed as she rolled her eyes. "We received word yesterday that the city would be doing work tomorrow. The animals were moved to the clinic. There's staff watching them there. We were here in case emergencies came in. Two litters of puppies were kept behind because they'd just been born."

The boy's expression crumpled. "They're still in back."

"Their owners picked them up while you and Josie went to get the pizza. You were gone for most of an hour." The blonde swung her fists wildly in the air. "That noise must have been pipes bursting."

"You never told us that." The brunette girl wiped away her tears, accusation rang in her tone.

The blonde bit her lip. "I didn't? Are you sure?"

I threw my hands in the air and eyed the burning building. Tongues of fire engulfed the structure as a column of smoke covered the sky. A series of small pops sounded behind me. With each additional explosion, a handful of debris arced into the night.

Two older couples had rushed out of the bar and grill in the strip mall. They herded us farther out into the parking lot.

I, for one, was more than willing to go.

The three teens huddled together. Raised voices filled the air as the fire raged on.

"How did you manage to get out in time?" A woman's voice rose above the others.

"The man told us to leave," the blond girl said.

Kevin stiffened beside me.

I was willing to bet that the city wasn't doing any work in this area tomorrow. Whoever had destroyed the building had made the earlier call to move the animals to safety.

"He called not five minutes ago," she continued. "Said there was a gas leak and to get everyone out of the building."

The boy stepped near, still staring at the blaze. "We were wondering if the lounge had gotten the call about evacuating when the building blew."

The dark-haired girl shook her head. "We barely got out in time."

"The sedan," Kevin whispered in my ear. His narrowed gaze focused on the corner at the end of the strip mall. At the top of a small incline, the commercial buildings ended, giving way to a dark area and what looked to be the fringes of a residential area. "Somebody was parked up there, waiting for them to leave."

I nodded. "The call must have come from the car that drove past us."

His gaze met mine. "Did you see who was in it?"

I grimaced. "I wasn't paying attention."

"Did you notice any details?" He spoke in a calm, low tone. No pressure. No hurry.

Knowing the police would ask the same question, I fought to recall the moment. Unfortunately, my memory didn't come equipped with a freeze frame. The car flashed by at its original speed.

"There were two of them." Best to start with a certainty. "The one in the passenger seat was thin. He was turned away from me, looking at the building. I saw a ponytail down the back."

"Could it have been a woman?" Kevin asked softly.

I replayed the memory, striving to see the figure more clearly. Though a corner of my mind wanted to agree, Crawford's stories about leading witnesses returned. He'd made it clear that it was amazingly easy to rebuild a witness's memory the way the cop wanted it to be. Citizens wanted to be helpful. They wanted to catch the bad guy.

I shook my head. "I don't know."

"Was he white or black?"

That was easy. "*He* was white."

The emphasis in my voice surprised me

Kevin gave me no time to think. "Who was black?"

"The driver." I looked around to see who had spoken. Crazy, I know. It was my voice. But I had no conscious memory to put with that answer.

I ran the scene again, focusing on the front seat. I got an impression of short-cropped hair, a glint of gold chain, a black T-shirt against dark chocolate skin.

Frustrated, I opened my eyes. The boy who'd tried to run into the burning building watched the blaze with an agonized expression. He put his hand over his face. A glint of light reflected off the class ring on his finger.

My arm shot out and pointed at the boy. "A ring."

Kevin crowded closer. "What about it?"

I closed my eyes and rewound the scene. The driver held his hand close to his cheek. I imitated the movement, to fix it in my mind. "He must have been on a cell phone. I saw a flash of gold with a dark center."

A firetruck's shrill alarm cut through the babble of voices.

A crash of stone and lumber wrenched me back to reality.

One wall of the animal hospital buckled. Fire clawed greedily at the law office, whose adjoining wall and roof had collapsed in the initial explosion.

Kevin hovered protectively at my shoulder, his gaze fixed on my face. "A gold circle? Like a wedding ring?"

"No." I pointed at the boy. "The ring had a circle of metal surrounding an emblem or a dark stone."

"Could you make out the emblem?" Kevin asked.

"Are you nuts? I'm doing good to remember the ring."

"Just asking." He held his hands up, palms out.

Was it live or was it Memorex? The old jingle ran through

my mind. I threw up my hands. "I don't know what's real anymore."

Kevin's squeezed my shoulder in a soft, affectionate gesture. "Forget it. You'll drive yourself crazy-- and you're close enough already."

I rolled my eyes. For a moment, I forgot the disaster. From Kevin's smug expression, I realized the teasing comment had accomplished his goal.

The inferno clawed at the building next to the hospital like a leopard would an antelope. Hungry flames devoured the sign for William Larson, Attorney-at-Law, letter by letter. Clouds of smoke seeped through the roof. The fire marched mercilessly toward the bar. The former occupants, some still sipping their drinks, retreated across the street. Their gaze remained riveted on the blaze. Probably waiting for the fireworks if those flames hit the alcohol.

The wail of sirens grew in intensity. Covering my ears, I watched a cavalcade roar up the hill.

Kevin glanced at the fire, then at me. He put his arm around my shoulders, stroking my cheek. Then we walked toward the Caddy.

Firetrucks roared into the parking lot. Firefighters rushed toward the destruction with the choreography of a ballet troupe. In moments, hoses were trained on the blaze as well as neighboring businesses.

Clouds of smoke thickened and grew. Thankfully, a slight wind blew most of it in the opposite direction. I caught a mouthful and gagged.

I leaned against Kevin's stalwart frame, comforted by his arms. As the buildings crumbled, an image of the animals trapped in their cages tugged at my heart. A growing anger took root in the marrow of my bones.

Maybe it was my Kentucky roots and growing up with the iconic status of horses, but despite Rickson's injury and

Henry Prushark's murder, what stuck in my craw was the trapped animals and cruel, senseless deaths.

More sirens interrupted my reverie. Two cop cars sped up the hill and parked on the street.

I brushed the weariness out of my eyes and settled in for the long haul. "This is going to take a while."

Kevin reached for his phone. "I'll update Rabi."

An image of Vandercoy's piercing gaze returned to haunt me. Air escaped between my teeth loud enough to catch Kevin's attention. "We should call Vandercoy."

Kevin stared at me like I'd lost my mind.

Lights from the cop cars lit his face. Behind him, gallons of water rained on the hissing fire. A rainbow formed a shimmering arc over his tall figure. A firefighter yelled for more hose. Another screamed at the people to get clear.

"How are you going to explain us being here?" Despite leaning closer, Kevin had to raise his voice to be heard. "No one on the Prushark estate knew about the dog, and we didn't mention Rickson's notes."

Frustrated, I raked a hand through my hair, a gesture that couldn't have helped my not-so-glamorous looks. "He's going to think we were holding out on him."

"We were," Kevin said.

"No, I wasn't. I didn't want to weigh him down with ramblings that made no sense."

Kevin raised a brow. "I doubt he'll appreciate the distinction."

More problems and no answers. "What could adultery have to do with destroying an animal hospital? Who would do this?"

Kevin stared at the shell of the strip mall. "Someone who doesn't care about the little guy."

He muttered the words as if speaking to himself. A determined glint took hold in the depths of his blue eyes. His whole being seemed to intensify.

"Don't get any ideas." An uneasy feeling grew from the pit of my stomach and spread outward. Kevin is one of the most easygoing people I know but get him riled and he can be hell on wheels. Though I didn't know the why, I could feel the fury building in his eyes.

"Our friends were run out of a hotel. A man has been murdered, and Rickson was caught in a bomb blast." His word reverberated in the air. His jaw tightened. "We need to go on the attack."

Without another word, he marched off. Ignoring the firetrucks and the flaming building, Kevin strode toward the teenagers.

So much for playing it safe.

10

8 Across; 9 Letters;
Clue: Pledged to a certain course
Answer: Committed

What the...? Caught off-guard by Kevin's sudden passion, I wasted precious seconds wondering what had set him off. I finally gave up and hurried after him as he strode toward the teenagers. The hissing flames and roaring water made yelling useless.

As I jumped over a hose, the wind shifted. Cold water doused me. I gasped at the sudden shower. My "power" blazer was so wet and wrinkled a five-year-old wouldn't hire me to build a sandcastle. At times like this, I wondered what I'd done to be on the losing end of the karma wheel.

Rather than ponder the possibilities, I grabbed Kevin's arm before the teens noticed his approach. "Hold it right there, buster."

He leaned in, inches from my face. His eyes gleamed like blue diamonds. "I was wrong. You were right."

Just my luck. "*Now* I get to be right?"

"Rickson was onto something. The dog and the murder must be connected." Kevin spread his arms wide like a preacher embracing a congregation. The whirling lights of the emergency vehicles and the roaring flames provided the fire and brimstone. "I'm going to get the people behind this."

I looked around to see if anyone could overhear us. I needn't have bothered. I could have screamed out a lung without drawing any attention. "Why are you going on the attack?"

Admittedly my father always said the best defense is a good offense, but why now? My buddy likes animals as much as the next person, but his family never owned a dog unless they needed one for a con job. "What happened to business as usual?"

"This setup is no different than a scam." The shifting hues of light hit his face. In the shadows cast by night, he had the look of an avenging Greek god. A vacuum formed around us. "Whoever is pulling the strings won't care who gets hurt."

A lead weight formed in my stomach. Kevin had spent his childhood learning to cheat marks and rob innocents. When his tortured conscience finally overrode family loyalty, he'd taken the good looks and charm that had added millions to his family's fortune and walked away.

Witnessing a con was the one thing that stoked Kevin's anger to the boiling point. He'd never let this case go.

And I would never desert him, but I had to consider my son's safety.

My heart weighed the two males in my life. I looked into the eyes of the man I loved. I couldn't abandon him. I wouldn't. I'd dragged him into this mess.

As he watched the tug of war between my gut and my

heart, the hard glint in his eyes softened. He looked more like a juggernaut at rest than an avenging Apollo. His gaze remained riveted on my face.

"I can't risk Marcus."

"You and he are the ones I'm trying to protect." Resolve shown in Kevin's eyes, along with a fierce love. His hands settled on my shoulders. "Whoever is behind this thinks we're players. They have your name and address. Trust me. Con artists don't quit. Neither will the people behind these bombs."

His words chilled my blood.

Two buildings destroyed. One man murdered. The smart move would be to grab Marcus and hightail it out of here. Except returning to Langsdale was no longer safe. Unless we solved this case, the problem would follow me home.

I fisted my hands to control their shaking. Righteous anger was all well and good, but life doesn't play fair. Ask any cop's family-- fighting for justice doesn't come with an invincible shield.

"Marcus's safety is paramount." I reminded Kevin. "I'm not leaving him an orphan again."

"I would never risk him or you." Kevin's fingers grazed my cheek. His determined expression didn't change, but his eyes burned with a different kind of fire. "If things get too hot, we'll go to England and adopt British accents."

A chuckle escaped me at the reminder of my landlady's mercurial changes.

"I'm not sure the British Isles could survive our merry band, but let's hang onto the walking away part." Now that we had decided on a course of action, the tension tying me in knots eased. "Until then, let's turn over some rocks and see what crawls out."

"I knew you couldn't leave a puzzle unsolved." Kevin

gazed at the teenagers like a pointer on a scent. "Let's start with the pooch you're so concerned about."

"I should have let the mongrel stay buried." I was almost sorry my hunch about the dog had been correct. Yet, even now, the bizarre clues and tangled threads called to me.

Solving a crossword puzzle is my way of making sense of the world. A crossword clue only has one correct answer. Find all the answers. Solve the puzzle. Life is good.

This whirlpool of crime and violence was no different than a blank puzzle. Questions galore, seemingly unrelated. But with the right facts in the right order, I could solve this case; just like I've solved every other puzzle I've put my mind to. I could get us out of here. Alive.

Moments later Kevin and I faced the teens from the animal hospital. I frowned at the young boy. "So, this guy brought in a dog that was already dead?"

We'd asked for odd happenings and this is what we got. It had taken several questions to get to this point and I couldn't swear we were on the right track. The encounter definitely sounded odd but was it what I was looking for?

The boy nodded. "The guy came in this afternoon. He asked about our limited staffing on weekends, like he already knew. I thought he was worried his dog having adequate care. Then, I found out the dog was dead."

"How long had the dog been dead?" Kevin asked.

The blonde had been studying the pavement, evidently determined not to look at the smoldering building. Her blank expression didn't change as she answered Kevin. "Doc figured two to four hours."

I faced her with a raised brow. "How did he know?"

"Rigor mortis. Internal damage." She shrugged. "He said in all the years he practiced, no one has ever brought in a dog that died so long beforehand."

That didn't surprise me. I clung to my goal of learning

facts. "What did the guy look like?"

"Just a guy." The blonde raised her gaze from the pavement. A spark of interest glimmered in her expression. "Five-eight or so. Sunglasses. Baseball cap. Either Hispanic or well-tanned. It was hard to tell. He said his daughter came home and found the dog. She was hysterical and he had to get rid of the body."

"Good story." An admiring tone underscored Kevin's voice as he glanced over his shoulder.

I followed his gaze. A couple of uniforms were talking to the owner of the lounge who pointed toward the teens.

The boy watched the firefighters aim a full jet of water at the red, smoldering embers. He answered without shifting his gaze. "As soon as I took the dog, the guy asked for the restroom and disappeared."

I checked over my shoulder. The cops were headed our way. "Did he come back? Did you see him again?"

"He walked out of the basement stairwell fifteen minutes later." The blonde's sorrowful gaze strayed to the remains of the building. "He said he got lost, which is nuts. The building isn't... wasn't that big."

She waved a hand toward the hospital and the adjoining building now little more than blackened frames. As she spoke, portions of the building's roof collapsed, spewing out a final burst of ash and smoke. Not much remained except the foundation.

Perhaps this was our guy. A bomb in the basement would be sure to bring the whole building down.

That left one burning question: why destroy an animal hospital? Was the reduced staffing the only reason to detonate it on Saturday or was it in conjunction with the Monroe explosion? What, if any, was the connection to the Prushark family? Was this connected with Rickson's dog story?

Okay, that's four questions, possibly five. Can you blame

me? All this work to find a nebulous connection and I had no idea what it meant.

"You three were in the animal hospital before it exploded?" A young, white cop and his partner stepped into our little circle. When the teens nodded, he gestured toward the black-and-white cop car. "I need you to step over here with me."

His partner, a solidly built black woman, eyed Kevin and me. "Were either of you here at the time of the explosion?"

"We were driving up the hill." Kevin paused. His next words would commit us to a drawn-out session of Q and A.

I cringed. My toes were screaming to be released from my pumps and my knees felt ready to buckle.

Kevin continued. "We saw a dark blue sedan drive away with its headlights off. It passed us going down the hill."

Interest sparked in the woman's eyes. "Before or after the explosion?"

"Ten seconds before," Kevin said.

Without shifting her gaze, the cop reached in her pocket and pulled out a pad and pen. "See the plates?"

Kevin and I shook our heads.

A flash of disappointment crossed her face but she spoke again quickly. "Can you tell me the make and model?"

Kevin nodded. "Ford SUV, dark blue, three to five years old."

"Step over to the car with me." The cop managed to nod, write, and wave us forward all at the same time. She scanned the street. "Jensen. We have a make and model on a possible suspect's car."

Her voice carried with little visible effort. Another officer, a white guy, hurried to us.

"These two saw the vehicle." She repeated Kevin's description. Jensen hurried away. The woman directed us to a cruiser a little way away from the crowded scene.

I trudged to the police car with Kevin at my side and the policewoman behind us. She directed us like a collie herding two prize sheep.

I met the woman's gaze. "We spoke to Detective Vandercoy at the Prushark estate a short time ago. It sounds crazy, but this bombing may tie to Vandercoy's case."

An aura of excitement built around her. I could almost see her mental gears turning. Any tie-in to a high-profile case could get her one step closer to a gold detective's shield.

I wasn't nearly that ambitious. I only hoped this case started to make sense before more bodies turned up.

Vandercoy's unlit cigar jutted out between clenched teeth. Though the clock was within waving distance of midnight, his slicked-back hair and neat mustache showed not one strand out of place. His gaze shifted between Rickson's notes, one in each hand. Finally, he tossed them to his desk and grabbed the cigar. "This is rambling. Why couldn't Rickson stick to the facts?"

No doubt the detective's case notes were neatly typed with bullet points.

I shrugged. "If you're expecting an explanation you've got the wrong people. The dog was our only solid lead, and that was a shot in the dark."

Kevin glanced at me.

Surely, he hadn't expected me to impress Vandercoy with my skillful deduction. He knew better. I rarely try to impress anyone. At the moment, I just wanted answers.

The detective bent closer to the loose pages as if further study would make them clearer.

I could have saved him the trouble. Closer didn't help. Re-reading also couldn't create logic where there was none.

"Some of this is obvious. The Prusharks and their insulated mentality. Quinlan. Linda, the daughter-in-law."

Surprise rippled through me. He had no reason to share information with us. Unless he thought if he talked we'd let slip whatever clue we might be holding back.

"How close is she to the family?" Kevin's attention seemed consumed with the toothpick he'd picked up somewhere. He rolled it through his fingers like a magician with a trick coin. But something in his tone set my radar bells ringing. "Do they get along?"

Position of trust. Anyone pulling off a con against a group as protected as the Prusharks would need inside info.

Vandercoy gave a shrug that made him look like a mountain in motion. "No obvious disagreements. Linda is the mother of the only grandchild. Proof of adultery might cost her the luxury she's grown used to. The Prusharks wealth could cost her custody of her son."

"That reasoning might explain Henry Prushark's murder, but Linda has no motive to bomb a contractor's office or an animal hospital." I couldn't get any of the threads to tie together.

Vandercoy stared at me with his piercing eyes. He evidently had no answers either... or none he'd share.

Kevin balanced the toothpick on his forefinger. "COC? Did Rickson call any of Crawford's old crew?"

"Not me or anyone else I've contacted." Vandercoy's double chins quivered as he clenched his jaw. His stubby finger stabbed at the notes. "What crime did Rickson plan to bring the police in on? Throwing a party for a politician? That's crazy?"

I'm the first to admit I didn't know, but, of course, that didn't stop me from speculating. "It's still extortion. Right?"

No one agreed. No one disagreed. No one had an answer.

"Any idea who Verdeen is?" Kevin broke the toothpick

between his fingers then leaned in. "The last name in the notes."

Vandercoy shook his head. "The name isn't on the list Quinlan provided. I ran it through the computer. No hits. I'll mention it to the family tomorrow, see if I get a rise out of anyone."

I frowned at the admission that Verdeen's name hadn't shown up anywhere. "Rickson's been on the case --what? Ten days?"

Kevin agreed.

"If Verdeen isn't associated with the Prusharks where did he come across the name? What did the notes say?" I fought to remember the brief strokes Rickson had used to paint each of his characters.

"'Verdeen – weakest link, wants out?'" Vandercoy read the note before throwing the pages on the desk. "Out of what? The planning or the execution?"

Kevin snorted. "We're past the planning stage."

Vandercoy studied the notes again. He took the unlit cigar out of his mouth. He looked like he might drop off, but his eyes were alert. "You can go. Bring the others in first thing tomorrow to sign their statements. We have a description of the men at the hotel. One Hispanic. One blonde."

I raised a brow. "Are they connected to the two we saw?"

"Two groups. Two bombs. I don't buy coincidences." He tweaked the notes. His jaw had the set of a bulldog in a fight. "I'll work on this and let you know what I find."

"Whoa, fella." I shot out of my chair and slapped my hand on the two loose papers. "These are the property of Crawford Investigations. The originals are going with me."

That sounded like my voice, but was even I crazy enough to start a pointless fight with our only ally?

Evidently, the answer was – yes.

11

6 Across; 6 Letters;
Clue: A recollection; Used to store facts
Answer: Memory

Vandercoy's jaw had a pugnacious stance that made him look like a poor man's Churchill. He eyed me with a fierce stare. "The pages are part of an ongoing investigation. They stay."

Even as I marshaled my arguments, I wondered why I'd started the fight. I had no clue whether Crawford had a legal claim to Rickson's notes. Besides, it wouldn't matter if I had the original or a copy. I'd still be clueless. I suppose, like the yellow box and the dog, the notes were one of the few solid things I could lay my hands on and, for some reason I failed to understand, my brain meant to keep a hold of them.

"You have no reason to keep the pages," I said. "Nothing links them directly to Mr. Prushark's death or the bombings. You can make copies if you need the information."

The detective's jaw was so stiff he'd have bitten through the cigar if he'd had it in his mouth. As it was, he edged up on his chair to within inches of my face. "These notes contain observations regarding an active homicide investigation. That gives me cause to retain possession."

"That gives you a right to the *information*." I dug in as well, completely clueless about whether my argument held weight. "The notes belong to Crawford Investigations."

Kevin remained quietly supportive. But a glimmer in his eyes told me he didn't understand my stubborn stance.

I didn't understand either. My body screamed at me to find a bed. But my mouth had gotten me into this and I make it a point to support whatever stupidity I talk myself into.

Like two dogs fighting over a bone, Vandercoy and I continued our silent stare down.

Finally, Kevin, the saner half of our partnership, spoke up. "We'll be in town. If you need the originals, call. Once Crawford returns, you can debate the matter with him."

I sat down with slow, deliberate moves. Worn out with the standoff, but unwilling to surrender, I hoped Vandercoy took Kevin's olive branch.

"Crawford said you were stubborn." The detective pushed off his chair and made a noise somewhere between a humbug and a growl. He pointed at Kevin and me. "If you find *anything*, you call me."

Kevin and I nodded in unison.

"Hold out and you'll rot in jail until Crawford bails you out." Vandercoy's tone left no doubt he meant it.

"All we want is to unravel this mess, so we can go home." Thankfully, Kevin spoke for both us and, as usual, he was more diplomatic than I would have been.

The clock struck midnight as we plodded into the Liverpool Hotel, my second hotel of the day. This time, I wasn't greeted by name. I also didn't get a smile.

The desk clerk heaved a sigh as he tore his gaze from his late-night movie long enough to hit a button then hand us two key cards. Instantly refocusing on the thirty-two-inch TV, he wished us good night with the enthusiasm of a man facing execution.

I stumbled to the elevator, glad I was still a free woman. Vandercoy's actions puzzled me. The detective not only shared information, he'd let us keep Rickson's notes.

I couldn't decide if he trusted us or if he was setting us up. I leaned against the wall of the elevator and debated taking off my shoes. "What's Vandercoy up to?"

"Covering his bases." Kevin eyed the doors with an annoying alertness. "He's got nothing to lose by having us poke around. We may get lucky."

His smoldering look added a double entendre to his words.

The affection in his eyes sent a slow warmth spreading through my veins. I answered with a smile. One of these days, we'd have time alone together, instead of stolen moments. For now, I reluctantly focused on the case. "If our track record is anything to go by, he's going to get more problems."

The elevator opened as I decided I didn't have the energy to pick up my pumps if I took them off. Luckily our room was close. When Kevin unlocked the door, the light from the hall showed two double beds.

Rabi, dark-skin blending with the shadows, stood in the open doorway of the adjoining room. He nodded once.

Kevin closed the door behind us. Together we walked over to Rabi.

"We cool?" Rabi asked.

"Nothing that won't wait until morning." I motioned to the room behind him. "Marcus?"

"Sleeping." His dry tone hinted that bedtime hadn't been an easy sell.

I smiled, glad to have missed that battle.

"Got you clothes." Rabi gestured toward the bed. "Guessed at the sizes."

"Thank God and thank you." Relief filled me at the thought of changing out of my dress and heels. The Prushark meeting seemed a lifetime ago.

"I'll take first watch." Kevin spoke to Rabi in a muted voice.

I couldn't smother a moan. If they stood watch, I'd feel obligated to take a turn and, God forbid, they might let me.

Rabi shook his head. "I'm sleeping in the chair. I'll wake if anything happens."

I don't care what anyone says: I love chivalry, especially when it's convenient for me. Still, good manners required a token protest. "You sure?"

Rabi's smile told me I didn't fool him for a minute. "You'll need your energy for Marcus tomorrow."

The reminder dissolved my pinprick of guilt. Breathing a heartfelt thank you, I walked to the far bed and kicked off my shoes. The clothes Rabi bought turned out to be a lightweight jogging suit. I took it and headed toward the bathroom.

"Five minutes," I whispered, passing Kevin.

"Sure you'll last that long?" he quipped.

"If I fall asleep in the shower, throw a towel over me." Fortunately, I made it to bed. The next thing I heard was Marcus's voice from the next room.

"She's been asleep for *hours*, five at least, maybe six."

Pale light beyond my eyelids told me it was morning. I snuggled under the covers. Six hours in a warm bed, not bad for one of Crawford's cases. Then I remembered Rickson lying in the hospital. My eyes popped open and a yawn escaped. But it was the stretch that gave me away.

"She's up," Marcus yelled. "She's awake."

"How could she not be?" Kevin's mutter sounded from the doorway.

I pushed myself upright and stumbled in the direction of the bathroom. "He's half right. I'm up."

Kevin smiled and held out a cardboard cup. "Coffee."

Marcus poked his head over Kevin's arm. "Flavored. I thought of you."

I snagged the cup with one hand and ruffled Marcus's silky black hair with the other. Fifteen minutes later I was curled up on a bed in the other room, sipping my second cup of coffee. I was almost alert and I felt halfway human.

Mrs. C sat in a chair, knitting away. Rabi was in the other one, silent and watchful.

Marcus bounced from one foot to the other while watching a bag of popcorn in the microwave. Opening the door, he grabbed the bag and landed on my bed. The enticing smell of hot butter filled the air.

"That's not a proper breakfast." My stomach growled. I eyed the bag and wondered when I'd turned into my mother.

Kevin, stretched out on the other bed, snaked a hand over and grabbed a handful of hot kernels. He obviously had no reservations about the nutritional value.

"I already had cereal, toast, bacon, three donuts, and a waffle," Marcus said.

My mouth watered.

Kevin spoke before I could comment. "I filled them in on the details from Rickson's notes and the bombings. I also called the hospital and got an update."

Apprehension skittered up my spine. "How is he?"

"Awake." Kevin's quick answer put my worst fears to rest.

"They don't think there'll be any permanent damage from the skull fracture. That's not the problem."

His tone caught my attention. Kevin has an annoying penchant for melodramatic buildup. "What is the problem?"

Kevin met my gaze with a glimmer deep in his eyes. "The concussion."

I shifted uneasily. "Why?"

Concussions are far more serious than TV dramas portray, but Rickson wasn't about to sneak out to solve the case.

Marcus shoved a handful of warm popcorn in his mouth. His gaze darted between Kevin and me like a moviegoer in a front row seat.

Kevin took a deep breath. "Rickson has short-term memory loss."

I took a drink of coffee while I digested the news. Who could think with Marcus eating buttered popcorn at my elbow? I grabbed some kernels and tossed them into my mouth. Then the implications hit me like a bat to my brain. "Are you telling me Rickson doesn't remember the case?"

Kevin nodded.

"Verdeen?" The name of the unknown in the notes.

Kevin shook his head. "Nada."

As disappointment washed over me, I realized how much I'd been counting on Rickson to provide answers. The man could be exasperating, but he had decades of detecting behind him. I didn't have thirty months of working solo.

I leaned in, hoping for some scrap. "He must remember something."

Kevin wagged his head from side to side. "Vandercoy showed him the notes-- not a glimmer. Rickson vaguely remembers talking to you in Langsdale though he's not sure what was discussed."

I slumped against the headboard. "The only one who knew any answers and he can't remember? I don't believe it."

Kevin snorted. "This is par for the course on your cases. And, now that you've had your coffee, Mrs. Colchester has news."

Alarm boiled up in my belly. Before I had time to imagine what new crisis had visited me, the older woman dove right in.

"Your apartment was broken into." She eyed me with a hint of excitement in her pale green gaze. "Me friends heard a noise last night and called the authorities."

"First, they took my car; now my home is under attack." I was getting ticked off. "How much damage?"

"Not a great deal," she reassured me. "Boxes cut open. Personal items strewn about. Part of your living quarters ransacked. They ran off when they heard the sirens."

It could only be one thing. "They were after the plastic box. Who knew I had it?"

Kevin shrugged. "Whoever targeted your car has your address. We can both be tagged through B & T Inc. Ferguson knew Rickson passed the box to someone in Langsdale. Pick your poison. Either Ferguson or someone else put the pieces together."

"At least it's hidden."

Marcus nodded before I finished speaking.

The little rascal probably knew all my hiding places. I ate more popcorn.

Marcus raised a brow. "That's not a proper breakfast."

I narrowed my gaze. That's what I get for trying to ensure he eats nutritious meals. I sipped my coffee as I dialed Vandercoy's number. Despite the fact that it was nine o'clock on a Sunday morning, the detective picked up on the first ring. Minutes later I repeated my directions.

"The blue chair in the main room has an empty base. The

rear panel flips off. The box is wrapped in a white towel." As if they'd find more than one towel there. "The people watching my apartment have keys. I'll make sure they're expecting the police."

Mrs. C dug into her massive bag. "I'll call them now. When will the bobbies arrive?"

Her formal mode of speaking made it sound like a tea party. I repeated her question to Vandercoy.

"Ten minutes ago," he said. "I want that box."

I relayed the answer to the older woman, then informed Vandercoy of the break-in.

"I'll get the burglary report when I call Langsdale." The detective clipped off the words. "We have your luggage. You can pick it up when you give your statements."

Covering the receiver, I repeated his offer. "Talk about blackmail."

Kevin's smile matched his easygoing attitude. "Be nice."

"At least I can expand my wardrobe." I uncovered the receiver. "We'll head there as soon as we get organized."

"Now we go see the coppers." Marcus lowered his voice in a fair imitation of Bogart in a fifties movie.

Kevin shot him an indulgent smile. "Start walking."

I hadn't seen Rabi move, but he was holding out his hand to Mrs. C. The older woman stuffed the yarn and needles in her oversized bag and let him help her up.

Eagerness grew in my veins. Parts of the puzzle seemed to be coming into focus, but the unknowns mocked me. For the moment, my stomach focused on a completely different issue. "Cops and criminals can wait until I have breakfast. Popcorn isn't enough."

Marcus walked over and pulled me up. "You can grab a bagel in the lobby. They have free breakfast. I need another donut. Hurry."

"You do not need more sugar." I wasn't sure I could take

his energy so early in the day. "We don't need to rush. Cops work twenty-four-seven."

"The sooner we get answers, the sooner we solve the case." Marcus hurried to the door. With his hand on the doorknob, he spun around. A horrified expression, too real to be feigned, covered his face. "Oh, no. The box."

I walked over and put a hand on his shoulder. "What about it?"

His shoulders slumped. His gaze fell before mine. It was several seconds before he looked at me. "When you were loading the car yesterday, I wanted to look at the box again. I had the back of the chair off when I heard you coming. I shoved the panel in place, but it wasn't straight. The burglars might have seen it. If the box is gone, it's all my fault."

For all the scrapes he'd been in, I'd never seen such a dejected expression on my son's face. I smiled and cupped his cheek. "The Prushark press release and Rickson led them to our apartment. If the box is gone, it's not your fault."

"That was our only clue," he protested. "The bad guys have the goods now."

"We don't know that for sure." Kevin came over and put a hand on the boy's shoulder. "As for clues, we're drowning in them, along with all kinds of suspects and crimes. Your mother can solve this case without that box."

"Absolutely." I forced bravado into my tone. Confidence, even feigned, will take you far. "The answers are here. We just have to find the pieces and put them in the right order."

A tentative smile touched Marcus's lips. The frown cleared from his brow.

"What about the animal hospital? Is it on the way to the station?" Excitement gleamed in my son's dark eyes as he put his worry behind him. "We should check out the scene of the crime."

The boy must have seen the interest in my gaze. His grin widened.

After grabbing some food to go, we bundled into the Caddy. I rode shotgun. Marcus sat in the rear between Rabi and Mrs. C. Balancing a full coffee mug and a makeshift egg, bacon, and bagel sandwich, I shut the car door. "If the box is there, Vandercoy should have word on it by the time we get to the police station."

"I wonder what the contents pertain to?" Mrs. C's British accent gave her question a formal tone.

"We have adultery, extortion, and murder. No way one piece of plastic can explain it all." I considered the options. "I'm going with hanky-panky. The proof Rickson was hired to find."

"Rickson should have turned it over to the Prusharks." Kevin wheeled the car out of the lot. "Why hide the evidence?"

Marcus stretched as far forward as his seatbelt allowed, completely recovered from his earlier dejection. "If the box was sealed when Rickson found it, he can't know what's inside."

"Good point, Watson." Kevin's British accent sounded as flawless as Mrs. C's. "Ferguson is hot for that box. Does he know what's inside?"

"Why the elaborate steps to hide the contents?" I bit into my cheesy egg sandwich before continuing. "Do the contents prove Linda's affair? Or the evidence Ferguson believes will clear him?"

"We should have drilled the box open when we had the chance." Marcus's voice held a note of accusation. "Then we'd know what was inside."

I offered a noncommittal smile. I wasn't about to admit I agreed with him. Besides, my brain was spinning like an out-of-control tilt-a-whirl. "How did Rickson make sense of this case so quickly? He had more answers than anyone, how did he find them?"

Kevin shrugged as he drove down the highway. The streams of cars on either side of us were laden with ski equipment. "He interviewed the players. Compared their stories against the facts. The usual routine. Nothing special."

"That depends on the investigator." Like the opening of a door, his words sparked a light in my brain. Excitement built in my veins.

In life, as in a crossword puzzle, to find the right answer, you need the right clue. "We've been asking the wrong question."

12

33 Down; 10 Letters;
Clue: Done intentionally
Answer: Deliberate

"What gave Rickson the edge in this case?" I clung to the question I should have been asking all along. "How did he find answers when no one else could?"

Marcus's shifted his dark eyes in my direction. "We've been driving for fifteen minutes and that's like, the tenth time you've said that."

"Because I don't have an answer."

Kevin turned into the access road that led to the Zenox Animal Hospital. "You think revisiting the scene of the crime instead of going directly to Vandercoy will point the way?"

"Call it an irresistible urge." A funny thing happened on the way to the police station, Marcus's idea of checking out the site of the explosion led me astray.

Admittedly, I'm easily led astray.

The blackened remnants of the animal hospital stood in stark contrast to the pale concrete surrounding it. The acrid smell hit me when I stepped out of the car. I grimaced at the stench.

"Look at this bomb crater!" Marcus rushed past me from the backseat of the Caddy. Running toward the rubble, he strained against the yellow crime scene tape. "It stinks."

"Don't cross into the crime scene." Kevin shut his door without taking his gaze off the boy. A long stride brought him to my son's side. Their black hair, one straight and silky, the other wavy and tousled, gleamed in the cool October sunlight.

My gaze lingered on my son and the man I loved. At many points in my life, I'd despaired of having either. A wave of contentment swept over me. I had my own little family and I couldn't be happier.

Well, at least, until I got some answers to this crazy mix of chaos.

Marcus hurried toward the foundation of the adjoining building, also destroyed by the explosion. "What was here?"

Kevin followed more slowly. "A lawyer's office. Older guy, William Larson, works alone. According to the locals from the bar next door he specializes in banking laws, trusts, civil law."

"He must be involved in the case." Marcus's inclination to view every fact through the filter of the current case never failed to make me smile. In the light of day, his idea seemed more than plausible. I shut the car door.

"Going after a lawyer makes more sense than targeting animals." Kevin cast me a glance over his shoulder. Then he returned to eyeing the bar and grill. The zone of destruction stopped just short of the third structure.

"Last night I was too exhausted to consider whether the

other building might be the real target." I walked over to Kevin and Marcus. "Can't hurt to check out a lawyer."

By now Rabi and Mrs. C had exited the vehicle.

Mrs. C remained by the Great White Beast, evidently opting to view the destruction from a safe distance.

Rabi strode the length of the crime scene tape, stopping in front of the untouched bar and grill. He seemed to be mentally mapping the scene, from the isolated position of the businesses to the amount of damage. His intense gaze zeroed in on the remnants of the wall that had once connected the hospital to the lawyer's office.

When the wind shifted and a breeze stirred his shoulder-length hair, his nostrils flared. Rather than turn away, he inhaled the lingering scent. He shifted his attention from the hospital to the untouched bar and grill.

Though his expression didn't change, an aura of certainty settled around him. "Overkill."

Kevin didn't bother looking at the bomb site. He focused on our own, personal Special Ops expert. "Explain."

"Too much." Rabi pointed at the deepest part of the hole, directly between the hospital and the law office. "Epicenter. The explosives blew outward in a controlled blast."

He spread his arms out, stopping, not at the farthest extent of his reach, but at a set distance. The bar and grill, completely intact in the early morning sunlight, provided stark evidence of Rabi's supposition.

"The lawyer *was* the target." Marcus's high-pitched voice carried on the wind and echoed around. "That's why that Monroe worker brought in the dog that Rickson heard about. They scoped out the place. Yesterday, they brought in the dead dog to put the bomb in place. Last night, they set it off."

Though there was no one around, I made a shushing gesture. My attention lingered on a handful of vans and

SUVs parked along the residential street at the top of the hill. After a second, I turned away. This case was making me paranoid.

"Quinlan did mention the Prusharks have been covering-up construction problems. Something in the lawyer's office could have tied them to the fraud." Possibilities raced through my head. I tapped Marcus's arm. "Check out the guy. See if you can find any connection with the Prusharks. I'm sure Vandercoy is working that angle but I doubt he'll share."

Kevin walked to where the office's main entrance had once stood. "The girl who worked for Zenox saw the guy coming up from the basement. Why go there?"

Rabi aimed two long, bony fingers at the deepest part of the pit. "Load-bearing wall."

I'd have to take his word for it. No amount of squinting helped me rebuild the twisted, melted pile of metal and concrete into a semblance of what had existed yesterday. "This mystery man could have carried a bomb into Zenox big enough for this blast?"

Rabi's sideways glance was enough to convey his surprise at my naiveté. "Small buildings. Shared wall. Pocketful is enough."

Bummer. Not that I wanted to toss away a lead, but… "Just once I'd like a clue that made sense."

"Much less suspicious to access an animal hospital than a lawyer." Mrs. C, who'd carefully remained outside the circle of ash and debris, picked her way closer. Though she risked damaging her pink slippers, excitement underscored her tone. "A law office could have alarms, security cameras, very difficult to get around, don't you know? I'd have thought Mr. Rickson would have mentioned the proximity of the attorney's office."

"He never made it this far." Kevin's hand shot out in time to catch Marcus's jacket as the boy ducked under the yellow tape. "He overheard the dog comment when he tailed the construction workers to a local bar."

"Just what I need, another farfetched lead." My defensive tone was half-feigned. Ever since I hit town, the violence had escalated.

"Feeling put upon, Belden?" Kevin's smile eased my unsettled nerves. Keeping a firm hand on Marcus, he walked the boy to Rabi before releasing his hold.

"When I create crossword puzzles, I know the answers."

"You'll make sense of this mess." Kevin returned to my side. When I leaned toward him, he put an arm around my shoulders. "We all know you won't stop until you have your puzzle completed."

"I wish I had a clue how this relates to adultery or murder." His confidence brought a comforting sense of security welling up in me. I straightened my shoulders. "Let's focus on what Rickson figured out and how he did it."

"We have the same clues." Marcus stabbed a finger at my purse, where I'd stashed the original notes. "We should be able to figure out the same things he did."

"We have his notes." Kevin faced the boy. "We don't have his experience."

"That's it!" I threw up my hands as the epiphany hit me. "Rickson recognized something from his past."

Energy burned through my veins. For the first time in thirty-six hours, I felt I was on the right track.

Mrs. C's reaction was an encouraging smile.

Rabi worried a toothpick in his mouth.

"What do we know about Rickson?" As Kevin voiced the question, his cobalt gaze turned thoughtful. "He knows Langsdale. He worked on the police force. The Prushark crew and the Lake Tahoe cops don't have that background."

"Don't forget Vegas." Marcus cast a wistful glance at the

destruction beyond the yellow tape. "He worked vice. He's told me stories."

Frowning at the probable content of the tales, I let my brain wander in circles looking for a spark of inspiration.

After a moment of silence, Marcus pointed at Rabi. "What are you thinking?"

The toothpick in Rabi's mouth had gone still. His eyes narrowed to slits. Gravel scraped beneath his shoes as he walked along the debris-strewn sidewalk.

"I spent time in Vegas." Rabi's low drawl moved with the speed of molasses down a maple tree. "Heard of a bookie who records his client's names in code. Uses initials and letters."

"Huh?" Nice to know my rapier wit never failed me. There was only one name that hadn't been identified. I dug in my purse for the pages, tightening my grip as they rippled in the pungent wind. A scrutiny of Rickson's notes proved Rabi's insight was spot on. "I'm going to have to re-work my crossword puzzle. That's why no one can find Verdeen. Rickson used code to hide the real name."

Marcus crowded close to my side, pulling at the notes. "How do you figure?"

"See here?" I pointed to the entry. "The V, D, and N are darker. He wrote over them several times. You can feel the imprint on the paper."

My son nudged me with his thin frame. "Those are someone's initials."

Mrs. C had moved upwind of the burned-out buildings. When she folded her hands over her belly, sunlight reflected on her parchment-like skin. "Why would Mr. Rickson hide the person's identity in his own notes?"

I paused for a moment, before admitting the truth. "I have no idea."

"He probably copied it from the bookie." Marcus quickly

jumped in to defend the big man. "He said you never know where a detail will lead. Now, we need to find Verdeen's real name."

The boy whipped out his smartphone, a Christmas present from Rabi, and started typing. Restrained energy simmered in the air around him.

I took a long drink of my coffee. The cold October sky overshadowing the destruction fit my mood. I'd come to another dead-end. "What do you think you can find with three initials?"

"V-e-r has to be part of the first name." Certainty rang in Marcus's tone. His face settled into a studious expression that always made me smile. "D is the middle initial. N is the beginning of the last name, and they must work for the Prusharks."

I wasn't convinced. "You seriously think that's going to lead to anything definite?"

"Google is your friend." The boy glanced at me over his phone. "Well... it is for most people."

I frowned at the top of his head. "I only broke one phone. Okay, and one tablet. It wasn't my fault. They wouldn't cooperate."

"They're machines, T.R." My son waved a hand. "Don't worry. That's why you have me."

"Oh, good." The wind shifted as I opened my mouth. I gagged as the lingering smoke caught in my throat.

Kevin touched my arm. "You okay?"

Warmed by his concern, I smiled. Together, we walked to the end of the animal hospital. With the wind behind me, I had a straight on view of the three buildings.

Mrs. C scowled in the face of the shifting wind and joined us.

Rabi had shifted out of the way after he'd noted the position of the blast.

Marcus, gaze pinned to his phone, walked toward me. He flicked through screen after screen. His scowl darkened with each failure. His mouth flattened, but the tight set of his jaw denoted his determination. Then, a light dawned in his black eyes. His lips turned up and he shot a triumphant grin my way.

Surprise swept through me. "You did *not* find someone."

"Verna D. Nelson, Executive Assistant for Todd Prushark." With a grin that stretched across his face, he focused on the phone's readout. "The article is three years old. She issued a statement about a construction project. With a name, I can find her background."

A silver dollar appeared out of nowhere and spun in the air on the edge of my vision. The coin glinted as it flipped end-over-end above Kevin's hand. "Never underestimate our resident computer genius."

Proud of my son's achievement, I wrested my attention away from the whirling disk. "I should know better."

The breeze ruffled Marcus's hair as he stopped by my side. "Verna Nelson has worked for the Prushark Corporation for fifteen years. Short-term jobs before that. Married twice. First husband died in a construction accident."

"What happened with the accident?" I pounced on his hesitation. "Another connection? What? What? Tell me."

Kevin chuckled. "Good thing you're a patient person."

I shot him a frown while trying to steal a look at Marcus's phone. "What did you find out?"

"The first husband was killed while working for the Prushark's. The accident happened after Mr. Henry Prushark insisted on a project being completed in a driving rain. The man's name was William Ferguson. Survived by his brother, David."

My lips pursed in a silent whistle. "We just hit the jackpot of motives."

Kevin snatched the coin out of the air, then flashed an empty palm toward the rest of us, waiting like a paying audience. "Verna is the inside connection Rickson mentioned in his notes."

Kevin's cynical tone harkened to his days of working with his family of grifters.

"A spy in the house could explain several details." I faced Kevin who displayed the silver dollar in his palm. The cool air seemed warmer with a tie between these seemingly random clues. "Verdeen could have known of the daughter-in-law's infidelity and shared the news with her brother-in-law years ago."

With ashes and soot as a backdrop, Marcus buzzed with excitement. "When David got fired for fraud, he used the information to get revenge. I bet the next letter asks for money."

"Possible." Kevin's shrug didn't interfere with his trick of weaving the coin in and out of his fingers. "How does this tie into two bombings?"

"I admit there are a few loose ends." Adultery. Murder. Explosions. I had too many clues to organize into a decent sized crossword puzzle. I waved my hand while the remains of the two buildings taunted me. "We need proof. I don't suppose the cops in Langsdale came up with something on my car being impounded? A name? Someone called it in?"

Marcus exchanged a co-conspirator's glance with Mrs. C. "Mrs. C's contact came through with the goods."

The older woman, who'd been eyeing her soot-speckled slippers with a tearful expression, raised her gaze to meet mine. "Evidently the local bobbies had your car impounded. A local patrol misread the license plate. The vehicle they were looking for belongs to a local drug dealer the authorities have been after. There were too quick to jump at the chance to harass him."

Marcus pocketed his phone. "It was just a weird coincidence."

With the sun shining down and the smell of smoke tainting the air, my brain screeched to a halt. "What about the conspiracy theory? Contractors being targeted?"

"Conspiracy?" Kevin flipped the silver coin in and out of view in rapid succession. A teasing smile stole over his lips. "You sound paranoid, Belden."

"Yeah." Marcus scrunched up his face. "The case is about extortion and murder. Who said Prushark contractors were being targeted?"

I growled and made a grab for him. "You did."

The boy laughed and ran away. His silky, black hair glinted in the sun. "I think the conspiracy theory is what they call a red herring in mystery novels."

One step forward. Two steps back. No solid answers.

"One more thing." Marcus jumped as if a jolt of energy had shot through him. "David Ferguson made bail two hours after he was arrested in the ER. He was out in time to be our burglar. Now, he could be anywhere."

"Probably behind those bushes, taping our conversation." Kevin pointed to a six-foot hedge that delineated the beginning of the residential area.

"I hope he's as confused as I am." My gaze tracked the quiet street. The row of parked vehicles sat where the dark sedan had been parked last night. "Marcus, did you find out anything about Rickson's movements or leads?"

"He called Crawford's office Thursday afternoon."

"About what?" Kevin had the question out before I could form the words.

Marcus eyed us with a smug expression. "He asked for the name and address of Linda Prushark's doctor."

Kevin and I exchanged puzzled frowns.

I felt as if someone had pulled the rug out from under me.

Of all the trails Rickson could have followed, this came out of the blue. "How could her health tie into this case?"

Marcus positively oozed satisfaction. "He got the doctor's name Friday morning."

"Did he think he'd get her medical history?" Kevin's skeptical tone made it clear I wasn't the only one at a loss. "Doctors don't give out information on their patients."

"Twelve hours after he had the doctor's name, he dumped the box in my lap." In the distance, snow-white paths wove in and out among the tall, dark pines. Sometimes close together, other times forking in opposite directions. Like the clues in this case. The stark beauty struck me as I sought for an explanation of how the daughter-in-law's health might prove crucial. "Nope. I got nothing."

"Rickson knew something." Certainty echoed in Marcus's voice.

"The clues are all over the board." Frustration bled into my tone. I'm good at puzzles, but the big guy had me beat. "Every fact points in a new direction. Which one led to murder?"

"Adultery strikes at the heart of the family." Mrs. C gazed at the blackened pit. An enigmatic expression settled on her features. "Mr. Prushark's murder was carried out in his home. An attack from within."

The older woman's certainty added force to her words.

Something niggled in my brain. When I tried to latch on, it scurried into the shadows. Though our clues spanned different cities and a seemingly endless parade of people, in the end, the man died surrounded by family.

Had a daughter-in-law's infidelity led to murder?

I only wish I had the answer.

13

12 Across; 6 Letters;
Clue: To gain entry to
Answer: Access

"Another day. Another police station." Kevin eased the Caddy to a stop in front of the Lake Tahoe Police Department. His carefree tone bordered on annoying.

A moment later, I held the door open for Mrs. C. "He makes it sound like all we do is visit police stations."

Marcus, having bolted ahead, now raced back. "This is fancier than any of the stations in Langsdale."

"Okay, maybe we have visited our share," I admitted, following my son through the entrance.

"Ma'am, is he with you?" A beleaguered looking cop eyed me from the other side of a glassed-in desk as soon as I walked inside.

Marcus's toes teetered on the molding six inches off the floor. His face was all but glued to the safety-glass. He jabbed a finger at the uniformed officer. "Where's homicide? We're here about a murder."

Putting on my professional manner, I walked up to corral my boy. Moments later, we exited the elevator and headed toward Vandercoy's office.

Sunday morning or not, the man was prepared. In no time at all, our statements were printed and signed. We also reviewed pictures of security guards at the estate.

None scored hits as the bombers.

After Marcus, Rabi, and Mrs. C were whisked off to work with sketch artists, Kevin and I faced Vandercoy in his not-so-spacious office.

I sat in one of two chairs. It was late morning and my stomach had already forgotten the breakfast sandwich. "Let's get the important things out of the way first. Where's our luggage? I'm tired of wearing clothes I slept in."

The detective waved a hand in the direction of the elevator. "Front desk. Ask on your way out."

Kevin sat back with a casual air, yet his gaze never left the homicide detective. "Any record of the Prushark estate calling 9-1-1 yesterday about shots fired?"

That would have been Rickson's Saturday afternoon run-in with Ferguson and the Prushark security guards. Hard to believe the big guy had been wolfing down pancakes in my kitchen a little over twenty-four hours ago.

"No call came in from the Prushark estate." Lips pursed around an unlit cigar, Vandercoy lowered his head until his double chins rested on his tailored vest. "When questioned, the guards did admit shooting at an intruder they identified as David Ferguson. They claim he fired first. Ben, the Prushark's grandson, was in the area. Rickson pursued Ferguson. Neither man returned."

"Why would Ferguson risk sneaking onto the estate?"

Only one of the many questions on my list. "He knew Rickson took the box to Langsdale on Friday."

The detective plucked the unlit cigar from his mouth. "I'll ask him when I find him."

"The box." I smacked my forehead. "Did the Langsdale PD open it? Do you know what's inside it?"

As soon as the words were out, my brain smacked me upside the head, reminding me that Marcus had left the panel off. I leaned forward, barely maintaining a perch on the edge of the padded chair. Hoping against hope the intruders had been blind.

Vandercoy arched a brow and gave me a fish stare. Light reflected off his carefully combed hair. "We may never know. The panel was off. The box was gone."

I slumped in my seat. Despair and regret warring within me. I steeled myself and fessed up to Marcus's actions. "I wish I'd drilled it open when I had the chance."

Vandercoy's accusing glare placed blame for the oversight squarely on my shoulders.

Kevin gave me a reassuring grin. Then his narrowed gaze drilled Vandercoy. "Any leads on the murder?"

I waited to see whether Kevin would have better luck with the detective than I'd had with Quinlan. She'd obviously left a lot of holes in her story.

"Nothing solid." The detective's tone left little doubt about his displeasure. "The preliminary autopsy states Henry Prushark died of injuries consistent with a fall; fractured skull, broken neck, internal bleeding."

"Nobody heard anything?" Kevin asked.

"Nada." Vandercoy finally took the cigar out of his mouth. He shifted a folder to the center of his desk but didn't look at it. "The attorney was in the conference room. After Sheila and Quinlan left you two, Sheila sent Quinlan to the kitchen to check on the refreshments for the meeting."

Kevin's gaze never left the homicide detective. "She couldn't just pick up a phone and call?"

"Evidently not." The detective plucked the unlit cigar from his mouth before continuing the countdown. "Sheila then went looking for her brother, who had an earlier meeting. The wife was upstairs retrieving papers for the meeting."

Vandercoy shifted and the chair creaked beneath him. He eyed us with the expectant air.

Kevin had acquired a pencil from somewhere and twirled it in his fingers. "They were *all* alone?"

"That doesn't help our cause." I resorted to my usual thinking device and chewed on my thumb. "What about Pete and Matt Monroe?"

"They stopped in a small office to talk." Vandercoy answered in a dry tone. "They alibi each other."

"Well, that's convenient, since Henry Prushark's death all but guarantees they'll regain controlling interest in their family company." My tone sounded a bit petulant, but, seriously, couldn't we get one decent clue? "What about the security cameras?"

Vandercoy paused. "Computer forensics is checking the tape. So far, the cameras confirm the story."

My jaw dropped open. "That can't be."

One side of Kevin's mouth curled up. "They're good."

I turned to him. "Who?"

He narrowed his gaze. "Whoever's behind this scheme."

Impatient for something solid to go on, I shifted in my seat. "What about the guards?"

"Accounted for," Vandercoy said.

"Someone else had to be in the house," I insisted.

"There was," Vandercoy confirmed. "Two strangers who hit town that day and got onto the estate with a bogus story of being contractors."

By the time he finished I realized Kevin and I were in the

crosshairs. Since my stalwart partner sat there with a gleam of admiration in his eyes, our defense was left to me. "We're the good guys. We're helping."

"We are?" Kevin quipped.

Admittedly violence and destruction followed wherever we went, but now was not the time to point out that fact.

"There's nothing on you." Vandercoy sounded disappointed. "You're not in the will."

I perked up. "Who gets the goods? Even better, who doesn't get the goods?"

The detective's gaze slid to Kevin.

"She has her moments," Kevin spoke in the patronizing tone he reserved to goad me.

I shot him a mock glare. A sly, knowing smile was his only response. In the whirlwind of uncertainty, the familiar give and take settled over me like a glowing sunset after a hard day.

"The lawyer sent over a copy of the will this morning." Vandercoy gestured at a pile of papers but didn't stir himself to find the document. "No surprises. The wife has her portion. The son and daughter will add a good chunk to what they already have in the companies."

"So, everyone profits and the old man doesn't take back control." I pondered the updates. No surprises. Same old motives. "What about William Ferguson's death? David could have blamed Henry Prushark for the accident that killed his brother."

Vandercoy blinked as if trying to stay awake. "Why kill Henry Prushark now, instead of fifteen years ago? Being fired give him a motive for the threatening letters. He and Verna could be working together."

I grudgingly agreed with his assessment, but blaming Ferguson for murder was easier than me trying to figure out this tangled web. I sipped the coffee. It wasn't flavored, but it was hot.

"What's the scoop on Verna D. Nelson?" I preened, proud of my son's success in uncovering 'Verdeen's' identity when the police had failed. I was also happy I could lock down at least one answer in my crossword puzzle. That made me feel more in control. A false sense of security, but it was all I had.

Vandercoy tweaked a slip of paper on his desk. "Verna D. Nelson packed her bags Thursday afternoon and left for a holiday in Brazil. Her family hasn't heard from her."

"That was the same day Rickson found the box," I noted. "Thursday was a busy day."

The pencil Kevin had been toying with stopped in mid-spin. "No extradition from Brazil."

He would know.

"Why is David here if she's there? What is he looking for?" As the interwoven strands spun through my mind, the light glinted off Vandercoy's watch chain. His three-piece tailored ensemble made me conscious that I was wearing clothes I'd slept in.

Kevin also wore yesterday's clothes, but his shirt was smooth as it tightened across his muscled chest. My outfit was so wrinkled I could've passed for a homeless person. With an internal sigh I gave up on comparisons. I was no more a model than I was a master chef.

Time to focus on the puzzle. "Which of the Prushark family oversees the security division?"

The detective arched a brow. "Since the old man's stroke, Todd Prushark is in charge. Girard reports directly to him."

Various implications spun through my mind. "Is Todd hands on? As in reconfiguring security logs?"

Vandercoy nodded in my direction as if bestowing a point on a pupil. "He's also in charge of the technology division. He has advanced degrees in computer programming."

"Oooohhh." My interest skyrocketed. "Slicing and dicing a computer recording would be child's play for him. Or Girard. Or Sheila most likely. No lack of suspects."

"We faxed the descriptions of the four bombers to Langsdale and Vegas." Vandercoy shook his head from side to side as if it took an enormous amount of effort. "No hits."

Kevin eyed Vandercoy. "What next?"

Good question. I gave up trying to smooth my top to a semblance of order and studied the detective. His poker face gave nothing away.

Vandercoy folded his hands over his stomach. "I continue my investigation into Henry Prushark's death and the bombings. You remain in town, go about your business, and stay away from explosions."

I kept a bland expression on my face and fought not to look at Kevin. The Prushark investigation was our only reason for being in Tahoe. Why would Vandercoy give us oblique permission to pursue an active investigation? Most cops arrest anyone messing with their case.

Pushing himself to his feet, Kevin pasted on a polite smile. "We intend to stay as far away from trouble as possible."

What a good line. Why hadn't I thought of it? Perhaps because trouble seems to find us like a magnet finds steel. "Thanks for recovering our luggage."

Vandercoy made no move to stand. He moved his tie half-an-inch, so it was dead center at his throat. "Your statements have your Langsdale addresses. Only my team and I know where you're staying in Tahoe."

I stilled. "Is there a reason for that?"

Vandercoy's shoulders rolled in a massive shrug that looked like a slowly building ocean wave. "Call me cautious."

After one murder and two bombings, caution was good.

He gestured toward the door. "Your friends should be done. If you think of anything, call."

Kevin planted his hand on the small of my back and unobtrusively pushed me toward the door. "We will."

As soon as he closed the door, I started down the hall one way, Kevin tugged at my sleeve. "Elevator's this way."

"They're coming." Marcus's yell echoed through the tile covered corridor. He started forward then stopped and stood by the desk with his hands by his sides, waiting politely.

"Funny, that looks like Marcus." He never stood still. Then I remembered his comment about impressing the police. "I wonder how long he'll stand there."

I slowed my steps.

Kevin chuckled and put a hand around my waist. "Play nice."

A moment later, Kevin and I stepped into the open area by the desk. Our luggage sat by a bench Mrs. C occupied. Since they'd already signed out, it was quick work for Kevin and me to finish the paperwork as well.

The cop behind the desk nodded at my son. "You have a bright young man there, ma'am."

Marcus beamed at him. "Thank you, sir."

Struggling to keep a straight face, I nodded before heading to the elevator. After the doors closed, I squinted at Marcus. "Who are you and what have you done with my son?"

He gave a devilish grin. "They love me."

"You're going to burst from the strain of holding it all in," I warned.

The elevator opened onto a busy main entrance. The late morning sun shining on the sidewalk outside had never looked or felt better.

"I'll take that." Marcus grabbed my suitcase and set it

back-to-back with his. Aiming them both at the Caddy, he took off at a running start and let them both fly.

Kevin paled as the missiles careened toward his pearly white car. "If you scratch the paint, I'll have your hide."

Fortunately, or not, first one then the other hit a rock. They bounced, teetered, then hit the concrete and skidded five feet. Good thing, I couldn't afford Gucci luggage.

"Leaving town, Ms. Belden?" A woman's voice sounded at my elbow.

Hearing the arched tone underlying the words, I put on my professional mask and turned to face Sheila Prushark. A limo was parked at the curb. Girard stood by her side Gathering myself, I nodded a greeting to her. "Leaving town is the last thing on my mind."

The sun lit up the dark depths of her black hair as her lips curled in a mocking smile. "Turning over rocks, are you? Or planning to start the reconstruction project?"

"I was never going to paint anything." I smiled in turn. This woman didn't want to see me with a painting roller in my hand. No one did, not even Kevin. It was a waste of good paint. "I came to help my colleague. Since he has been injured, I'll take over the case."

Girard, silent until now, raised a brow. "Murder and extortion are matters for the police, not amateurs. You'll find Mrs. Prushark has canceled the contract with Crawford Investigations."

Sheila gave a slight, knowing nod. "Your business in Tahoe is done. Time to go home."

It took all my self-control to keep a tight rein on my tongue. These two thought they could be rid of me so easily? I fixed Girard with a long stare. "I don't leave a fallen man behind."

I paused to let the words sink in. He was former military. I was sure of that much. I met his narrowed gaze for several seconds. A subtle tightening around his eyes signaled my arrow had struck home. Too bad I didn't know if I'd antagonized a killer or won an admirer. Time would tell.

I shifted my attention to Sheila, the daughter who'd watched her less talented brothers earn the recognition she deserved. "I'll be in town until this case is solved. Whether I get paid not, I *will* find out who hurt my friend. I'll turn over any rocks I have to, but someone is going to pay."

Though Sheila's expression remained composed, the other woman raised her chin.

I held her gaze before giving a nod. "You two have a nice chat with Detective Vandercoy."

I turned on my heel and walked away without a backward glance. Inwardly seething, I concentrated on the car.

The luggage was out of sight, obviously stored in the Caddy's cavernous trunk.

Kevin, leaning against the closed trunk, watched me approach. He knew how I felt about people telling me what to do.

I stopped in front of him with my fists clenched. "If those two or anyone involved with this case think they're done with me, they better think again. And you better hope I find the answers, because I'm staying in Tahoe until I nail somebody for these crimes."

Kevin put his hands on my shoulders. "I never doubted that, or you."

As I watched him walk toward the driver's door, my irritation dissipated. I was left wishing I had a small dose of Rickson's experience; in investigating, in spotting crimes, in...

The thought stopped me cold.

Police. Crimes. Lightning coursed through my brain. What if--

"Hey, lady." Marcus stuck his head out the car window.

Everyone in the car eyed me expectantly. "You riding with us?"

I pulled out of my stupor. "Sure."

Kevin waited until I buckled up then pulled the Caddy out of the parking lot. "Well, Sherlock? Any new insights?"

I ignored his irreverent tone. "I have a thought."

Kevin gazed heavenward. "I hate to ask."

I ignored him. "What if family politics or adultery aren't the motives for this chaos? What if Rickson discovered evidence of another crime?"

14

8 Across; 5 Letters;
Clue: Multiple tracks laid down
Answer: Paths

"Murder and blackmail aren't enough? You want to add another felony?" Kevin's incredulous tone matched his expression. With a sideways glance in my direction, he drove the Cadillac away from the police station.

Lake Tahoe's busy traffic filled the streets around the Great White Beast like a rushing stream. Ski-poles and skis adorned the tops of cars. It seemed as if everyone but us planned to hit the snow-packed slopes.

With my talk-first-think-later motto in hand, I forged ahead. "I think Rickson uncovered something more serious than adultery. Quinlan said Ferguson has sworn he was innocent from day one. Think about it, if he's guilty and they have evidence, why isn't he in prison? Also, someone blew up a construction headquarters and a law office. That's a bit much for photos of an affair."

Marcus slid a glance at Kevin. "She may be onto something."

Kevin grimaced as he met the boy's gaze in the rearview mirror. "I hate to admit that out loud. It will only encourage her."

I smiled at their teasing even as I fought to grab hold of my nebulous logic. "Say somebody had a racket going."

"Has." Rabi's single word cut across my statement.

His unexpected input silenced me for a heartbeat.

A matching certainty crossed Kevin's handsome face. "If somebody's making money, they won't walk away unless they have to. The explosions were an attempt to cover their tracks."

"I hadn't thought that far ahead." I was building my crossword puzzle on the fly. "The Prushark company has been in flux. One son dies. Sheila jockeys for power. The father has a stroke. Amid the confusion, someone saw a chance for quick money. Fraud. Theft. The crimes Ferguson was framed for."

"Stealing materials or diverting shipments." Marcus thumped the soft leather seat with his fist. His enthusiasm was heartening. "Kevin said a Vegas project lost millions."

Kevin's handsome profile hardened. "Lynam Construction. Rumor had it they got taken big time. Insider job."

My son waved his hands wildly. "Maybe Verna was in on the thefts with someone else. That's why she took off for Brazil."

Kevin executed a sweeping turn and a lane-switching semi would have challenged a lesser driver. As it was, he didn't pause in the conversation. "That's a possibility."

Mrs. C's gnarled fingers pulled a long piece of yarn from her bag. "This theory would tie several loose threads together rather nicely."

Silky black hair flew about Marcus's face as he looked from person to person. "This would be grand theft."

"Hard time." Rabi's soft drawl cut across all other noise.

"Which would justify murder and bombings more than a five-year-old adultery case. This is what we've been missing." The pieces shifted, neatly connecting another errant clue. "Whoever is committing the thefts would need their own records and a place to hide them. That could be where the law office comes in. Older guy. Works alone. No computer system. Destroy the building. Destroy the records."

"I saw a movie where the incriminating evidence was kept in a safety deposit box. But why bomb places now?" Though Marcus's dark eyes shifted to the ski trails snaking through the trees, he didn't appear to see the view. "And what about the letters saying the daughter-in-law had an affair? That started the case."

Kevin snapped his fingers. "That's where a six-foot-nine-inch monkey wrench entered the picture."

"Of course!" I love it when crossword answers bump up against one another. "Mrs. Prushark brought Rickson in under the guise of doing a security audit. The thieves had successfully framed Ferguson. Then, Rickson is given free rein to interview the staff and check the files. Word got out."

"Panic." Rabi's derogatory tone made it clear what he thought of such a weak-kneed reaction.

Kevin's snort wasn't far behind. "They lost their nerve."

"I never let a guilty conscience bother me." Marcus's carefree expression froze when he met my gaze. "Until I met you, T.R."

"Good save." Kevin's stage-whisper held an admiring undercurrent that had the boy preening. "Whoever's running the scam believed Rickson was on their trail."

"Ferguson must have thought they'd destroy the real evidence. So, he sneaks in, sees the toolbox, and grabs it."

Marcus uttered the words with a note of drama. "I bet he doesn't even know what's in it."

"You may be right." The boy sounded like an ad for a cheap thriller, but the timeline fit. "I wonder if Henry Prushark had recovered enough to look at the accounts. If he found a problem and asked for a review, that might be the motive for his murder."

Marcus thrust his hair away from his eyes. "Were the bombs for the threatening letters or the fraud or one for each?"

"The explosions have to be connected to the same crime." I frowned, annoyed at how quickly the threads became tangled. My eyes tracked the crowded, colorful storefronts outside the windshield. "I'll buy two crimes, but I draw the line at two groups of bombers."

"As well you should, dear." Mrs. C sounded morally offended at the very thought.

I was oddly comforted by her agreement, but there was a stumbling block. "The fraud angle doesn't explain who sent the blackmail letters."

Rabi's brow shifted by a hair. "Inside job."

"Good catch." Marcus thumped the man's arm. "The adultery angle had to come from in the house. I bet Quinlan knows."

I considered the possibility of Quinlan's duplicity. "Why would she keep information from me?"

Mrs. C paused in her knitting. Her gaze focused on the mountains, where the slimmest of paths wound through thick, green pine forests. "Most people are motivated by self-preservation. I would wager Ms. Quinlan fears someone in the household."

Kevin turned onto the main thoroughfare that led to the Liverpool, our latest hotel. "Quinlan can't be blamed for snitching if you or Rickson discover the culprit."

"Threats. Theft. Murder." As Marcus recited the litany of crimes, his interested gaze darted from the shops to the throngs of people. "The Prusharks are messed up. Would his wife or kids have killed the old guy to keep power?"

How could I answer that?

"The thirst for power and money are all some people have inside of them." Kevin's voice held a cynical note reserved for his family of grifters. "For those people, too much is never enough, certainly not enough to share."

"The killer just dumped the old man out of his wheelchair and watched him tumble down the stairs." Marcus's breathy tone held a note of horror.

The sheer callousness of the murder chilled me. "A personal attack within the fortress he built."

"Opportunity." Rabi's ashen skin and stillness made him seem like a statue, but the waters in him ran deep. "No record on camera."

My brain filled in the picture Rabi's abrupt mode of speech painted. "Todd or Girard both have an insider's knowledge to reprogram the security tapes. I'm betting Sheila could handle that maneuver as well."

"It's the people closest to you that you have to watch most carefully." Mrs. C let go a long, slow exhale. "One never sees the blow coming."

Her somber words offered a chilling insight into why the police always question family and friends when looking for a killer. They also provided a glimpse into her psyche.

As the unexpected door opened into her past, my brain jumped tracks. To heck with the Prushark's problems, this was my chance to find answers to the older woman's history.

As I thought of my lead-in question, Kevin pulled the car into a slot at the Liverpool Hotel. He'd barely parked when every car door opened but mine. Rabi was already outside assisting Mrs. C.

I watched a perfect chance to dig into her past slip away.

Marcus nudged my arm. "Let's eat. I'm starving."

I opened my mouth to call them back, to extend the journey and recapture the moment. No sound came out. No words. They were already walking toward the hotel. My brain screamed for them to stop.

When Kevin opened my door, I was stuttering. He offered me a knowing smile. "The timing is never right for your personal crusade, is it?"

I shook my fists in the air before taking his offered hand and pulling myself out of the vehicle. "Why couldn't you get lost for once in your life? Drive around aimlessly for an hour or two?"

He simply shrugged.

"Someday, I am going to dig up the truth about her." I huffed my disappointment. Then, the warmth of his calloused hand against mine distracted me. I brushed my thumb against his palm while sorting through the latest setbacks. "My home has been vandalized. The burglars stole the box. Whatever evidence it contained has likely been destroyed."

"I wouldn't be so sure of that." Kevin fixed his gaze on the distance as we headed toward the hotel's main entrance. "The thieves wanted that box for a reason."

My shoulder brushed his as a cool October breeze stirred the pine trees lining our path. I chewed my lip. "Ferguson made bail and was in Langsdale when my apartment was ransacked."

"Time for a new topic." Kevin's commanding tone brooked no argument. He took my hand in his and faced me. "I want to discuss something near and dear to your heart."

I put my hand on my chest as my heart jumped. "Is this topic what I think it is?"

He gave a solemn nod. "Food."

"You're my hero." I wasn't kidding. The man knows me well.

The front door of the hotel opened with a whoosh.

"What's taking you two so long?" Marcus's yell carried throughout the parking lot, perhaps to the next block. "Have you been talking about the case without me? What's for lunch? I'm starving."

I'll fast forward several hours. Past more guesses. Past the unpacking and the shower - which was heavenly. I will linger over the wonderful lunch. We ate in a glassed-in dining room with a dazzling view of the snow-capped mountains surrounding Lake Tahoe. I was wearing clean clothes and I had a full stomach. I could have sat there all day watching the sun glint off the crystal blue water.

Then, Kevin clapped his hands together. "Now for the next item on our agenda."

Marcus swirled a fry in ketchup then pointed the red-tipped potato at Kevin. "The case. New leads. We're going to see what's left of the Monroe offices bomb crater. All of the above?"

"None of the above." Kevin's mouth tilted up. "We're going bowling."

Yes, bowling. Next to Friday night board games with buttery popcorn, an afternoon of bowling and running to the snack bar is one of the favored outings of the Belden Detective Agency.

The skill level begins with one player who's lucky to crack a score of one hundred.

Don't laugh. Those pins have minds of their own.

The other four players vary from the low one-twenties to well past two hundred depending on the day.

Yes, the case was discussed.

Nothing was resolved. The clues knotted and crossed like

a vining plant on steroids. With my one solid piece of evidence gone, my questions continued to multiply.

What Rickson had kept hidden, I had unwittingly let loose.

Question of the hour... What did that blasted box contain?

Though I'd never be able to fill Rickson's size twenty-two shoes, I could follow in his footsteps. On the heels of that thought came the familiar fear of endangering my son.

Finding the box had unleashed a whirlwind. What would my search for a murderer bring forth?

A tsunami?

15

7 Down; 5 Letters;
Clue: Lure another into a trap
Answer: Decoy

"Another day, another bomb crater." Marcus studied the remnants of the Monroe & Sons Construction headquarters. Monday morning's heavy cloud cover that hovered over the site had managed to hold in the smell of smoke. "This is way better than going to school."

I started to nod. Then, I wondered if that made me a failure as a mother. But, at eleven, anything was better than school, especially visiting the aftermath of an explosion.

An interested bystander might ask why I was here. The answer?

I had nowhere else to go. Stumbling around blindly is basically my strategy for investigating. Besides, I can only lose at bowling so many times before even cheesy nachos fail to perk me up.

Rabi won the first game. Marcus surged to second place on a trio of strikes in the final frames. He missed a turkey, four strikes in a row, due to a seven-ten split. Kevin scored high for game two. Mrs. C wrapped up the day with a big finish in the third game. At seventy-plus, she's a spry old lady.

Now, with breakfast behind us and a cloud covered Monday morning, we were hitting our second bomb site in as many days. Marcus's ghoulish reason for insisting we visit the crime scene was simple. He was eleven.

He, Kevin, and I had seen Rickson in the hospital first thing this morning. The big guy still had no memory of the case. So, no help there.

Rabi and Mrs. C had driven to the Monroe site in the car Rabi rented after they were chased out of our fancy suites and returned the "borrowed" car.

I heaved a big sigh for my lost luxury. I was in a second-rate hotel and my investigation had been reduced to grabbing at straws. Even they were slipping through my fingers. Marcus and Crawford's office were both working on the lawyer's customers, looking for possible connections. I'd left Vandercoy a message asking for information, but I doubted he would be forthcoming.

As a weak sun sought to break through the clouds, Rabi followed my son to the edge of the crime scene, where familiar yellow tape cordoned off the site.

"Oh, dear." Mrs. C chose to survey the damage from a safe distance. Her pink bedroom slippers had suffered from the ash and soot yesterday. She was taking no chances with the purple backups. "Rather a total loss, isn't it?"

Standing between the older woman and Kevin, I could only nod.

Kevin studied the scene with an intense gaze. "No other buildings this time. The bombers opted for total destruction."

"They got it." A sweeping look at the burned, crumbling walls and an ashy debris field confirmed the large parking lot had insulated the other buildings in the area from damage. The roar of a car engine pulled my gaze to the access road. My gut clenched.

My feet moved before my brain fired a command. Rabi had Marcus. Protect Mrs. C.

Kevin touched my arm with a restraining gesture. That's when I saw red and blue lights through the black SUV's windshield.

I exhaled in relief.

A moment later, Vandercoy, in yet another flawlessly tailored three-piece suit, complete with a navy vest with gold threads and a watch chain glinting across his rotund form, fixed me with a disapproving stare. "Is touring my crime scenes going to be a daily occurrence with you?"

While I puzzled over the detective's jibe, a gleam shown in Kevin's eyes. "You had a surveillance team on the hill yesterday, or is it a security camera?"

Marcus skidded up to us in time to catch the exchange. He crossed his arms across his chest. "Keeping a lookout is a good idea. Criminals always return to the scene of the crime."

The detective's narrowed gaze had no discernable impact on my son's enthusiasm. "And here you are."

"It's not us," Marcus assured him with a breezy air. "We're on the job. Besides, we'd be way sneakier."

"Good to know." Vandercoy, fiddling with his ever-present cigar, shifted his eagle eyes to me. "You have been to both bomb scenes. Why is that?"

I opened my mouth, totally unaware of what I planned to say, when the sun's reflection off another vehicle distracted me. "More visitors. Were you planning a party? Our invitation must have been mislaid."

A flush of excitement colored my son's golden skin as he studied the sleek, black limo. His eyes snapped with a sudden decision. "I have to reconnoiter with Rabi."

The detective frowned as my son's small frame darted away. "What is he planning?"

Kevin chuckled. "There is literally no telling."

The limo's progress toward us seemed achingly slow. Would they never park the car and get out? Was it Todd? Sheila again? Mrs. Prushark? A little family reunion?

I craned my neck around Vandercoy's wide frame then simply stepped to one side. My gaze remained glued to the limo. "Would you prefer we leave?"

The man tucked the unlit cigar in his vest pocket. "Would you go?"

"Not far," Kevin assured the detective. He crossed his arms over his chest, straining the shoulder seams of his jacket. "Marcus has listening devices in the trunk and Tracy has the hearing of an owl. I'm also pretty sure she's taken a lip-reading course."

"That is not true." I drew myself up to five-foot-nine-inch height. "It's a gift."

As for my son having listening devices in the trunk? More likely he had them in his pocket and was even now recording every word.

Mrs. C had drifted to a nearby stone bench where the breeze blew in her direction.

Her casually indifferent attitude didn't fool me. I knew from personal experience how well conversations carry on the wind.

Rabi and Marcus had moved to one side of the site. Within hearing distance of the boy's keen ears.

Kevin's quick gaze took in the positions of the players.

"Do you expect me to believe you being here is dumb luck?" The detective made no effort to hide his skepticism.

"Well, it's not a plan," I assured him, sneaking a glance at the limo, now parked by the detective's SUV.

Kevin snorted. "I can vouch for that."

"Stay," Vandercoy ordered as he followed the direction of my gaze. "I can use a lightning rod."

Girard was the first to exit the vehicle.

"He was with Sheila at the police station yesterday." Did he accompany the family whenever they left the house? Perhaps he didn't want to miss any updates. The stout form of Todd Prushark came next. Both men turned and, with a solicitous air, held out a hand to the next occupant. "It can only be Mrs. Diana Prushark. Evidently, no one can refuse you, Detective."

A thin white-haired woman emerged. At first glance, she looked like a piece of Chinese porcelain, translucent and fragile. Then she turned. Pale blue eyes, hard and cold as diamonds, swept over me as she scanned the area.

My guard went up and my spine stiffened.

When Mrs. Prushark walked forward, Girard followed two steps behind. Ramrod straight, the epitome of a marine on duty.

"Who arranged this meeting?" I whispered. "You or them?"

Vandercoy grunted. "Information gathering on both sides."

"Why here?" Kevin moved to my left side, leaving me standing between the two men.

Kevin had his reasons. Don't ask me what they were. The man knew all the nuances of body language and positioning people for maximum effect. Me? I charge in blindly, hoping to stir up a bit of chaos.

Vandercoy, his gaze fixed on the Prushark party, paused before answering Kevin. "I chose the location. There are multiple layers to this situation."

Could that be a reference to our fraud theory? When Vandercoy went to meet the advancing Prushark party, I followed the rotund detective, as did Kevin.

Todd stiffened like a dog on point when his gaze landed on me. His scowl deepened as his hands formed fists.

I have that effect on some people. I don't know why. His sister hadn't appeared to be fond of me either.

As soon as he got within arm's length, Todd addressed the detective. "Why are they part of this interview?"

I maintained a polite mask from long practice.

"They were on site when I arrived." Vandercoy spoke in the same lazy manner he used with Kevin and me. "Would you rather they leave?"

"Please, stay." The old lady's eyes had lost their diamond hardness. Though she held herself erect with the air of easy grace, weariness haunted the depths of her gaze. "We never had the chance to meet the other night."

The woman was a hard read. Dry-eyed and stoic, she made no reference to her husband's death.

She struck me as a go-getter. She'd been a successful athlete and entrepreneur at a time when that wasn't common for women. Yet, she'd spent decades in the background, as had her son and daughter. Since the patriarch's stroke, they had each moved to secure control. Had one of them killed him to keep their power?

Kevin's expression turned somber. "Mrs. Prushark, I can't imagine how devastated you must feel at the death of your husband."

I inclined my head in a gesture of sympathy. "I'm sorry for your loss."

Todd's jaw stiffened as he eyed me. "My mother is under a great deal of pressure. In consideration of her feelings, don't you think it would be a thoughtful gesture if you left?"

"Definitely." However, while my Kentucky bred grandmother had taught me good manners, I didn't go out of my way to follow them if it wasn't to my benefit. Especially if I needed answers. "I'm pretty sure everyone knows I'm not leaving, so we may as well share information."

As Todd's frown hardened, a calculating gleam in his eyes gave clear evidence of the intelligence and determination that had helped take the Prushark company to new heights over the past two years. "You're employed by Crawford Investigations, same as Rickson. The contract with your employer has been canceled. You have no authority to investigate."

With the smell of cordite still wafting on the breeze, I marshaled my brain for a battle of wits with what was left of the Prushark clan. "Crawford will never walk away from this case until he finds out who's responsible for Rickson's injuries. Neither will I. I intend to finish what my colleague started. No matter who that convicts."

Mrs. Prushark raised a delicately painted eyebrow. A glint of admiration shown in her pale blue eyes.

A deep flush painted Todd's neck a splotchy, unattractive red. "You two are paid private investigators."

Kevin held up a hand. "For the record, I'm not being paid."

"That's true." Which is one reason I wished our job to refurbish the ballroom had been real. I felt responsible for dragging him into this case. To be honest, I wouldn't mind getting that paycheck myself. At the moment, I was just kicking rocks to see what lay underneath. "Now that we know who's who, let's get back to business. I understand Mr. Prushark had recovered from his stroke and planned to take control of the company. Is that true?"

I steeled myself as Mrs. Prushark's clear skin lost color.

Her downcast eyes lasted less than a heartbeat. When she met my gaze, her expression was composed. "My husband had made great strides. His faculties. His speech. That makes his death all the more tragic and heartbreaking."

She drew in a small gulp of air before clamping her lips tightly shut. Her mouth thinned to a narrow line, tightening the skin over her high cheekbones.

Todd's glare would have sliced me in two had the fire been real.

While I understood her pain, I refused to back down. My brain was focused on the puzzle. "Mr. Prushark's first step would have been to review the reports on the current projects. Did he have a chance to offer input on any of them? Was he aware the ballroom renovation had been awarded to a female-owned business?"

"Though he wasn't strong enough to attend a meeting, my father had been in contact with several directors regarding various projects." Todd's too quick reply had the smell of a canned response. "We were all eager for his input."

As someone who has skated around the truth more than once, I admired the way Todd provided facts without answering my question. Which actually told me what I needed to know. "So, he was already over-seeing your decisions."

A muscle jumped in Todd's jaw. "My father had a lifetime of experience in business. I valued his opinion."

"Ms. Belden, in light of my husband's death, your question is in poor taste." Mrs. Prushark arched a brow at her son as she smoothly took control of the conversation. "My husband and my children all know--knew--their own minds. Any business disagreements they may have had, never detracted from their respect for each other."

Judging by the victorious smirk Todd shot at me, he

evidently thought this conversation was over. Did he truly believe no one else had ever pointed out my lack of tact?

"I have one more question. Detective Vandercoy probably covered this topic, but I wasn't at that meeting." I glanced at the silent detective, who was probably hoping I'd hang myself with the length of rope he was giving me. "Have either of you ever heard of the Larson Law Office that was destroyed Saturday night? Did you have business with William Larson? Set up secret accounts? Hide assets? Misplace money?"

Stunned silence greeted my questions. Vandercoy's cigar went completely still. Mrs. Prushark's eyes widened in an unladylike display of emotion. Girard broke his marine-like control for a double take. If Todd's eyes fired lasers, I'd be a cinder.

Even Kevin, who had to have known it was only a matter of time before I put my foot in my mouth, cast me a sideways glance. Veiled amusement danced in his eyes.

No one said a word, though I sensed everyone had something to say.

"Well?" How would I know if I didn't ask? Besides, what did I have to lose? I wasn't on their payroll.

Nothing but silence.

"Okay. Just thought I'd ask." I shrugged, disappointed but not surprised. "Would you like to jump in here, Detective?"

Chubby fingers once again set the cigar twirling. He fixed me with a pointed stare. "Thank you."

It might be me, but I don't think he was sincere.

Vandercoy waved a meaty paw at the charred pit. "As majority owners of the Monroe & Sons Construction company, were you notified of the explosion at the offices?"

Mrs. Prushark cast a discerning look at the destruction. "I was dismayed to learn the Monroes had suffered yet another blow. I contacted them personally this morning to express my regret."

Was not answering direct questions a family trait?

Vandercoy was not deterred. "Any information you have pertaining to the business would be helpful. A large portion of their records were destroyed."

The idea of construction fraud loomed larger.

"We have records of our dealings with the company." Todd's shoulders lost their stiffness. "I doubt that would be of any help to your investigation."

Though Vandercoy's polite expression didn't waver, the atmosphere around him seemed charged with an aura of challenge. "I'll judge what will help my investigation."

A muscle jumped in Todd's jaw. When he opened his mouth, his mother put a hand on his arm.

"We'll be happy to cooperate." The old woman's gaze remained locked on the detective, sparing not a glance for her son. "Our business office will forward everything we have to you."

"The sooner the better. This may be connected with Mr. Prushark's murder." Vandercoy fixed Todd with a telling gaze until the younger man pulled out his phone and keyed in a message. Then, the detective turned his attention to the older woman. "I've had reports of thefts from Monroe sites that haven't been reported to the police. Covering up a crime could leave your family open to charges of being accessories in the losses."

The clan matriarch's expression tightened. "Sheila found irregularities. She met with the foremen and project managers from Monroe & Son Construction to follow up."

Vandercoy's frown deepened. He tucked the cigar into his vest pocket. "Has evidence of fraud been uncovered?"

As the wind shifted, Mrs. Prushark blinked several times against the dust and ashes. She held out a hand as if she could command the elements themselves to cease. "The investigation is ongoing. My daughter is in charge. She would have apprised my son and me of any details of the theft."

I caught the slightest trace of a snide undertone, but even I knew that was a lie. According to Quinlan, they had solid evidence of Ferguson's guilt.

"I need all records pertaining to her internal investigation. A number of them would be downloads from the Monroe main computers over the previous year." Vandercoy added a touch of steel to his tone, just short of threatening a court order.

Would the Prusharks force him to contact a judge or would they play nice?

Girard, standing at the woman's shoulder, stiffened. The man evidently resented the encroachment on his territory. Or was he worried what the police might find?

"We'll cooperate with the police any way we can, of course." Todd's agreement held a note of condescension.

Mrs. Prushark met the detective's gaze straight on. "Your analysts are welcome to come at any time."

Vandercoy gave a short nod before looking over his shoulder at a plainclothes detective who stood a few feet away. "Send a team to the Prushark estate to go through the files and Sheila Prushark's computer for any and all records from Monroe & Sons Construction. They can update Sheila when they arrive."

As the younger detective scurried away, the matriarch's hand clenched. Spidery blue veins showed through the skin. The older woman pursed her lips, etching deep lines around her mouth.

Todd's eyes tightened. He shot a quick, hard glance at his mother, but their hands were tied. Vandercoy had smoothly prevented the Prusharks from warning Sheila.

Check and mate. I watched with an increased admiration for the detective's cunning.

Fiddling with his watchchain, Vandercoy turned his now lazy-looking gaze on Mrs. Prushark. "Any further contact with your extortionist?"

Her jaw tightened. She shot me a withering look.

Like the fraud, the woman preferred to handle the blackmail on her own.

Yes, I wanted to say, I blabbed. I wasn't about to lie to the police about a possible motive in a murder case.

She gave an infinitesimal shake of her head, but her son, after a searching look at her rigid expression, shifted his attention to the detective. "Another threat arrived this morning."

Mrs. Prushark shot her son a look of... fury? Her expression reminded me of Quinlan's comments regarding the older woman's zeal in protecting the family from scandal.

Todd hesitated for a moment before continuing. "The letter warns that our failure to comply with the instructions will cost us. Further instructions will arrive soon. If we contact the police, they will release the alleged proof to the media."

Vandercoy's attitude changed from a thrust-and-parry with suspects to a protector of victims. His eyes narrowed as Todd reached into his pocket and withdrew an envelope in a sealed plastic bag.

After the detective took the bag, he launched into a series of rapid-fire questions regarding method and time of delivery.

I leaned close to Kevin. "For the letter to arrive on Monday, it had to be mailed on Friday or earlier. The box was stolen from my apartment Saturday. Was the blackmailer so certain they'd have the evidence back? Or are they bluffing? Or do the contents tied to the fraud?"

Even as the blackmail took center stage, I couldn't ignore what I'd learned about the struggles within the family.

Alive, the family patriarch would have disrupted the lives his son and daughter had created. Now, both were safe to consolidate their power. Had one of them cleared the path? Or had the old man stumbled onto fraud and been silenced before he could make trouble?

16

33 Across; 9 Letters;
Clue: Turning from expected course
Answer: Diversion

As Mrs. Prushark entered the limo, I caught Girard studying me. The chief of security's gaze darted to Vandercoy, then Kevin, only to return to me. A frown marred his brow as if I were a puzzle *he* was trying to solve.

Semper Fi. I knew the depths of Rabi's loyalty to my son. Who commanded Girard's loyalty? Todd? Mrs. Prushark? Sheila? Or was the man playing by his own rules? Was he the insider behind the fraud or the loyal family protector?

If the security system had been tampered with after the murder, Girard and Todd both had knowledge and opportunity. Did they have a motive?

Extortion and murder. Fraud and adultery. I juggled the crossword clues to make them fit the puzzle while the blackened remains of the Monroe offices taunted me.

A crunch of gravel at my elbow startled me out of my reverie. Vandercoy was in my face before I could move.

"Learn anything?" The detective asked in a droll tone.

"Not nearly enough." Privately, I had a growing feeling I had the clues to complete the puzzle. However, arranging the questions in the right order with the requisite symmetry was proving to be a mammoth task. "Did you get my message about the lawyer, William Larson? Any customers connected to the case?"

Vandercoy took time adjusting his cuffs, then straightened his vest. "You're as pushy as Crawford said you were."

I gave him a cheeky smile. "I try."

All I got in return was a flat stare before the ringing of a phone sent him burrowing into his pocket.

"Vandercoy." His expression stiffened, then a thundercloud descended. His gaze snapped to me. "Ferguson? You're sure?"

Kevin rushed forward, exuding a ready-for-combat aura. "Where? When?"

The detective held up a hand. "Did he get to Rickson?"

My breath caught in my throat as a skid of gravel alerted me to my son's presence. I felt more than saw Rabi close in. Holding still so as not to miss a word, I didn't take my gaze off Vandercoy.

"On my way." The man's bulk didn't slow him as he pocketed his phone and hustled toward his SUV. "Rickson's unhurt. Ferguson ran off when a nurse recognized him. Security has the place locked down."

"Which will only help if Ferguson is still in the building." My cynicism was showing again.

Marcus snorted. "Security guards haven't caught Rickson or Ferguson all weekend."

Fortunately, Vandercoy had his sirens on and was aimed toward the street by this time.

With the immediate danger past, my heart rate settled. "Why does Ferguson keep trying to break into places? Doesn't he know how to lay low?"

Kevin and Rabi stood poised on the balls of their feet. Their tense forms reminded me of boxers after the bell has sounded.

"Go check on Rickson." I waved them toward the Caddy with one hand while holding out my other to Rabi. "Give me the keys to the rental. I'll take Marcus and Mrs. C to the hotel."

"Be careful." Kevin was already jogging toward his car with his keys in hand. "You're sure you can get to the hotel?"

"There's a map in the glove compartment." I gestured toward the rented Toyota. "And I have a navigator with GPS on his phone."

I pointed to Marcus, who saluted sharply.

Kevin gave a decisive nod, then he ruined the effect by glancing at Marcus. "I'm a phone call away. Good luck."

Worry for Rickson fueled my irritation. I pointed at the Caddy. "Get going."

I never thought I'd be sorry to see the Great White Beast leave my sight, but as Kevin and Rabi sped away, my heart went with them. I tried to hide my concern behind levity. "Drive a guy into a gang fight once and he never lets you forget."

Marcus shook his head. "Some people."

I thought I detected a hint of sarcasm, but his expression gave nothing away. By the time I settled in the driver's seat the Caddy was out of sight. As I fastened my seatbelt, my son thrust an earpiece at me.

"This is connected to your phone." He pointed at my purse. "You can't use your phone while driving. You have to be ready for anything."

"I hate these things." With my protest on record, I

adjusted the device in my ear. Moments later I headed toward the hotel.

"How about we stop at a burger place for lunch?" It was late morning, but I worry better on a full stomach.

"Fries, a greasy burger, and a strawberry shake," Marcus said.

I smiled at him and shifted my gaze to Mrs. C. Ripples of yarn cascaded over her legs and to the floorboards. "What are you knitting?"

"An afghan for me godson. He's getting married soon. It's a family tradition to make a personal gift for the newlyweds."

I perked up. Godson meant friends, which meant background.

All thoughts of meetings, mayhem, and murder fled. A crossword puzzle, older and emptier than the current case popped up. Nailing down the origins of her English accent would be a good distraction. "Where does he live?"

"Dorchester," she said.

A straight answer. I perked up. "Really?"

"Turn right at the next light." Marcus's voice sounded in my ear.

"Sure thing." I agreed absently and moved toward the median in the center of the street. "How long has he lived there?"

"His whole life." She glanced up from her needles. "Born in the village. The only boy. With two older sisters, the little nip is a bit spoiled."

Marcus leaned over the seat. "Turn *right*, T.R."

"I will," I said with a touch of impatience. Didn't he realize this could be my only chance for information? If I asked later, she might claim amnesia. Flipping on my blinker, I pulled into the turn lane. Facing two lanes of oncoming traffic, I settled to wait for the green arrow.

"I meant your *other* right." Marcus pointed in the other direction. "That way."

Images of Dorchester and English cottages grew hazy as I followed the direction of Marcus's arm. The cobwebs brought on by Mrs. C's secrets dissipated. I was in the left turn lane. "How do these things happen to me?"

Marcus shot me a long-suffering look. "At this rate, Kevin and Rabi will get to the hotel before we do."

"I'll get us there." The boy should learn to take these side trips in stride. "It will only take a minute to turn around."

"I have absolute confidence in you." Sincerity rang in Mrs. C's voice.

"See?" I said to Marcus. "Have faith."

The green arrow flashed, and I made my turn. "I should get some credit; I'm on the right street."

"Headed in the wrong direction." Marcus's words held a dampening tone.

I waved a dismissive hand. "Not for long."

The street was heavily traveled. I watched for a convenient place to turn around.

An unfamiliar trill from my cell phone filled the air. "Must be Kevin. He's probably lost."

"Yeah, right," Marcus muttered.

I shot him a sideways glance. "I'm not the only one who gets lost, you know."

The boy chuckled. "Between you and Kevin, you are. Besides, that's not his ring."

Between driving, being lost, and trying to hit the button on my earpiece, his comment slid by me. The phone rang again before I answered it. "You didn't have to call. I'm doing fine."

Instead of a smart-aleck quip, silence greeted me. "Hello?"

"Ms. Belden?" The familiar female voice hesitated.

I frowned. How many people had Rickson given my number to? "This is Tracy Belden."

"We're going in the wrong direction." Marcus held up the map displayed on his phone.

I waved him to silence. But since we were at a corner, I turned right.

"This isn't the way either," Marcus whispered.

Some people are never happy.

"Ms. Belden." The woman spoke again. "This is Victoria Quinlan. I think I'm in danger."

Her breathy voice sounded nothing like the cool professional of the previous evening, but I suppose having your boss murdered would upset anyone.

Before I could say anything, she hurried on. "I have to speak with you."

"About what?" David Ferguson and Quinlan both make a move in less than an hour? Was everyone coming unglued?

"I'll explain when I see you," she said. "You're the only one I can turn to."

Well, yeah, everybody else was getting bombed. I chewed my lip. I couldn't lead her to the hotel. If Vandercoy wouldn't tell his people where we were, I wasn't about to trust Quinlan.

Realizing my know-it-all navigator hadn't been spouting directions I glanced in the rearview mirror. Big mistake. Marcus was on me like a tick on a bloodhound.

He leaned forward. "We have to go."

His tone made it sound like it was our God-given duty instead of his crazed obsession to uphold the detecting honor of the Belden clan.

We did need answers and a scared Quinlan seemed a much surer avenue than a still-concussed Rickson.

I was supposed to be headed *away* from the action. I glanced at Mrs. C.

The older woman smiled. "Don't worry about me. I'm happy to go along for the drive."

Marcus thrust himself so close he was practically in my skin. "We have nowhere else to go."

How had I gotten stuck with a geriatric knitter and a boy detective? I shut off the voice that said it had been my idea.

Never let reality interfere with a pity-party.

"Why don't you call the police?" I asked. What did she think I could do that the police couldn't? "Vandercoy--"

"No." Her shrill tone cut across my words, not to mention my eardrum. "I can't go to the authorities. You have no idea what's going on or who is behind this."

Well, she had me there. I realized I'd ended up in a left turn lane again. How could I be expected to find my way in a strange city with a hysterical woman on the other end of my phone? What if this was my chance to get some solid answers to this stupid case?

She must have sensed my resolve weakening. "I didn't tell you everything last night."

"Thanks for the confession. I figured that out." I came out of the turn on a residential street. It did nothing to mellow my mood. "Did you have anything to do with Rickson being hurt?"

"Of course not." Her hurried words had a ring of truth, not that she merited a lot of faith at this point. "I thought he could help clear things up, but..."

I nodded at the phone as if that would encourage her to continue.

"He knew too much. I don't know how he figured it out." She spoke so quickly I had to concentrate to understand her. "He's only been on the job a week."

"He's a detective." It felt good to use Crawford's frequent comeback on someone else for a change. Her words added weight to my growing certainty that Rickson discovered more than anyone bargained on. However, it was hard to pat myself on the back and drive at the same time.

"If you meet me, I'll tell you everything." Her voice receded on the final words as if she'd pulled away from the phone. When she spoke again, it was in short gasps. "You have to hurry."

I searched the tree-lined boulevard for something familiar.

The guy driving the SUV planted on my bumper evidently knew where he was going and from the hand signals he was giving me he was in a hurry to get there.

"Heck with it." There was no sense getting any more lost. I pulled to the curb behind a parked Lexus and stopped.

The SUV's motor roared as it rushed past then faded into the distance.

I turned my attention to the phone. "Where are you?"

"I can't tell you," she answered.

I put my hand to my forehead.

"That's going to make it difficult to find you." I spoke slowly so she'd understand the dilemma.

Her breath became even more hurried. If she hyperventilated and collapsed, I could hang up and drive to the hotel - if I could find it.

"I can meet you somewhere." Quinlan's voice rose in excitement at the novel concept.

"Great idea." My sarcasm was lost on her.

She continued as if she hadn't heard me. "Where would be a good place?"

She obviously had no idea who she was dealing with. At this point, I couldn't find my own hotel. For that matter, I didn't have the faintest clue where *I* was right now.

"There used to be some lovely little shacks tucked away on a manmade lake north of the city. Blue Mountain Beach was the name." Mrs. C chimed in as if we'd been discussing a spot for a family get-together. "Privately owned. Rarely visited this time of year. And, unless I'm mistaken--"

I knew she wouldn't be.

"I believe the area closed for re-development years ago." Mrs. C smiled over her knitting. "The place should be quite deserted."

"She's right," Quinlan said. "That's perfect. Who's with you?"

As if I'd tell her.

"How long will it take to get to these cabins?" I asked, trying to gauge how far away Quinlan was now.

"It depends," Quinlan said. "Where are you?"

"Not me." My voice came out brusque. Maybe she'd take it for confidence. I wasn't about to admit I was lost. "When can you meet?"

A moment of silence greeted me.

"Half-an-hour," Quinlan answered.

I glanced at my comrades. Marcus nodded without hesitation. Typical male. The place could be on the other side of Nevada for all he knew.

Mrs. C met my gaze with a thoughtful look. "That should do nicely, ducks."

"I'll be there." Admitting defeat, I could only wonder where this road would lead.

To answers? Possibly.

More likely? Disaster.

17

*3 Down; 8 Letters;
Clue: Empty of people
Answer: Deserted*

"Do you have a gun?" Marcus sat in the backseat. He had the map clutched in one hand while his gaze remained focused on the road ahead. Lack of reception in the mountains made the phone useless.

Too late, I regretted my decision not to contact Kevin and Rabi. At the time, I figured they had their own worries. Now I was getting more concerned about me, er... us.

Thanks to Mrs. C's directions and Marcus's navigation, it took twenty minutes to get to our rendezvous. According to the signs, Blue Mountain Beach was at the end of the gravel road I was driving on.

"You know I don't carry any weapons." I slowed to handle a sharp curve. The rearview mirror showed no one behind me.

My son shook his head. "We should've brought Kevin."

Annoyed at being so easily replaced, I frowned. "He doesn't have a gun either."

The boy stared at me via the rearview mirror. "Rabi does."

I didn't say anything. Rabi always carried when he helped on a case. That fact usually reassured me. Though I didn't want Marcus to view guns as a way to solve problems, the isolation of our meeting place had me wishing for a bit of insurance.

Mrs. C put aside her knitting and sat watching the scenery.

Marcus rested his chin on his crossed arms and eyed the road ahead.

I fought to appear confident while I steeled my gut against the knots coiling inside me.

We were in the middle of nowhere, headed toward God knew what calamity. Why had I brought an old woman and a young boy to meet with someone who'd already lied to me?

Quinlan could have security guards lying in wait. Or the foursome from Saturday night's bombings might be with her.

I weighed the possibilities. If I turned around, how would I ever get to the bottom of things? I didn't want to worry about someone targeting my family and friends.

Marcus patted me on the shoulder.

I jumped.

"Don't worry," Marcus said. "We'll solve the case."

I forced a confident smile and winked at him in the rearview mirror. "You bet we will. While I'm talking to her, you two can keep an eye out and guard the car."

His thin shoulders slumped. "You need backup. Besides, we'll be sitting ducks in the car."

Why did he have to argue about everything? I winced, realizing my mother used to say the same thing about me.

"You can drive the getaway car if we need to make a quick exit."

"Really?" His eyes lit up.

I frowned. Why had I said that?

"That's a very good idea, luv." Mrs. C patted my arm. The older woman clasped her hands in her lap. "The buildings should be around this next turn if I remember correctly. It must be twelve years since Alfred brought me here. Stayed right on the lake, we did."

Her lilting accent and quiet reminiscences managed to dampen even my worry. I smiled, imagining her husband loading the car and driving here on a moment's notice. "Is that the only time you were here?"

"Oh, heaven's no," she said. "I first saw it decades ago. I used to run up here for the odd weekend."

My ears perked up. Perhaps she'd been a spy for MI-6. That would account for her British accent. "Were you here on business?"

Sadness filled her eyes. "The original episode began as a personal outing, but it quickly became far more."

"There it is." Marcus's shout brought me back to the present.

The brush and trees that had been thinning on the right cleared to show a long line of undulating sand dunes. Beyond them, a rolling beach met a manmade lake. Scraggly weeds poking up through the sand marred the scene.

My gaze followed a long pier out to the surface of the lake. Other than a few ripples and a decrepit looking rowboat riding low on the waves, nothing moved.

On the left, gray shacks poked through the trees. Missing shingles left the interiors open to the elements.

If I wanted deserted, I'd come to the right place.

Not a soul in sight.

Or a car for that matter.

"Where is she?" Marcus asked.

I scanned the wind-sculpted sand. No tire tracks marred the surface. At the end of the row of shacks, a large white building sat high on an outcrop. An overhanging eave sheltered a wrap-around porch.

Worry skittered up my spine. Admittedly we'd made good time. However, Quinlan had grown up in this town. Shouldn't she have beaten us here?

Marcus shifted position. "What's that big building?"

Mrs. C leaned in. "It's the pavilion. It used to be quite the place in its heyday. Dances every weekend. Music and lights spilled into the darkness and livened up the moonlit beach."

For an instant, melodies wafted on the wind and ghosts waltzed into view. Then the breeze rattled a shutter and the dancers and the memories vanished like smoke on the wind. Today's empty landscape solidified.

"Maybe she parked around the side," Marcus suggested. "If she's scared, she wouldn't want anyone to see her."

"That makes sense." I followed a dirt road around the building. Sure enough, a small red Porsche sat in the shade of the pavilion. I sighed in relief.

Marcus pulled himself straighter and smirked at me.

"Don't get too full of yourself," I said, but I was relieved we hadn't been betrayed.

An ancient rock garden lay across the most direct route to the parking lot. I was forced to take a winding path to park next to the fancy sports car.

A soft intake sounded from Mrs. C. "Ms. Quinlan must be waiting inside."

Her overly casual tone set off alarms.

I turned in time to see her pull her attention away from the Porsche. From this angle, she had a direct view of the interior. The warning in her eyes made my stomach clench.

Marcus glanced at the Porsche through the window. "Her car's empty. Can I come with you?"

"No," I said, trying to keep my tone light. "You're the lookout."

"Of course, ducks. We have to watch the flank or what it is military people call it." Mrs. C pointed out the window toward the line of scrawny pines.

"It's the rear." Marcus's tone was resigned but he obediently scanned the slope behind us. "There's nobody there."

As she turned to follow his gaze, the older woman slid a metal knitting needle across the seat toward me. "We have to make sure the area remains clear. Any sign of movement, we'll honk the horn to warn your mother."

My heart thudded so loud it was all I could hear. Picking up the needle, I slipped it up my left sleeve, with the point cupped in my palm. I wondered if Crawford and Mrs. C had studied under the same teacher. I could almost hear him now. "The best weapon is one no one knows you have."

I'd started the undercurrent of espionage to humor Marcus. But it suddenly carried very real overtones. I drew a deep breath to still my nerves. "I'll check the place. You keep a lookout. Honk and I'll come running."

I stepped into the open before I could lose my nerve. A few steps brought me to a wooden walkway set into the sand and marked by overgrown grass. I studied the hood of the Porsche but saw nothing to explain what had put the older woman on edge.

So, what if the car was empty? It seemed natural for Quinlan to wait in the building. Maybe the isolation of the place had played havoc with Mrs. C's nerves.

Sure, and the winning lottery ticket was tucked inside my shoe.

A cool breeze blew against the sweat on my upper lip. Nerves of steel, that's me. Toying with the point of the knitting needle, I swept my gaze across the building, nothing out of place. To the left, the beach remained deserted.

I raked a hand through my hair and fought to relax. My worry would be for nothing. Quinlan would be inside and I'd get my answers. Stepping into the shadow of the building, I eyed the interior through the dusty windows. Empty.

Deserted picnic tables sat in a mix of sun and shadow in a large open room. Coming to the side door, I touched the knob. Before my fingers closed around it, my gaze rested on a bloody handprint.

It was at eye level, smeared on the doorjamb in perfect view. Talk about overlooking the obvious. In my defense, the wood was dark and the print was in the shade.

My hand moved upward of its own volition.

"Don't touch anything!" Crawford's dictum sounded in my mind loud enough to jerk my hand away from the stain. "Why do people always touch stuff at crime scenes?"

Why did the man yell even in my memory?

All five fingers and a full palm print, red and glistening.

I was no expert, but it had the thin, smeary quality of blood. I matched my fingers against it from a few inches away. The imprint was a good inch shorter.

Just like Quinlan's smaller hand.

I grimaced and glanced at the Toyota seven yards away.

Mrs. C gave me an encouraging nod.

Marcus peered intently over the seat.

I held up a hand, palm out to make sure they stayed put. I wished I could wait with them. Since I couldn't think of a good excuse, I reached for the knob. If it were locked, maybe I'd give up and drive away. Unfortunately, it turned easily.

Stale air slapped me in the face. I waited for my eyes to adjust to the dimness. On the right, a small raised dais looked ready-made for a band. Nothing but dust motes danced in the room now.

I crouched to view the floor at an angle. No footprints disturbed the dust. No blood. I checked the way I'd come but saw no dark spatters there either. I straightened and swept the room a second time.

"Quinlan?" My voice fell flat in the dry air. One heartbeat. Two. Three. They thundered in my ears. Every nerve in my body was on high alert. The blood was fresh, incriminating.

I shut the door.

The pier was the only place left to search. I looked at the car and pointed toward the lake. Once clear of the building, the sun offered little warmth. No breeze greeted me. No one else did either. No Quinlan. No attacker.

I gripped the knitting needle in my hand. False courage if ever there was any. What could I do? Challenge my opponent to a knitting duel? I wasn't that good of a knitter. My mind returned to the problem.

The Porsche was here. Quinlan *had* to be here. Somewhere.

The water was the final place left to look.

Heart pounding in my throat, my heels hit the wooden planks with a solid thud. My pace increased with each step. I was a sitting duck trying to outrun myself.

Halfway down that endless pier, I realized I could hardly search the entire lake. I also realized I didn't want to find the woman. Yet, I couldn't bring myself to retreat.

My gaze scanned the shining blue water. Nothing moved but the glistening waves, tossed by a soft wind. The dull thud of wood hitting wood overrode the beating of my heart.

With a sinking feeling, I remembered the rowboat tied to the end of the pier… the low-riding rowboat.

My stomach tried to crawl up my throat to join my heart.
Sam Spade, I'm not.

The thumping sounded again.

I told myself the dingy was empty. My feet slowed to a

crawl. With my toes on the end of the pier, I screwed up my courage and looked over the edge.

Quinlan lay in the boat, legs akimbo. Her eyes stared blankly at the sky. One hand clutched a bloody wound high on her left chest.

Lightning shot through me. I caught a shaky breath and swallowed again.

She blinked.

My knees buckled. I grabbed the wooden post for support. I may have screamed.

Her eyes met mine. "She… believed him."

18

17 Down; 8 Letters;
Clue: Careful to avoid problems or dangers
Answer: Cautious

The blood oozing through the wadded-up scarf all but eclipsed Quinlan's words. Each wave that slapped the rowboat against the pier sent a fresh wave of pain across the face of the injured woman.

"I... I'll get you out." I couldn't speak for her, but I felt very little comfort at my promise. I grabbed my cell phone and stabbed 9-1-1.

No service. I shoved it in my pocket.

An old rope, stretched to the end of its ten-foot length, connected the boat to one of the wooden posts. No ladder in sight. Nothing but sand and the surf slapping the beach at the land side of the pier.

An idea glimmered through the shock that held my brain

captive. If I untied the rope, I could pull the rowboat onto the beach.

When I looked at Quinlan, her eyes were closed.

Panic stole through me. Was she dead? The shallow rise and fall of her chest calmed my worst fears.

"I'll get you out of this." I repeated my useless words. Unsure whether I was talking to her or myself, I dug at the knotted rope. Hard and crusted from years of baking in the sun, it remained impervious to my efforts.

As my hands tore at the ungiving cord, the thought of the shooter stole into my mind. Anyone at close range would have shot her again and finished her off. The bullets had to have come from a sniper.

Perhaps they'd assumed she was dead, or they had a bad angle. Either way, there was only one location they could have used.

My gaze darted to the pine-covered hills above the lake.

A gunman hidden up there could have shot her from a distance. That same gunman could shoot me. Or he could be on his way to finish us both off.

My hands tugged at the stubborn rope. The knitting needle rattled in my sleeve. Cursing my slow wits, I grabbed the metal needle and forced the slender point between the strands of the caked rope.

"Come on. Come on. Loosen." I pleaded with the rope, the knot, the wind, and everything else I could think of to cooperate. All the while I could feel a bullseye on my spine.

Sweat dripped into my eyes. I darted a glance over my shoulder. Marcus and Mrs. C were distant figures in the car. How long could I struggle to save Quinlan at the risk of those two innocents?

Facing the unanswerable choice, lent a desperate strength to my sore fingers. The coils loosened. Breathing a trembling sigh of relief, I tugged until the knot gave way.

Once I freed the rope, I pulled the boat to the side and started toward the beach. The pier, which had seemed too short moments ago, now looked far too long. Feeling conspicuous, I kept a tight hold on the hard, scratchy rope. My gaze raked the green-gray hills behind the building.

I waved the bent knitting needle at the Toyota then pointed toward the beach. Unsure what I expected, I left the choice to them.

No doubt, Mrs. C would come up with something.

By the time I ran off the pier and jumped onto the sand, my heart was racing and I was puffing. I struggled to pull the rowboat onto land.

Up close, the injured woman looked paler than before.

The roar of a car engine sounded absurdly loud.

Sand shot out as Mrs. C skidded to a stop. Parked parallel to the water, several inches of soft sand buried the tires.

Marcus jumped out and craned his neck to see into the rowboat. His eyes widened. "Is she dead?"

His voice reverberated across the waves.

Water soaked through my running shoes. "Help me get this out of the water."

Marcus grabbed the edge of the boat and pulled. "What are we gonna do with her body?"

"She's alive." My voice sounded harsh against the lapping of the surf.

"Did you call the cops?" Marcus asked.

"No signal. We have to get her to a hospital." Between our efforts and the surf, the boat ended up halfway out of the water.

"What do you need, luv?" Mrs. C was all business.

I swiveled to face her, lost my footing, and hit the cool sand butt first. "Look for towels or cloth, anything to stop the bleeding."

The older woman hurried to the car.

I turned to Marcus. "Give me your belt and your outer shirt. Then open the rear door and move the front seats up as far as you can."

Marcus shoved the clothes at me and took off.

I put my palm against Quinlan's cheek. Her skin was cool and clammy.

Sand sprayed my leg. Mrs. C's shoes stepped into my vision. I met her gaze across the boat. "She's been shot, probably from the back. The wound on the front looks big."

What little I knew about gunshots I'd learned from Crawford. Twenty-five years on the force adds up to a lot of war stories. He'd mentioned more than once that a bullet's exit wound is larger than its entrance.

I peeked inside the scarf Quinlan had used as a makeshift bandage. A gaping wound of blood and torn skin greeted my gaze. Wincing, I levered her shoulder up. The folded square of Marcus's shirt hovered into view.

Like a perfect surgical assistant, Mrs. C handed me the cloth. Slipping it inside Quinlan's jacket, I covered the entry wound. Seeping blood dampened it immediately. I held it in place then reached out again. "Did you find--"

Mrs. C held out a skein of yarn, doubled for extra padding. She clutched a second one in her other hand.

Images of weddings and a white satin gown popped into my mind. When I hesitated, she raised a brow. "I don't think we should linger, eh?"

The soft-spoken words spurred me to action. Between us we added the yarn as further padding to the wound. They were awash with blood by the time I secured the belt over the bulky bandage.

"The door is open." Marcus's excited voice sounded from beside Mrs. C. His dark eyes met mine. "Now what?"

Despite the race against death and the worry of the

gunman taking another shot, I studied Quinlan's pale face. *Don't let her die.*

"T.R.?" The urgency in Marcus's voice broke through my stupor.

I pointed to my side of the boat. "We'll lift her out and carry her to the car."

Marcus shot me a wide-eyed look. "We're going to carry her?"

I got my feet underneath me. "It's our only choice."

Mrs. C gestured toward Quinlan. "You had best cross her arms over her chest or they'll be flopping about like chicken wings."

I grimaced at the image but did as instructed. The yarn and the belt were already covered in blood. I frowned at the make-do bandage then at the hills rising behind the beach.

This was taking too long.

Fortunately, Mrs. C had parked close by. As long I didn't lose my footing in the soft sand, we should be fine. "I'll take her shoulders. Mrs. C, you and Marcus get her hips and legs."

Mrs. C gave a nod. "You're doing a grand job."

Unsure I deserved the vote of confidence, I looked over my shoulder. It almost proved my undoing.

A seventy-something woman and an eleven-year-old boy stared at me. A dying woman lay before me. The desperate nature of our situation descended. How was I supposed to get them out of here safely?

"One step at a time." My father's voice floated up from my memory.

Unlike me, my brother and sister had inherited his and my mother's gift for handling horses. When I asked him time and again how he could train such large animals, he'd always answered the same way.

"One step at a time." He'd lean on the fence, his foot on the bottom rung and his gaze on the animal. "Too many details overwhelm the horse and rider. You take one step, then the next, then the next."

Hearing his voice in my memory, gave me renewed confidence.

Marcus had his gaze riveted on my face. A frown furrowed his forehead and his gaze grew uncertain.

I released the breath I'd been holding and gave him a small smile. "Ready, cowboy?"

He straightened his shoulders and nodded. His fingers tightened around Quinlan's knees.

I looked at Mrs. C. "I'll lift her shoulders first. Then we'll raise her together."

Leaning over Quinlan, I maneuvered both arms underneath her torso. With my feet braced, I nodded. "One. Two. Three."

I pushed myself upright. The strain of her dead weight threatened to overbalance me. I put a hand on the bow to keep from falling.

Quinlan's head lolled. With only my right arm supporting her, she slipped out of my grasp.

A moan escaped her lips.

"T.R.?" Worry sounded in Marcus's voice. He scrambled into the boat and put his shoulder under Quinlan's waist.

The strain on my arms eased. I steadied myself and repositioned both hands under Quinlan's body. I cast Marcus a grateful smile. "Good job."

He shot me a grin. "You'd be lost without me."

"In more ways than one. Can you get out of the boat okay?" If anyone went down now, we'd all go.

For an answer, Marcus stepped over the side of the rowboat and pushed it away with his foot. "Ready."

"Let's move." My feet sank several inches into the sand with every step. Remaining upright while holding Quinlan proved harder than I'd imagined. Even with Marcus and

Mrs. C helping, the pull on my arms began to tell. My breath came in heavy puffs.

"I need to start working out," I muttered.

Moving as carefully as a snail on stilts, we finally reached the car. Maneuvering her inside proved even more awkward. By the time I laid her on the backseat, my arms felt like noodles. I sat on the edge of the seat next to the injured woman as Mrs. C shut the door.

The rowboat was already several yards out on the lake, bobbing on the waves.

Marcus stared at Quinlan from the front seat. Chalk-white with ragged breathing, she could have been a poster child for trauma care. Her cheeks were cool beneath my palm.

"That's not good," I whispered.

"She gonna die?" Marcus asked.

I jerked my head up. "Not after I hauled her up that beach, she's not. Close the door."

He flipped around and slammed the door.

Mrs. C had already settled herself behind the wheel. The car roared to life. "Ready?"

I gritted my teeth and held onto Quinlan. With her head and shoulders in my lap, the injured woman's body lay wedged in the valley formed at the back of the seat.

The wheels tossed up a steady stream of sand. The car slipped deeper into the soft beach.

Just when I was sure she'd bury the axle, the car gained traction. Gradually at first, then with a steady speed, we gained level ground. Sighing with relief, I watched the water fall away.

A half-circle brought us to the red Porsche and the only road out. I glanced in the window of the other vehicle as we roared past. Though I didn't have time to study it, I caught a glimpse of broken dials and a shattered dash.

If Quinlan had been shot from behind as she stepped outside, the bullet would have buried itself in the dash. When I'd walked by the car, I'd studied it head on. Mrs. C would have been at the perfect angle to see the damage inside.

"She could've warned a person," I whispered to the unconscious woman. Her breathing was no better but her cheeks didn't look as waxen as before.

"What did you say, ducks?" Mrs. C asked.

If I hadn't gone to the pier, Quinlan might be dead even now. "Her color is a little better."

Mrs. C nodded. "Having her legs raised should help and the pressure on the wound will stem the blood loss."

"I hope so." I pressed harder on the makeshift bandage.

Clouds of dust from the gravel road followed our retreat.

Marcus craned his neck around the headrest. "They should've shot her again."

I frowned at the insensitive comment. "Marcus."

He shrugged with the nonchalance of the streets. "Why take the chance she'd live?"

Mrs. C murmured, "I wondered that very thing."

I'd been trying to avoid discussing the gunman and these two were dissecting the crime.

Marcus tried 9-1-1 again with no luck. "We saw the blood on the building. Even if she ducked inside the car after the first shot, once she was on the pier, she would have been a sitting duck."

That's my boy, always practical.

Mrs. C was more than willing to discuss the shooting. "Unless they thought she was already dead."

Marcus twisted around to face the older woman. "Or they couldn't get a clear shot."

"The angle, the sand. If the door was open she might have fallen inside the vehicle." Mrs. C put her finger to her lips. "Many people don't appreciate the art of being a sniper."

Having made the declaration, she added a soft sigh of disappointment for this apparent lack.

Marcus agreed. "Three-fingered Louie always said long shots were the easiest to miss."

I shook my head. "I don't believe you two."

Marcus shrugged. "You're the one who wanted to know what happened. We're trying to help."

I opened my mouth to defend myself.

Mrs. C veered around a corner without slowing.

With my feet and knees braced to keep the pressure on Quinlan's wound, I kept my position. But my shoulders swayed.

The white sand and blue-gray bushes swept by in a blur. A cloud of dust billowed behind us. Mrs. C pulled out of the curve smoothly.

If I'd been driving on this gravel, I'd have put us in a ditch. I looked at Quinlan, fearing what I'd see. The yarn was a sodden mess. Blood seeped through my fingers, leaving them wet and sticky. I'd read somewhere how much blood the human body contained but I had no wish to have it wash out over my hands.

The injured woman, though pale, looked no worse than when we'd put her in the car. She wouldn't live if she kept bleeding.

A hollow formed in the pit of my stomach. I glanced up to find Marcus eyeing Quinlan with a furrowed brow.

"Is there anything in the glove compartment we could use to staunch the flow of blood?" Not that it would last more than a millisecond, but I had to do something.

Mrs. C slapped the steering wheel. "How stupid of me. Use me afghan."

Marcus bent over. When he straightened, he held an armful of knitted yarn. He wiggled out of the safety belt.

Mrs. C gestured at the blanket. "Do take the needle out first."

He fished it out then leaned over the seat.

I grabbed at Mrs. C's carefully woven creation. As soon as I released the pressure, warm liquid flowed over my fingers. With trembling hands, I bunched a corner of the afghan behind Quinlan then shoved more over the wound.

A new wave of blood spread over Quinlan's skin. I locked my elbows and pushed on the bullet hole with all my strength.

Marcus thrust the rest of the afghan between my arms. "You can grab it when you need more."

I looked at him, hanging in the backseat only inches from my face. "Good idea."

He gave me a quick kiss on my cheek then swiveled around hurriedly and plopped in the front seat.

A warm glow filled me at this display of affection from the once-wary street shark. I smiled at Quinlan over the billows of knitted yarn. "Hang in there. You *are* going to make it."

"Hold on." The older woman's words sounded more like a tally-ho than a warning. The car careened to the side of the road. "Sorry."

Her apology held an excited ring.

"She doesn't sound sorry," I muttered to the shooting victim.

"They didn't kill her with the first shot and they couldn't shoot her again because they had the wrong angle." Marcus's disembodied voice sounded from the front seat.

What a little bulldog.

"They should've checked," Marcus continued.

Pulled into the reconstruction, I frowned at a hole in the scenario. "Why bother to take a distance shot? Why not drive in behind her?"

Marcus leaned forward. "Here's the highway."

"Thank, God." I felt relief. "Now we can make time. We need to find a hospital."

Mrs. C's gray-haired head bobbed. "There's one heading into town. We should be there in no time."

I didn't doubt that, considering how she drove.

"You're right, T.R.," Marcus said.

"Oh, good." I love being right. "What am I right about?"

"The shooter had to know where she was going," Marcus said.

A chill froze my blood. We'd only spoken of our destination by cell phone, which meant... "They tapped her cell phone."

Anyone with the proper equipment can do it. Cops don't even need warrants because cell phones don't use wires. They use airwaves.

"They knew we were coming." Marcus peered around the headrest. His eyes narrowed. "Why not shoot us all?"

My breath caught in my throat at the image of his body lying on the sand. I swallowed hard. "They couldn't count on all of us getting out of the car."

Only me, I thought with something akin to relief. Once I'd been shot, Mrs. C would never have let my son get out. She'd have high-tailed it out of there.

Marcus nodded. "He should have followed her in, then he could have got us. This road is the only way in or out."

The car slowed as we reached the highway. Mrs. C looked both ways. "I'd forgotten that was there."

Her voice held a thoughtful note.

"What?" I glanced toward the road.

"The construction site?" Marcus asked.

I remembered now. Piles of equipment and supplies had been stacked just before the turnoff to Blue Circle Beach. A construction company's sign marked the materials. I couldn't understand her interest.

She turned onto the highway but continued scanning the area on the other side of the road.

"What are you looking for?" I asked.

"Construction companies have reported an increase in incidences of equipment being stolen from building sites," she said.

"Kevin mentioned that. Some companies have started posting cameras." I stopped short. My mind spun with the possibilities.

"There's a camera. On that pole." Marcus pointed. "That one, too."

"That's why they didn't follow her," I said.

"Or us." Marcus looked over his shoulder. "They'd have been recorded. Shooting the cameras to disable them might have alerted someone."

"They *had* to shoot from a distance." I spoke softly. "If they couldn't drive in after her. They didn't stay in the hills to shoot us. Where did they go?"

My heart thudded in my chest. I glanced at the highway. A couple of trucks drove by headed in the opposite direction. "Maybe they assumed they'd killed her and left."

Call me an optimist.

"I wouldn't," Mrs. C demurred. "Especially if Ms. Quinlan shifted as I fired."

"If they couldn't get a second shot, it would explain why she's still alive." As Marcus spoke, his gaze shifted out the window. "What kind of car did you see at the animal hospital?"

"A dark blue SUV. Four doors. Tinted front window," I answered by rote. A cold feeling crept into my stomach. "Why?"

Marcus pointed out the window. "It's behind us."

19

41 Across; 4 Letters;
Clue: Move swiftly, as in a competition
Answer: Race

Mrs. C checked the rearview mirror with a darting glance. "The car does resemble the one fleeing the explosion."

Apprehension slithered through my veins. The sedan's presence confirmed why the shooter hadn't killed me on the pier. He'd left the high ground to guard the only exit.

"Let's find out if it's us they want." The older woman's comment ended on a challenging note.

The car lurched without warning. The motion threw my weight onto Quinlan's wound which still oozed. "Shouldn't this have clotted by now?"

Marcus screwed up his face in thought. "When I saw a guy shot in the street, years ago, the bleeding didn't stop until he was dead."

An image of Quinlan, pale and waxy in death, flashed before my eyes. Though we hadn't exactly bonded, I shuddered. "That's not what I needed to hear."

Mrs. C nodded. "I'm afraid he's right, ducks. Ms. Quinlan needs a hospital rather badly."

Tell me something I don't know. I bit my tongue against the comeback. The woman's life was slipping through my fingers and nothing I did helped.

"We'll be in the city in a jiffy." Determination mixed with excitement in Mrs. C's voice. "Marcus, be a dear and look on the map. I believe I saw a hospital marker just before we turned off the main road."

"'kay." Marcus swung around in his seat. A rustle of paper followed.

I grabbed for all the composure I could muster. Outside the window, the evergreens around the city of Tahoe whirred by at a dizzying rate. I tried to forget the car chasing us.

Mrs. C felt no such qualms. She glanced in the rearview mirror. "Those people must be in a terrible rush. They're doing close to ninety."

Marcus spun around. "Are they gaining?"

"Not for long." She hit the gas.

The Toyota sped down the highway.

A tan house with manicured landscaping rushed by in a blur, a gas station and an office building followed in close succession. The ride reminded me of *The Wizard of Oz* tornado scene except this time it was our car swept up in a whirlwind.

Marcus looked up from the map. "The hospital is a mile away. Exit here."

"Turning." Mrs. C spun the steering wheel.

Gulping as we crossed in front of a semi, I bent over

Quinlan to reduce the centrifugal force. The Toyota fishtailed, righted itself, then picked up speed.

My son pointed straight ahead. "Stay on this road. After the third stoplight, turn right."

We were among civilization. Buildings, businesses, and traffic thickened with every block.

"They have to back off now." Only Quinlan heard my attempt at reassurance, and only one of us needed comforting.

Marcus swiveled around. "Still on us."

Mrs. C wove in and out of the city traffic with a skill that would have challenged Kevin. She zoomed through one, possibly two intersections.

I studied the street with a frown. We *might* have dropped to sixty miles an hour. No way could we keep up this speed. Mrs. C would have to slow and when she did…

"They're gaining." Marcus uttered the announcement without a trace of worry.

I eyed Quinlan's still form. Fury burst through my veins. Hadn't they done enough? Were they going to shoot her again before she bled to death?

Amid the chaos, the puzzle portion of my brain pondered another question. What did she know that was worth this much effort to silence her?

Marcus, dividing his attention between the obstacle course in front of us and the car behind us, gave a slight sound.

I jerked upright. "What?"

The wail of sirens made his answer unnecessary and almost drowned out his single word.

He grinned and pointed behind us. "Cops."

The crazed woman behind the steering wheel settled into her seat. "It's about bloody time. They've had two cars speeding along a main thoroughfare for several minutes."

"And we're one of them," I noted as the scenery outside continued to zoom by us.

"*We're* rushing to a hospital." Self-righteousness rang in her tone. "The gentlemen in the other vehicle have no such excuse."

Marcus pumped his fist. "You tell 'em."

"I'm not sure the police will appreciate the distinction," I muttered. Assuming we survived to plead our case.

"Oh, dear," Mrs. C clicked her tongue. "This is a bit of a bother."

Trepidation filled me. Did I want to know what could worry her? I glanced past Marcus's bobbing head.

The stoplight at the intersection showed bright red. Stopped cars blocked every lane in front of us. I braced myself for a hard brake.

The Toyota didn't so much as slow down.

"There must be ten cop cars now." Marcus, grinning wildly, stretched his neck for a better view out the rear window. "They're all over the street."

I never thought I'd say it, but cops were the least of my worries.

"Mrs. C, the cars in front of us are stopped." I spoke extra loudly to get the point across.

"Hold on," she ordered.

The Toyota swerved into the empty lanes on the wrong side of the road. The older woman laid on the horn as our vehicle barreled toward the traffic facing us from the opposite side of the intersection.

My mouth fell open as I pushed into the backseat. I had no illusions the maneuver would save me.

Our light flipped to green. A clear patch appeared in the cross traffic.

Mrs. C hit the intersection doing fifty. She pulled the

steering wheel into a hard turn that sent the car careening directly toward the row of headlights facing us.

I braced my legs and held Quinlan steady with stiff arms.

A woman in a green Mercedes opened her mouth in a silent scream. She raised her hands in a vain attempt to forestall disaster.

I gritted my teeth. Our tires screeched. Horns blared. A smell of burning rubber hit my nostrils.

Then, slowly, amazingly, the Toyota slowed, straightened, and gathered speed. We shot up the hill.

Too stunned to speak, I concentrated on letting out the breath I'd been holding.

"The hospital is at the top." Marcus's voice sounded over the seat.

A parking lot flashed by outside. Blue signs pointed the way to the Emergency Room.

Hope rose in my chest. I dared to breathe. I glanced out the window. Every car in the intersection sat frozen in place. "I can't believe we weren't hit."

"Way to go, Mrs. C." Marcus patted her on the shoulder. "Those other guys will never make it through there."

I studied the injured woman. Her face looked like pale mocha instead of rich cocoa, but that might be due to the contrast with the afghan and my clothes, now painted a lurid crimson. "Hang on, Quinlan. Don't let them win."

I shoved the last dry corner of the blanket over the wound. A giddiness bubbled up from my stomach to my chest.

We had survived. We were alive.

"More cops." Despite his words, Marcus wore a grin. "They're chasing us."

Let them catch us. I'd sic Mrs. C on them.

"Here we are, ducks." The older woman drove up a curving drive and stopped under a wide arch.

I met Marcus's gaze. "Get some white coats."

He bolted out the door, yelling before he hit the ground. "Gunshot wound! A lady's bleeding to death."

The sirens that had been our calling card reached a crescendo as they surrounded us.

Mrs. C turned off the engine and exited the Toyota with a speed I found hard to credit. "I'll speak with the bobbies."

I twisted my head in time to see her march into the path of the oncoming police cars.

She held her arm in front of her, palm out. While the police vehicles raced toward her, she stood without flinching.

Safely inside the Toyota, I cringed as the black-and-white units screeched to a stop within inches of the gray-haired figure.

I released the air I'd kept locked in my lungs. Before I could see more, the rear door of the Toyota was flung open.

A black man in scrubs took one look at the sodden mess that used to be an afghan then yelled over his shoulder. "Gurney. Pressure bandages. Stat."

His orders didn't stop him from checking Quinlan's pulse with a no-nonsense efficiency.

The next minutes passed in a haze of noise and movement. Between the hospital personnel and the cops, I found myself hustled into the ER. Once they realized none of the blood was mine, they abandoned me. The last thing I heard before I closed my eyes and sagged against the wall was an order to call the OR and page a surgeon.

"This is so cool." Marcus's voice sounded at my side.

I opened my eyes.

"Mrs. C's talkin' to the cops." Face flushed with excitement my son peered up at me. "Can I go help? Ple-ease?"

I had a flash of sympathy for the men and women in blue,

but by now they outnumbered the old lady and the boy ten to one. The odds were even. "Go ahead."

The words barely left my mouth when he spun on his heel and ran out the door. In the drive, the Toyota sat deserted and open to the world. Not one of us had closed a door behind us. What would our mothers think?

"Tracy?" The voice sounded in my ear as before someone grabbed my arm and spun me around.

Jolted alert, I stared into a pair of cobalt blue eyes. As the color leeched out of Kevin's face, warmth flowed through me. I'd forgotten all about Rabi and Kevin racing to check on Ferguson's appearance in Rickson's room. Mrs. C, Marcus and I had ended up at the same hospital where Rickson had been admitted.

I raised my arms to throw myself at Kevin. The sight of my crimson colored hands stopped me. From my fingers to my elbows, I was red with blood.

His gaze searched my clothes, sticky and stiffening. His grip tightened. "Where are you hurt?"

His presence sent a wave of strength pulsing through my veins. "This isn't my blood."

"Whose is it?" Kevin stepped closer. His steady strength offered a well of support that never failed.

I gathered my wits. "Quinlan's. She's been shot."

"I can't leave you for a minute." The tension in his shoulders eased as shock gave way to curiosity. "What happened?"

"Quinlan called me on my way to the hotel." I shrugged. "I have no idea who pulled the trigger. She was down when we found her."

His hands rested on my shoulders with a welcome weight. He looked out the doors then at me. "I assume this parade of sirens is for you."

My lips lifted in a sheepish grin. "Marcus and Mrs. C helped."

Our gazes met, then we burst into laughter.

After a moment, I caught my breath and gestured toward the outer drive. "They're explaining things to the police."

Kevin laughed harder before he pulled me along the corridor. "Here's a bathroom. Clean up while I get you some clean clothes at the gift shop."

Hot water sounded like heaven. I pushed open the door then glanced at Kevin's retreating form. "A comb, too. I don't know where my purse ended up."

He raised a hand in acknowledgment.

As I locked the bathroom door, I remembered throwing my purse on the floor of the car. I wasn't going after it now.

For the next minutes, I felt like Lady Macbeth. Despite a steady stream of hot water and handfuls of soap, the blood held on stubbornly. I could deal with that.

Quinlan was alive.

Kevin was here.

All was right with the world.

He returned with a sack in one hand and a cup of chicory hazelnut coffee in the other.

I was more grateful for the latter. Especially after I donned my new outfit.

"A muumuu?" I fisted my hands on my hips and faced him in the corridor. "Do I look like a muumuu type of woman to you?"

"There aren't a lot of options in a hospital gift shop." His appreciative gaze sent a tingle through me. "You look good, Belden."

I refused to admit the vertical flow of purple and brown mixed with whirls of burnt orange did look and feel nice. I also liked the fact that it was floor length. Thankfully, the leggings would keep my legs warm.

"The shoes are cute," I admitted, admiring the woven leather sandals. "How did you pay for this?"

Kevin shrugged. "Credit card. I'll put it on the expense account. Crawford can pay."

"It's the least the bossman can do," I said. It served him right for taking off for the wilds of Canada.

"Is Rickson under guard?"

"Yes." Kevin hugged the wall as a man and woman in green scrubs hurried down the tiled corridor. A nurse pushing a patient in a wheelchair followed on their heels.

"Did they catch Ferguson?" I knew the answer. Ferguson had too much experience with quick escapes for the redheaded man to have been caught.

"He got away." Though disgust sounded in Kevin's tone, a serious look crossed his face. "He asked Rickson one question."

My interest shot off the scale. Crossword puzzles are full of questions. Which lead to answers. With enough answers, I solve this puzzle.

Kevin tilted his head in my direction. "Where's the evidence?"

I stopped in the middle of the corridor, forcing hospital personnel, patients, and families to flow around me. My hands balled into fists. "It's that blasted box."

Kevin waffled his hand. "He might have meant whatever was in the law office. Or the Monroe accounts. No way to know. Rickson is clueless."

"So am I." I rejoined the river of people. When we reached an intersecting corridor, I started right. A pair of strong hands gripped my shoulders and turned me the other way. "Evidence of what? Adultery? Fraud? Which one is the motive for the old man's murder?"

"You're asking the wrong person." Kevin could spot a scam a mile away, but his mind didn't bend to solving puzzles. "I'm the muscle in this gang."

"I had you pegged as the chauffeur." I tossed him a teasing

smile. Then, my mind veered back to untangling clues. "Ferguson believes Rickson has proof."

The final word resonated in my mind. It snagged on one thought, then another.

"Proof. Action. Exposure." My voice escalated with each word. By the time the last one echoed off the walls, I was too excited to care about the looks I was getting.

As I turned to Kevin, he put a hand around my waist and pulled me to one side as another group of white coats rushed by. "What are you babbling about?"

"I've been wondering all weekend about the timing of Prushark's murder. Why now?" When we started walking, I put my arm around his waist. Slanting him a smile, I fell in step with him. "If Henry Prushark learned of the fraud and planned to investigate, that could be why he had to be silenced."

Kevin's hand felt comfortable as his fingers beat a rhythm on my hip. His blue eyes darkened in thought. "Any other ideas?"

"Plenty." A tired laugh escaped my lips. "Sheila and Todd may have feared losing their positions. The daughter-in-law has no guarantee that proof of adultery won't oust her from the estate and from her son's life. Someone involved in the fraud could have bribed a guard to kill the old man."

It was like a movie-of-the-week, everyone had a motive, and I wasn't done. "Pete and Matt Monroe may have seized their chance to kill the man who tricked them out of their own company and would have blocked them from regaining control."

Kevin's expression grew somber. "Did you learn anything from Quinlan?"

I sketched a quick overview of the administrative assistant's call and the plan to meet. Our desperate drive through town brought him up to speed.

"'She believed him.'" Kevin repeated her words with a raised brow.

I pictured Quinlan lying in the rowboat. "Could have been she or Sheila. Watching her bleed to death wasn't the best circumstances for a conversation."

Kevin stared at the floor with a thoughtful gaze. "Even assuming 'him' is Prushark, it doesn't help. We need more information."

"It's all I've got."

"Tracy Belden, return to the ER." An official sounding voice spoke from the hospital PA system. "Tracy Belden, return to the ER immediately."

20

10 Across; 7 Letters;
Clue: To take back a possession
Answer: Reclaim

"They found you." Kevin's dramatic tone brought a smile to my lips.

Another demanding summons came over the hospital PA system before I arrived.

Marcus met us halfway down the hall from the waiting room of the Emergency Room. "The cops told them to page you. They want to talk to you."

Rabi greeted us with a nod. For the first time in a week, Mrs. C's hands lay idle, the yarn and knitting needles sacrificed to save Quinlan.

Marcus hung by Kevin's side. "Rabi said you were around. I figured we'd find each other."

Mrs. C's eyes lit up when she saw my muumuu. "What an attractive outfit."

Kevin glanced at me with a superior smile.

When I stopped, the smooth fabric swirled around my legs "What do we know?"

"The other car got away." Marcus's frown matched his disgusted tone. "The cops're still looking, but if they haven't caught 'em by now they're not going to."

I had to agree.

"The nice police officer said they're not going to give me any tickets." Mrs. C spoke in a light tone. "A few bobbies were rather upset, until I mentioned how embarrassing it would look if the media found out they couldn't catch one old woman."

If she hadn't been on my side, I'd have been tempted to lock her up myself. As it was, I just smiled. "That's good news."

Marcus pointed toward the door. "That's the detective who wants to talk to you."

A white guy in a wrinkled shirt and a loose tie ambled toward us. His gaze narrowed. "Ms. Belden?"

I straightened my shoulders and tried not to look like an escapee from a luau. "That's me."

The guy opened his wallet to display a gold shield. "Detective Swafford. I'd like to ask you a few questions."

I gestured to Kevin. "This is my partner, Kevin Tanner. It will save time if he joins us."

Despite the dark blue jogging outfit, Kevin looked like a business-type and he could have passed for a lawyer.

It took a bit of doing, but we brought Swafford and his partner, Hoang, a slim Asian woman, up to date. After a brief call to Vandercoy, Swafford's partner told us we were free to go.

Then we promised, once again, to go to the station and sign our statements. Soon I'd be able to find the place on my own.

The female detective had a parting shot. "Keep in touch and *try* to stay out of trouble."

"That's always the goal," I said as we walked away.

"She just doesn't accomplish it very often," Kevin muttered.

Moments later, our troop exited the ER. The Toyota sat outside the entrance where we'd left it. Unwilling to abandon my purse, I steeled myself and opened the door.

Amazingly the pale gray interior was... gray. "What happened to the blood?"

Kevin snorted. "Did you see yourself?"

An image of crimson colored hands and the blood soaked clothes I'd taken off flashed through my mind. I couldn't suppress a shudder.

Mrs. C nodded. "I'm rather afraid you did get the worst of it; you and me afghan."

A mournful sigh accompanied this last bit.

I patted her on the shoulder. "The next one will be even better and we'll make Crawford buy the yarn."

Receipts for a muumuu, knitting needles, and a dozen skeins of yarn might win the annual award for most bizarre expense report. On this happy note, I turned toward the Caddy, a few parking stalls away. The Great White Beast and its soft leather interior beckoned like an old friend.

Kevin jiggled the keys in his hand. "We can grab some lunch, then reconvene at the hotel and plan our next move."

My stomach growled in happy anticipation. Quinlan's call had interrupted my brunch plans. Now, it was mid-afternoon. "Lunch sounds wonderful."

Rabi detoured to the driver's side of the Toyota.

Marcus hung back. "I'm riding with Rabi in the death car."

"Quinlan is alive." My response came out sharper than

intended. I took a deep breath and consciously relaxed. "The nurse said she's going to make it."

Kevin put a reassuring hand on my arm. "That's the good news. The bad news is we have another witness who can't tell us anything."

I ran my fingers through my hair. "Our leads do seem to disappear as fast as we find them."

"Not to worry," Kevin said. "We have guesswork to fill in the blanks."

I had a retort all ready, but the shrill ring of his cell phone stopped me.

"If that's Vandercoy, don't answer it," I warned.

He frowned at the readout then stabbed the screen. "Tanner."

Silence fell. The wind died and the rustling of the pine trees ceased.

Kevin's phone usually has a lot of bleed through. I moved so close to his side I could feel him breathe.

Not wanting to be left out, Marcus sidled up on silent feet.

"Is this Kevin Tanner of Crawford Investigations?" The male voice was muffled.

Kevin's response mixed a snort with a rueful chuckle.

Who would ask him that? Kevin doesn't work for Crawford.

"Who is this?" Kevin asked.

For a heartbeat no one answered then-- "David Ferguson."

I caught my breath. The redheaded man who'd chased Rickson in the ER. The construction foreman Sheila Prushark fired. The rat who'd stolen the yellow box.

Marcus stood on his tiptoes, straining to hear.

Ignoring my son and me hanging on him like ornaments,

Kevin's gaze focused on the mountains on the horizon. "Where did you get this number?"

"From Rickson. He said you and Belden were his backups."

Marcus glanced at me, then gave a sharp nod.

Rickson could never remember my number. The big guy always gave Kevin's cell number, which only had three different digits in it. The fact added credibility to Ferguson's story.

I tried not to breathe so I wouldn't miss a word.

"When did he tell you this?" Suspicion rang in Kevin's tone. "You've been chasing him all over Nevada."

"Saturday. He caught me when I tried to see Sheila." Ferguson's strident tone rose in volume.

Kevin's eyes narrowed. "Why sneak into the Prushark house?"

"To get the proof to clear my name. I know it exists." Ferguson shot back.

"Why trust Rickson?" Kevin repeated my muttered question.

"Rickson discovered the kickbacks and fraud didn't stop when I left." Impatience sharpened Ferguson's insistent tone. "He was getting evidence to expose the real offenders."

When the other guy's voice became harder to hear, I leaned closer to Kevin.

Marcus pulled on Kevin's shirt. "Where was Rickson going Saturday after he chased Ferguson?"

That's us. Interrogation by committee.

Kevin repeated the question.

"He was headed to Monroe's to get evidence. The final nail, he said." Ferguson's voice rose in volume, as if he'd pulled his phone closer to his mouth. "We planned to meet Sunday. Now, I learn he doesn't remember anything.

Prushark's dead. The Monroe evidence is destroyed. I need to talk to you and Belden. Now."

The man sounded desperate, but with this case, I wasn't trusting anyone.

With his free hand, Kevin fiddled with a quarter he'd pulled out of thin air. "What do you want from us?"

"Compare notes. Clear my name." Ferguson's demands came through loud and clear. "Get my life back."

Marcus took half-a-step back, his expression intense. "We have to go."

Ever cautious, he whispered the words.

Kevin and I exchanged nods. As bizarre as Ferguson's story sounded, it had a ring of truth. If he hadn't spoken to Rickson, he wouldn't have Kevin's number. I must admit, the allure of finding answers for my crossword puzzle was already burning through my blood like an elixir.

Moments later, the details were set. We would meet at a café on the road leading to the Prushark estate at three o'clock. His insistence that he couldn't come earlier was fine by me. The episode with Quinlan had eaten up my lunchtime. I think better on a full stomach.

I tried to bury the worry of the weaselly-faced Ferguson setting a trap. What would the man gain by attacking me and Kevin?

Kevin hung up, then glanced around. His serious expression faded before a smile. "Breathe people. Breathe."

I retreated, stunned. "I did not see this one coming."

Marcus rubbed his hands together. "When do we leave?"

"You're not going." I ignored the boy's groan and the stubborn set to his chin. "You and Mrs. C have to sit out this interview."

"She's right, dude." Kevin glanced at Rabi, who gave an infinitesimal nod. "Belden, Rabi, and I will get the lowdown. You'll be our backup in case of an emergency."

Sensing defeat, Marcus punched Rabi in the shoulder. "Call if you need me."

I felt relief that my son and Mrs. C would be safely behind the front lines. "Now let's talk lunch."

At three o'clock, the Winston Pub was dark wood, tinted windows, and dim lights. Kevin and I arrived thirty minutes early. We dropped Rabi off two blocks away.

Rabi's sole text consisted of "No Ferguson. No backup."

Happily, that moved the possibility of a setup to the rear burner.

I sat next to Kevin in a booth. Looking past his handsome profile, I had a clear view of the main entrance. With our thighs touching from the knee to hip, the tingling in my blood could have been from his nearness or the case building to a head. Or both.

Kevin checked the front door, then met my gaze. "Alone at last."

A silly grin touched my lips. "It might not happen often in our relationship, but I like it."

As if on cue, a faint whoosh of air signaled the front door opening.

Kevin and I turned as one. When the bright sunlight invaded the dim interior, he shifted his face to one side.

I kept my gaze trained on the entrance. For an instant, I saw the black silhouette of a slim man against the outside light. The quick snap of the closing door obliterated the profile.

I lost him as my eyes readjusted to the inky darkness. Too late, I understood why Kevin hadn't stared into the outside light.

My buddy refocused on the main entrance. "Red hair."

By slight gradations, I made out the man's image and coloring. "That's the guy who chased Rickson into the ER Friday night."

Had it only been three days? It seemed as if the short space of time had been packed with a month's worth of violence and intrigue. Hopefully, this meeting would fill in some blanks in my crossword puzzle.

After a quick scan of the other occupants, the guy headed straight for us. He hesitated briefly, studying first Kevin, then me before he slipped into the booth, facing us.

Even in the dim light, I could make out his tanned, leathery skin. I'd grown up with enough horse people in my native Kentucky to recognize the signs of a life spent in the sun. Though on the skinny side, he had corded muscles that spoke of long labor on construction sites. Like Kevin, Ferguson hadn't earned his muscles in a gym.

Moments later, after the waitress had taken orders and delivered drinks, Ferguson checked over his shoulder for the third time. The gesture pulled the zipper on his jacket down a few inches. "You alone?"

"We're the only ones here." In the building. Since Rabi could be anywhere, I figure my response counted as the truth. Besides, Ferguson had nothing to fear from our side. I only wanted answers. "Tell me why you think I should help you."

"Because I'm innocent." Ferguson stabbed his chest with a bent finger. "I stumbled onto the losses from the construction projects months ago. I traced them back five years. Small at first, then bigger and more widespread."

His voice rose as his agitation grew.

As he flung out his arms, I caught a flash of yellow inside his jacket. Exactly where an inner pocket would be. A pocket big enough to hold a small, plastic toolbox that had gone missing from my apartment.

I nudged Kevin's leg with my knee.

When he nudged me back, I could only hope he was

thinking theft rather than footsie as Ferguson continued ranting.

"I worked with the Prusharks and the Monroes for years, but for all I knew the old man or one of the kids did it, to grab more of the Monroe company. I planned to find the people responsible." After another glance around the deserted café, Ferguson hunched over the table and continued in a softer tone. "Just as I was ready to take the information to the police, Sheila and Pete Monroe laid out proof *I* was guilty."

While I noted the name, Ferguson launched into a fluid and colorful string of curses for the people who'd framed him.

I inched forward. "Were Sheila or Pete in on the fraud? Did they frame you?"

"They're legit. The evidence is so good, I'd have believed I was a thief." The guy pressed his lips together. His pinched face took on a haunted expression. "The guilty ones are Ulesh, a construction manager with the Monroes, and his cronies. They oversee the thefts."

Kevin spun a fork in his fingers like a baton. The spinning utensil came dangerously close to the glasses on the table. "You're certain Verna Nelson isn't part of the scheme?"

"Verna's my sister-in-law. She was the only one I could trust." Ferguson's defense was instant and convincing. "She helped me track the thefts. She's innocent."

That didn't mean I believed him. "She just happens to go to Brazil when extortion, explosions, and murder take center stage? What a coincidence."

"I told her to leave." The older man's expression turned mulish. "I was ready to make my move and I wanted her safe. She only got involved to help me."

Kevin spun a fork on his fingertips before laying it flat. "Does that include helping you murder Henry Prushark?"

The red-haired man froze with his glass halfway to his mouth. Puzzlement blanketed his face. "Why would I murder the old man? He has nothing to do with my problems."

My guy shook his head in evident disbelief. "Your brother died because Henry Prushark insisted the crew finish a project in the pouring rain."

Ferguson snorted. "My brother died because he drank four beers with supper. Everyone knew he shouldn't have returned to the construction site. Verna and I never blamed the Prusharks. Besides, it was fifteen years ago. If I wanted the old man dead, I'd have murdered him then. Ask Victoria Quinlan. She knows the truth. She helped Verna with the records."

Drat the man's sincerity. Another grand theory, shot down in flames.

Kevin spun his glass in the condensation on the table. "Why would Quinlan help two outsiders prove the Prusharks guilty of a crime?"

I love my man and his insightful comments.

Ferguson snorted. "Verna and Quinlan graduated from the same high-school, years apart. They were good friends. Verna warned her not to trust anyone."

With my poker face firmly in place, I digested this latest news. "Quinlan didn't cover her investigation as well as she thought. She got shot this morning."

Another string of curses lit up the air. When the weaselly-faced man wound down, the dim light reflected off the beads of sweat on his lip. He seemed to have aged just hearing about the shooting. "Ulesh and the others are getting desperate. If they were smart, they'd pack up and leave, but they have families here."

"Do you have proof of the fraud?" I moved closer, though I was certain of the answer. "We need something that incriminates these men."

"They're too careful." The other man swept his bony finger through the air. "I thought I had it. Verna saw... Last week I made it into Todd Prushark's office and..."

"And what?" Something in Kevin's tone brought the yellow box to mind. Perhaps the other man realized he'd been on the verge of incriminating himself.

"Didn't pan out." Ferguson's beady eyes shifted. "After Rickson left me Saturday, he planned to get the files on the Monroe server. He wouldn't say how he got the sign-on information, but he had to be in their offices to use it."

I waited for more. "And?"

"The. Building. Exploded." Ferguson spoke through clenched teeth. "Rickson is in the hospital."

I seethed in the face of his sarcasm and my own slip. "Any proof on the Monroe computers is up in smoke now."

"You have to do something. I'm innocent." After taking a long drink, he slammed his glass on the table. "When Rickson hit the scene last week, everyone figured the game was up."

Kevin's lips turned up in a cynical smile. "Too many guilty consciences."

Ferguson spread his hands, offering a tantalizing glimpse of yellow inside his jacket. "Ulesh and the foremen, the men tied to the thefts and fraud, panicked."

"Are you saying foreman as in a mid-level shift leader? Or *four* men?" I held up the appropriate number of fingers.

A laugh burst out of Ferguson's mouth. "Both. There are three divisions in the Monroe organization and Ulesh has one man in each division, plus him is four."

Kevin spun a plastic swizzle stick. "Is one a demolitions expert?"

Ferguson nodded as his nervous gaze scanned the bar. "Either Wilson or Sanchez."

Quinlan's shooting sprang to mind. "What about a marksman? Former military? A sniper perhaps?"

Ferguson's brow furrowed. "Ulesh is ex-army. Whenever he had a few drinks, he bragged about his marksman medal. Krause is the fourth."

I met Kevin's gaze. "We've identified our bombers and the sniper that shot Quinlan."

"What do you want from us?" As Kevin spoke to Ferguson, his foot tapped mine, twice in quick succession.

Time for action. All I had to do was follow my buddy's lead. First, we had to get out of the booth. Not even my sticky-fingered guy could slip the box out from across the table.

"I want my life back." Ferguson's sweeping gesture barely missed his almost full glass. "Ulesh has stopped the thefts and covered his tracks. If he kills me, the investigation will end. You're buddies with that police detective. I want protection."

Why do people contact me instead of going to the police? If Ferguson's plan rested on the belief that Vandercoy and I were friends he was doomed. Before I could utter a denial, Ferguson stabbed his bent finger at me.

"You call him. Explain and get me protection."

"Don't talk to her like that." Kevin batted the guy's arm away, again swinging dangerously close to two of the drinks.

This was it. His reaction was out of all proportion to Ferguson's comment. Besides, he knows I can outtalk anyone.

I subtly moved my glass closer to the wall. I could see where this was going. While I was willing to sacrifice to get the yellow box, I preferred not to get soaked in a mixture of drinks.

"Go to the cops on your own." Kevin's voice held a dismissive tone. "We're done here."

He stood abruptly, jostling the table with his hip. The mugs tilted and spun.

"Kevin," I growled through gritted teeth and slid to the outside of the booth. "Wait."

Ferguson shot a dark, dangerous scowl at my bud. Then, he grabbed my arm. "You're not leaving me here."

Twisting free of the man's grip, I clenched his wrist in turn, locking my fingers. I hadn't grown up wrestling with an older brother and a posse of cousins for nothing.

"Calm down. I'll call Vandercoy." With my body half-turned out of the booth, I braced my feet. "Kevin, get over here."

I launched myself up and out, dragging Ferguson with me. My hip caught the table as I lunged at Kevin. The three glasses crashed to their sides.

Liquid splashed on Ferguson's legs.

I snagged Kevin's arm and pulled him around, dragging the other man with me.

Ferguson struggled against my grip, while cursing at getting wet.

"Belden, this is your problem." Kevin jerked against my hold. "I'm gone."

I set my legs and swung them both toward me. I faced Kevin. "Don't you run out on me."

Then, I thrust myself at Ferguson, until we were nose-to-nose. "I'll make sure Vandercoy sends someone to pick you up."

Still scowling, I released my holds and we all took a step away. I hadn't seen Kevin take the box. I didn't need to. Ferguson's jacket was more zipped up than it had been in the booth. And he hadn't touched the zipper.

I made the call to Vandercoy, who was thrilled to get a hold of Ferguson. Then I waited for a plainclothes detective to take the guy off our hands.

I figured Ferguson would miss the box. I didn't realize that he was so worried about being the next murder victim that an elephant could have sat on him without him noticing.

We were on the road again with Rabi in the backseat, when Kevin tossed me the elusive prize.

I clutched it my hands. "What is in box number one?"

21

37 Down; 5 Letters;
Clue: Value highly; Covet
Answer: Prize

I finally had Marcus's McGuffin. The box had wreaked havoc on my life for three days. Would it hold the answers to my questions?

Not likely.

I had a *lot* of questions.

"Are you going to open it or stare at it?" Kevin's voice pulled me from my musings.

"I was basking in the moment."

"Bask later," he said. "Open it."

"I'll need a knife to cut through the glue." I flipped up the tab in preparation. The lid eased away from the bottom half. "What the…? Ferguson looked inside."

"Who wouldn't?" Kevin's confident hands eased the

Caddy into traffic and headed toward town. "Except you, evidently."

I thought I heard a snort of amusement from Rabi, but I ignored it. Curiosity was zinging through my veins. My hands gripped the lid as the theme music from *Sherlock* sounded from my purse. Marcus's ringtone. "Seriously? Now?"

Fighting a rush of frustration, I held onto the box with one hand while I answered my phone with the other. "This better be good."

As I spoke, I snuck a peek inside the box. Wrinkled white tissue was wrapped around what looked to be several photos.

"Pictures?" I inched down the tissue paper to get a glimpse of the photographs.

"Rabi's car exploded." Marcus's high-pitched tone carried through the Caddy.

My heart dropped to my stomach. I shut the box and dropped it in my purse.

Kevin's hands throttled the steering wheel in a death grip. The Caddy rocketed forward with a force that thrust me against the seat.

Rabi's expression froze to a stony façade. His gaze took on a cold, murderous glint.

Though my lungs seemed to have seized up, I had enough presence of mind to put the phone on speaker. "Are you and Mrs. C okay?"

"We're good," Marcus assured me. "We were in the restaurant in the hotel lobby. We saw the explosion through the window."

My whole body sagged with relief. "What happened?"

"A lady was in the parking lot walking toward the Toyota. She clicked her remote and ka-blooey. Ball of flame."

A hand squeezed my heart. I closed my eyes against the image of Mrs. C turning the key in the ignition.

"Her remote must have been on the same frequency." My stomach was doing somersaults of fear, but my voice sounded amazingly steady.

"That's what we figured," Marcus agreed in a know-it-all tone. "She froze, then she turned and ran inside."

"Smart woman."

"I know who set the bomb." My son lowered his voice to a stage-whisper. I could imagine Marcus pushing his jet-black hair off his forehead as he scanned the café for eavesdroppers. "The guy walked past the hotel wearing sunglasses, but I recognized him."

Marcus paused. Just when I opened my mouth to prod him, he continued. "He was one of the bombers we followed to the Monroe offices Saturday night."

His words slammed into my chest. For a second, I couldn't breathe. "Keep your heads low. We're on our way."

"What's your ETA?" Marcus asked in an official tone.

I rolled my eyes. Nothing gets this kid depressed for long.

"We just passed the estate. It'll be twenty minutes." Even at this speed, I added silently. "Stay put. Stay out of sight."

"Sure," he answered blithely, then hung up.

With my son and Mrs. C safe, anger lit a slow burn in my gut. I glanced at Rabi. "How did they find us?"

A worry line cracked the lean man's icy mask. He inclined his head, resembling a stone monument. "GPS."

"The ER." Kevin's fist hit the steering wheel hard enough to make it shake. "One of them must have planted a tracking device on the Toyota when we were inside."

"What about the Caddy?" My stomach lurched at the thought I might be sitting on a bomb waiting to explode.

"Tracking? Probably." Kevin raced around the slower moving traffic as if we were riding a rocket. "Bomb? Evidently not."

"ER is high traffic. Cops in and out." Rabi spoke in a business-like tone. "Hotel is quiet."

"Ferguson's ex-buddies are tying off loose ends." I tossed my cell phone in my hands, trying to plot the next move. When it rang, I nearly dropped it.

Kevin laughed. Even Rabi smiled.

I caught my breath before I answered. "Hello?"

"How's me favorite Yank?" Mrs. C's carefree tone did little to soothe my jangled nerves. "Roxie called. She tried to reach you and Marcus, but your lines were busy."

"News from Roxie." As I spoke I turned on the speaker. Crawford's office administrator must have an update on the case. "Where's Marcus? I don't hear him."

I get nervous when he's quiet.

"Watching through the door, luv. Quite a crowd has gathered to watch the spectacle." She made it sound like the gladiator games had come to life.

"Okay." I relaxed a notch. "What's the news?"

"Roxie received an e-mail Mr. Rickson sent Saturday evening. She has no idea why the message was delayed for two days." Like any good storyteller, Mrs. Colchester paused for effect. "It was evidently lost in cyberspace."

I watched Tahoe's landscape zip by in a blur as hope leapt in my heart. "The problem is that server Crawford refuses to update. It's fine for most things, but large attachments confuse it."

"I dare say that might complicate a transmission." The older woman could have been discussing a gardening question. "According to Roxie, there is a rather large file attached which the computer person is attempting to open."

"Rickson got the Monroe records." That filled in more blanks in my puzzle. "That should be enough to incriminate Ulesh and his three criminal buddies."

Kevin's expression remained somber as he maneuvered the powerful car past a semi then squeaked through two cars to find an open stretch of road. "I don't care about evidence. I want Marcus and Mrs. Colchester safe."

"Priority. Secure family." Rabi's words could have been carved in stone. "Then, attack."

"Marcus is here," Mrs. C said.

"We have to go." Marcus's rapid-fire words came clearly over the line. "The man is headed this way. I don't think he saw me."

I stiffened, instantly on edge. "The bomber man?"

"Oh, de-yar. I believe the boy's correct." The older woman made it sound like a slight setback instead of a major calamity. "He's on the front walk. A white man. Straight blond hair combed to one side, over his forehead. Not an attractive look on his round face."

I stared at the phone. She's dissecting his haircut at a time like this? Then, I caught Rabi's infinitesimal nod. A chill traveled up my spine. I would *not* want to be that man if Rabi got a hold of him.

"Act casual, but hurry," Marcus said in a stage-whisper. "We can go through the kitchen. Then to the lobby or sneak around the building."

Kevin's eyes narrowed. "Stay where there are people."

"I heard," Marcus said. "I'm trying."

Kevin's jaw tightened. The car shot into warp drive.

Mrs. C's hurried voice sounded over the line. "We're in the kitchen. I see no one following."

"This better not get back to his social worker. She frowns on bombs, not to mention murders and shootouts." I spoke as clanging pots sounded over the phone. I was rambling. Sue me, I was nervous. Okay, I was petrified. "Can this car fly? How much farther?"

"Fourteen miles." Kevin ground out the words through gritted teeth.

"Why are we going to the kitchen, ducks?" Mrs. C asked.

"A second bomber out the rear. The Hispanic guy. Goatee. Red and yellow shirt." Marcus's tone was steady. "I've got a plan. You'll need both hands."

"I see what you're thinking." The older woman's admiration roused my curiosity. "Good show. Later, luv."

With a sign-off that sounded like a tally-ho, I found myself staring at a silent phone.

I ran my fingers through my hair. The thought of grabbing my son and leaving town held definite appeal. I'd go anywhere to keep Marcus safe, but we were running out of places to hide.

Kevin wiped a hand across his face. "We need to go to ground. Fast."

"No cops." Rabi's expression seemed to harden even more at Kevin's words. "We get our people. We go."

I was agreeing right up until his last restriction. "I have to abandon my clothes again?"

Kevin's sideways glance carried more than a trace of disbelief.

"I'm kidding." Sort of. "Not that I want to sound like the whiner of the group."

Kevin gave a ghost of a smile. "Then quit whining."

The banter did little to distract me. I reached over and squeezed his shoulder. His hand covered mine with a comforting strength.

When the phone played Sherlock, I jumped on it like a lifeline, clicking the speaker. "Marcus?"

"I'm back." The boy sounded cheery. "Where are you now?"

"Eleven miles away." Kevin supplied the answer in a steady tone.

I swallowed and fought to keep my voice calm. "Where are you? What did you do?"

"Started a fire." The answer came in stereo, but not from the phone. Rabi and Kevin supplied the response simultaneously.

"It was easy." Marcus crowed. "Smoke. Sprinklers. Evacuation. We're in the lobby. I lost sight of the guys stalking us."

"I'm a fool." I thrust my phone at Rabi and motioned toward Kevin. "Your phone."

He dug it out and handed it over. "Who are you calling?"

"Vandercoy." I clipped off the detective's name. "We need reinforcements."

"Hey, Bro." Rabi's voice came out cool and collected. "What's up?"

I stabbed at the numbers with shaking fingers. Licking my parched lips, I urged the phone to ring.

"You know T.R.," Rabi said in the background. "She's checking on something. We'll be there any minute. We're flying down the highway."

I'd thought Mrs. C had done a good job of speeding through traffic. Kevin wove in and out of the lanes without touching the brakes. He could give lessons on racing circuits.

I pounded the seat, mentally screeching at Vandercoy to pick up. All the while I listened to Rabi's level tones, wishing I could adopt his attitude.

"He's off the speedometer," Rabi said in a sleepy tone. "Hell of a ride."

"Vandercoy." The detective's voice pulled me away from my eavesdropping.

"My car just exploded at the Liverpool Hotel." I spat out the words. "Two bombers are after my son and Mrs. Colchester."

"Hold."

Something in Vandercoy's tone cut through my adrenaline high. The lone, sane corner of my brain put the brakes on my border-line hysteria. Resting a hand on Kevin's shoulder anchored me. I swallowed a lung full of air and waited with bated breath.

I braced my feet. The freeway flew past in a blur. In seconds, we'd left it behind. At over ninety miles an hour, the city streets rushed to meet us.

Kevin threaded the traffic without blinking an eye.

"T.R. is lining up the cavalry," Rabi sounded unconcerned. "You still in the lobby?"

Despite his tone, Rabi's eyes were hard as stone and cold as glaciers. "You and Mrs. Colchester get the chance, go to the firetrucks, you hear?"

Satisfaction ran through my veins. If anyone could save my son, it would be Rabi. The man would battle an army for the street orphan who'd adopted him as a surrogate uncle.

"Belden?" Vandercoy's voice sounded in my ear.

"Here." I bit off the word and turned my attention to the phone. "They're going to the firefighters."

"Tell them not to go with anyone else." Urgency filled the detective's voice. "I'm on my way."

And hell was sure to follow. I don't know where the phrase came from, but he sounded ready to do serious damage.

Me? All I wanted was to grab Marcus and Mrs. C and head for the hills.

Handing Kevin his phone, I spun to face Rabi. "Vandercoy will find them with the firefighters. Only him."

Rabi repeated the instructions, then, "The bombers? Get away from them."

Rabi's voice rose for the first time. He handed me my phone. Screams and shouts erupted from the cell.

His high-pitched yell rose above it all. "I wanna see the firetrucks."

"Marcus, wait for me." Mrs. C's scream hurt my ears. Anyone standing close by might have been deafened. "I will not stop. I must catch the boy. That man is not security."

A thud followed her words. Her purse was heavy enough to be considered a lethal weapon. With luck, she'd laid somebody out.

Sirens wailed in stereo. I looked at the readout, but the call had disconnected. Were we that close to the hotel?

A block ahead of the car, a pillar of gray smoke darkened the sky.

"Get ready." Kevin pointed to the right. "The main lobby is through the trees. I'll put you on the grass."

With shaking fingers, I texted Marcus. "Rabi's coming."

Images flashed between the pine trees like a slide show. Cops shielding evacuees. Firefighters wielding massive hoses. EMTs bending over a gurney.

I gagged on the smell of smoke.

Rabi was by the door, crouched low.

The Caddy slowed, jumped the curb, and swung onto the grass.

I waited for the car to stop. Rabi didn't.

The door opened, then slammed shut.

By the time I looked toward the hotel, all I saw was an empty swath of green and a few branches on an evergreen tree twitching in a non-existent breeze.

Rabi was gone.

I still expected the Caddy to stop. To my surprise, the car sped up and swerved into the street. "We have to get Marcus."

Kevin reached out blindly to grab my hand with unerring ease. "Rabi's on it."

I returned his clasp with white-knuckled pressure. I'd never been so close to losing those I loved.

"If the Caddy's being tracked, we can't tip our hand." His narrowed gaze scanned the street ahead. "They see our tracker stop, the bombers will come running. We'll go in from the front. What's the strategy?"

I throttled back my roiling emotions. I had the clues. I had a hazy image of answers. This time, I was going fill out my crossword puzzle no matter what it took.

"Distraction is my usual go-to." As the car sped toward the long drive that led to the hotel, I focused on my options. "I need their attention on me. A loud, noisy confrontation."

"Go with your strength."

Lights and sirens filled the air and flashed through the landscaping on the right. "My plan involves a cop car and a microphone."

He released my hand with a final squeeze and a wry laugh. "Scary thought."

A moment later, we were in position.

"You'd think the police would keep a sharper eye on their vehicles." It had been amazingly easy to make off with a cop car. That's where Kevin's training as a thief came in handy.

"In their defense, they're dealing with a car bombing, a kitchen fire, and an evacuation." Kevin eased the black-and-white vehicle into a wide, slow circle around the other police cars that cordoned off the sweeping driveway leading to the hotel.

"It's kind of cool sitting in the front seat." A multitude of switches, gears, and equipment faced me. Being in the backseat of a cop car is no fun. Trust me on that. I grabbed the microphone. Time to go on the attack. "I've always wanted my own PA system. You do the lights and sirens. I'll handle the talking."

Billows of black smoke rose from an ever-expanding

pillar in front of the hotel. Red firetrucks spewed water. Police lights whirled in a mad kaleidoscope of color. People ran from the hotel in a steady stream, while others gawked at the firefighters battling the burning car.

Talk about bottled chaos.

Kevin's hand was poised over a switch on the dashboard. "Tell me when."

I girded myself, wondering what I was going to say. Reason with them? Attack? Threaten? No doubt my mouth would be ready when the time came. "Go."

The discordant wail of sirens reverberated directly over my head. Bracing myself, I keyed on the microphone. "Ulesh. Wilson. Sanchez. Krause. We have the evidence of your fraud."

With me yelling at the top of my lungs into the microphone, the words echoed in the air as I paused for breath.

"You can't bury your involvement any longer." A metallic tone underscored my voice. "It's over."

"Why're you shoving me down?" I released the button on the mic. I'd drawn a lung full of air when Kevin's strong arm propelled me to the floor. "Hey, there's a crack in the window."

"Sniper." Kevin's stern expression matched his steely tone. "Keep talking. You've got their attention."

"Aren't you supposed to sit up to drive?" From my position crouched on the floor, I gripped the microphone like a lifeline.

"Relax, Belden. I got this." Kevin drove with one hand while half-laying on the seat. His head was high enough to see over the dashboard. "Keep talking."

Drawing in a lungful of air, I raised the mic as if in slow motion. "Listen, you idiots. Shooting at me will not shut me up."

"I could have told them that."

I ignored Kevin's muffled comment. "Rickson downloaded the Monroe files before the building exploded. They've been sent to the cops. You're on the hook for theft and fraud."

I paused to let the facts sink through their paranoid minds. "Save yourselves by cutting a deal with the police."

That's my motto, squeal first, get the best deal.

When I rose to look out the windows, Kevin pushed me low again. "You don't need to look them in the eye. They can hear you."

He was right, of course. It was just reflex.

"You have information to sell. It's your only chance. You're not walking away. You have nowhere to go." I thumbed off the mic. "Do you see Vandercoy's SUV?"

He'd kept the car moving in a zig-zag. I'd watched the treetops slide by, but I had no idea where we were in relation to the hotel.

Kevin angled his head up enough to peer over the dash. "By the fire engines. We're getting close."

"Detective Vandercoy is on site," I screamed at the top of my lungs while gripping the mic in a chokehold. "Rickson and Quinlan will recover. None of you had a hand in Prushark's death. I know who's guilty, but if anyone dies now, you'll go down for murder."

The ominous word hung in the air as I paused for air. I deliberately lowered my tone and spaced out the next words. "Save yourselves. Surrender."

I met Kevin's gaze. "You think they'll listen?"

"No new bullet holes." With a firm hand on my shoulder, he eased our police cruiser to a stop.

An eerie, almost deafening, silence descended.

A long minute passed.

"Throw down your weapons." Vandercoy's delivery sounded a touch more controlled than mine, but he'd done this before. "Come out with your hands up. I guarantee your safety."

What are the sweetest words to a cop?

Two-word answer.

I surrender.

22

16 Across; 10 Letters;
Clue: Previously unknown fact
Answer: Revelation

In a weekend full of police interviews, what I hoped would be the last was more confusing than the others. It started when Vandercoy asked me about the murderer's identity. I answered him with a shrug and a frown.

He gave me a strange look, complimented me on my bluff, and said to come to the station in the morning.

I was so wrung out, I wasn't sure how long the arrest and the aftermath took. It may have been one hour or several. It seemed endless, but it was finally over. I whispered the mantra to myself as the elevator doors closed. The sun's golden glow, partially hidden by the lacy spires of a pine tree, was the last sight I saw.

I leaned on Kevin's shoulder, happy to have him close.

"The Belden Detective Agency strikes again." Marcus

smacked the button for the third floor. "That was so cool. I was on top of the firetruck and saw it all. Mrs. Colchester laid out the blond dude with her bag. Rabi ran through the smoke like a ninja. He dropped Sanchez with one blow."

I expected Marcus to complete the rundown. The cops got a third guy in the lobby. SWAT got Ulesh, the sniper, in a nearby building. He asked for a deal before he got to the patrol car. Instead, Marcus paused for breath, or perhaps to relive the moment. I wasn't sure. I only know silence descended.

"Who killed Prushark?"

Though I couldn't decipher who spoke, the question forced a sardonic response from me. "If we knew that, we could turn them in and go home."

It was only when four pairs of eyes stared at me with matching frowns that I realized I'd missed something. I reluctantly raised my head off Kevin's shoulder. "Why are you looking at me?"

Mrs. C raised a delicate brow as she pushed a disheveled curl into place. "Luv, you broadcast to everyone within four city blocks that you knew the identity of the murderer."

"I did?" My gaze flicked from one to the other, lingering on my son before landing on Kevin, who confirmed the older woman's surprising claim with a nod.

"You yelled it into the mic." Marcus flung out his hands. "You told the bombers they were only on the hook for theft and fraud."

I pointed a finger at the boy. "I remember that part."

"You said they wouldn't go down for murder because you could identify the killer." My son wrapped up the replay with an expectant look on his face.

I felt my expression freeze.

"You were bluffing?" Shock rang through Kevin's tone. He knows how bad I am at poker.

I cast my eyes toward the elevator's ceiling. I wasn't sure whether I thought the answer might be written there or if I hoped heaven would provide. Either way, it didn't work. "If my brain knows the killer, it's not sharing with me."

Only Rabi's expression remained undimmed. "It'll come."

Kevin gave my hand a reassuring squeeze.

I heaved a long, dark sigh as the elevator opened. Though I'd found some answers for my crossword puzzle, one entire section remained blank. The one dealing with murder. If I already had the answer, why were those empty squares taunting me?

Rabi, walking at the front of the group, scanned the empty hall. "New crash-pad."

"We need to stay ahead of the killer." Amusement threaded through Kevin's agreement. "This hotel attracts the wrong kind of people."

I mentally groaned. I didn't want to move again.

Kevin shook with laughter.

I cast him a sideways glance. "Did I say that out loud?"

His blue eyes danced with glee. "Yes, whiner-of-the-group, you did."

"That will be our third hotel in three days." A note of pride filled Marcus's voice as his undersized frame sauntered ahead of me. "That's a new record."

"Oh, goody." Despite my pathetic attempt at sarcasm, I couldn't help but laugh as my son tossed me a grin. If only I were an energy leech, then I could siphon off some of his boundless enthusiasm. Instead, I trudged to my room.

I was the first one ready. It helped that I never had the chance to unpack.

I threw my purse on the bed then plopped down next to it. Kevin and Rabi discussed our next destination but I paid them no heed. As the others gathered their things, my mind wandered. My gaze followed. A flash of yellow in my purse caught my eye.

"Oh, my gosh!" Energy surged through me. I gripped the plastic box with both hands. "I forgot I had this."

A babble of questions and answers brought Mrs. C and Marcus up to speed regarding our meeting with Ferguson coupled with Kevin's pickpocketing trick. As I spoke, I tore the white tissue paper off the photographs inside the box.

"Pictures." Half-a-dozen to be exact. Four-by-six-inches. As I scanned the top two, Marcus snatched the other four from my fingers. My two showed a head and shoulders shot of the same three people. "This is Sheila Prushark. The man has to be Paul, her deceased brother. He looks like a younger version of Todd. The blonde is Linda, the daughter-in-law. Who would hide these? They aren't incriminating."

Ferguson had hinted at a secret, but these photos were bland tourism.

Disappointment washed over me. I'd been running around all weekend for this? I checked the back of the photo. Perhaps there was a secret code.

Nope. Nothing.

"Three people standing on a bridge." Disappointment filled my son's voice.

I handed one picture to Kevin. I held the other out to Rabi, who stood by the window alternately eyeing the parking lot and the door. He shook his head.

Didn't the man have an ounce of curiosity? I'd been itching to find out what was in the box since Friday. I passed the second picture to Kevin, who was leaning against the headboard, on the same bed as Mrs. C.

My son had shared his prize with the older woman.

"Why, this is the Charles Bridge in Prague." Mrs. C spoke with a nostalgic tone that meant a tale lurked in the background. "I visited there as a young girl."

Kevin flipped between the two views he held. "The date stamp in the corner is over five years ago."

Mrs. C glanced at me. "Didn't you say the grandchild's fifth birthday is coming up?"

Busy trying to puzzle out why these pictures were worth hiding, I almost missed her question. "He'll turn five soon."

Marcus had shifted to Mrs. C's side. "So that lady's not fat. She's pregnant."

Though curious to see the pictures in the other woman's hands, I was forced to admit they wouldn't tell me anything new. "That would be Linda Prushark, before she gave birth."

Kevin gaze narrowed. "According to Quinlan, Linda and her husband visited infertility specialists in Europe. Sheila joined them a few months later when her brother fell behind on setting up the European office."

"You did say the Prusharks have a strong family resemblance?" Mrs. C's soft British accent held a hint of suspicion.

I frowned at the odd question. "Yes, Paul looks just like Todd and Sheila."

Mrs. C arched a brow. She fanned the four photos out like playing cards. When her pale green eyes peeked over the tops, she looked like a card shark holding the winning hand. "Unless the youngest Prushark married his twin, some of your facts may be in error."

Kevin stilled. Our gazes met.

I all but threw myself on the other bed. I managed to squeeze between Kevin and the older woman as he shifted to look at the pictures.

Throwing aside all claim to politeness, I grabbed the photos out of her hands. "I was cheated. These are full body shots."

Kevin crowded close and tilted the photo in his direction. "Linda didn't give birth to Ben. Sheila's the pregnant one."

I studied the threesome frozen in time. The blonde was

the same tall, thin cheerleader type I'd seen at the Prushark house. That Paul Prushark and the pregnant woman. Both with round faces, black hair, and green eyes. My mind spun with the implications. Pieces of the puzzle rearranged into a new view.

"Wow," I muttered in a soft tone.

Yes, it's true. My razor-sharp comebacks never fail.

Kevin tapped the images. "Next time you drag us into a case, get a cast of characters with descriptions."

"Like in Perry Mason books." Marcus, now on the other bed, thumped his heels on the floor. "Why did Sheila Prushark give them her baby? Didn't she want it?"

"There's more to it than that." Kevin didn't go into detail. Instead, he tapped the photos. "Sheila must have been in Europe for most of her pregnancy."

Something clicked in my brain. "Nancy and Josh, at the Pine Trail Inn, said old man Prushark promised Sheila a vice-presidency if the European launch went well. When she succeeded, he reneged."

Mrs. C eyed the photo with a sad expression. "'*She* believed him.'"

The message Quinlan had struggled to deliver. Could her words be tied to this old secret? The final answers in my mental crossword puzzle remained stubbornly blank.

"Why would her father care if she had a baby?" Marcus, a child of the modern era, frowned. "That doesn't make sense."

"The man was born in a different time." I knew the rigid style of thinking all too well. "If he was like my uncles, Henry Prushark would never have let an unmarried mother be an executive. Sheila may also have realized she wasn't ready to be a mother."

"She gave up her baby and he still passed her over for her younger brother." Kevin's tone took on a hard edge. "She must have been furious."

"This all happened five years ago." I studied the photos. "Someone had these taken, but they were never revealed."

"Maybe Todd, Sheila's other brother, didn't want her in charge either." With his elbow on his knee and his chin on his fist, Marcus looked like the statue of the Thinker. "If their father gave Sheila the promotion, Todd could tell him she had a baby."

He made it sound like a childish squabble.

The motive sounded weak, but who knew what the addiction to power did to someone's soul? "According to local gossip, Sheila has the best head for business of the children. When their father denied her the promotion, the pictures weren't needed. So why keep them?"

Somewhere in my brain, a pinball ricocheted madly, looking for a possible answer, a pattern, anything.

"Ferguson stole the box because he thought the contents would clear his name." Kevin held up the photos. "These don't clear or incriminate anyone for fraud."

"They prove the daughter-in-law's been lying. Nope, not even I buy that as a motive for murder." Fortunately, the shrill ring of my phone interrupted my theorizing. "Hello?"

"Thank, goodness." Mrs. Prushark's voice quivered in relief. "Miss Belden, I must warn you. I overheard my daughter on the phone. She knows where you are. She sent someone to your hotel."

Questions flooded my mind even as a fresh wave of fear swept through me. I covered the mouthpiece. "Sheila knows where we are. Someone's coming here."

Kevin stood, motioned to Marcus, then held out his hand to Mrs. C.

"Why would Sheila come after me?" How could she know I had the photos? "I have no proof of her guilt in either the fraud or murder charges."

The figures in the photos stared back at me. I did have a

possible motive. Had Henry Prushark discovered the pictures? Had he threatened his daughter's power?

"Sheila believes you are a danger. I've called Detective Vandercoy," Mrs. Prushark's commanding tone interrupted my thoughts. "I'm on my way. Sheila won't hurt you if I'm there."

"Coming here will put you in danger." I surged to my feet. Was she nuts? "Vandercoy will alert his people. The police may still be around."

"Cops cleared out." Rabi, from his station by the window, inserted the update in a low drawl.

Of course, the police were gone. Why should my luck change now? "Sheila won't risk a direct confrontation."

I hoped.

Rabi's hand went into his jacket. "Limo pulling up."

A vise seized my heart.

Kevin and Marcus turned as one toward the window.

"Old woman getting out." Rabi's narrowed gaze remained locked on the view. He gave a quick nod. "Alone."

What? No Girard? No escort?

"I'm at the hotel entrance," Mrs. Prushark said. "Where shall I meet you? I have to explain."

Like my conversation with Quinlan, this discussion had spun out of control,. Hopefully, this time no one would get shot. Since I had little choice, I gave in gracefully. "Come to the third floor. Kevin will meet you by the elevator."

"Very good." The phone call ended on her hurried, but authoritative, agreement.

Kevin strode toward the door. "One blue-haired rescuer coming up."

Marcus turned to follow. "I'm with you."

I grabbed his jeans and pulled him to me. "No, you don't, mister. We wait here."

Marcus flung up his hands. "She's an old lady. What can she do?"

Considering his friendship with Mrs. C, he should have been more cautious, but I decided to stay on topic. "At this point, I'm going to frisk squirrels for acorn-grenades."

Marcus rolled his eyes.

With a hand on the doorknob, Kevin winked at the boy. "Humor her. She's had a long weekend."

"Ain't that the truth?" I sat on the bed and wondered how I'd gotten to the point of being paranoid about a grandmother. Especially when the case was almost over.

But anyone who grew up in horse country could tell you-- most races are lost in the homestretch.

Kevin glanced over his shoulder. "If I knock, don't open the door."

With that warning, he pulled the door shut behind him.

Evidently, I wasn't the only paranoid soul. I eyed Rabi. "Any movement?"

He shook his head without turning around.

Tension built inside me like a volcano ready to blow. Sheila wouldn't risk a frontal assault, I repeated silently. I realized I had the bedspread in a death grip. The photos lay scattered on the bed. Too bad Vandercoy hadn't seen them first.

Guilt sliced through me. "I never told Vandercoy we stole the box from Ferguson."

I grabbed my phone then hesitated. The detective should be here soon. An image of his massive bulk running to our rescue flashed through my mind. The visual alone was enough to throw me off my feed. More likely, he was sitting at his desk leading from the rear.

Pushing aside my procrastination, I dialed his number. The ringing seemed to awaken an alert in my brain. I felt as if I'd overlooked a piece of the puzzle.

Jealousy. Envy. Power.

Prushark family dynamics. The possible motives teased me.

"Vandercoy."

I started at the abrupt tone. So much for him riding to our rescue.

"Tracy Belden." I fought to ignore the sense of dread clawing up from my toes. "I know you're on your way, but I wanted to tell you I have the box. Kevin and I --"

"I'm in my office."

"Didn't Mrs. Prushark call you?" The temperature in the room took a nosedive. I wasn't sure what was happening, but I didn't like it. "She's on her way up to my hotel room."

Mrs. C's resigned expression gave me the impression she'd expected this turn of events.

"What the--" Vandercoy's voice cut off almost before the word was uttered. "Stall."

The card reader at the door clicked in answer to Kevin's key card. The knob turned.

I turned to ice. I surged to my feet, pulling Marcus with me. "Rabi."

The lean, black man met me in mid-stride. He hustled Marcus to the far corner and thrust him beside the bureau then planted himself in front of the boy's slim form.

The door opened.

The matriarch of the Prushark clan glided into the hotel room. Shorter than me by a head, her translucent skin suddenly recalled the intense heat and pressure required to forge clay into the hard shell of porcelain. The pale blue eyes seemed to hold depths as dark as the deepest ocean.

Kevin walked in behind her. When his gaze met mine, his easy athletic stride faltered. His cobalt blue gaze paused at Marcus's empty place, then he took in Rabi's protective stance, and the small feet behind him. Recovering quickly, Kevin shut the door then quietly threw the deadbolt.

Seizing the initiative, I took the lead. "Mrs. Prushark, I appreciate your concern. However, I'd feel better knowing you were safe at your estate. The police should arrive at any minute."

She stepped closer and patted my arm. "Ms. Belden, I couldn't live with myself if anything happened to you or your friends."

Anyone else would have scoffed at the thought of fearing the old woman. Fortunately, Mrs. C had taught me not to underestimate the blue-hair population.

Since the police station was on the other side of town, I had to stall long enough for Vandercoy to arrive. Uniformed officers might do for inner city malcontents, but one of the state's wealthiest citizens demanded a lead detective. Besides, it wasn't like she'd pull a gun out of her designer handbag and mow us down.

I hoped.

What could Sheila have planned? Was Mrs. Prushark an accomplice, a dupe, or a protective mother? Was she trying to save me or cover up a crime?

While my brain frantically rearranged the crossword puzzle, I fell back on etiquette. Though Miss Manners lacked an entry on how to entertain a possible criminal in your hotel room, my grandmother had impressed upon me that good manners are never wasted.

"You've met Kevin." Stepping to one side, I deliberately turned Mrs. Prushark's sharp gaze away from Rabi. "This is Mrs. Colchester."

Mrs. C stood from the bed and returned the introduction with a graceful nod. She sidled past the other woman then walked to the swivel chair by the desk. "Let me move out of your way."

This two-bed hotel room was certainly no suite. In fact, the walls seemed to be closing in with every passing second. I smiled at Kevin. "Would you get Mrs. Prushark a chair?"

Kevin obligingly moved a paisley upholstered chair to the open area at the bottom of the beds. This conveniently limited my opponent's movements.

With a start, I remembered the plastic box and the pictures. Though unsure what part they played in this drama, I didn't want to be the one to expose their secret. A quick scan showed no trace of them on the bed.

Mrs. C met my gaze then put her hand over a bulge in her pocket. Thankful for her swift thinking, I sat on the end of the bed to Mrs. Prushark's right. "What is Sheila planning?"

"I didn't hear everything." The matriarch sat as stiff-backed as any queen on her throne. "I caught the name of this hotel, then she said, 'Get over there. The Belden woman must be silenced. She can identify the murderer.'"

No, actually, I can't.

The other woman clasped her hands to her chest. "You must tell me. Who killed my husband?"

23

21 Across; 9 Letters;
Clue: A sudden and unexpected reversal
Answer: Turnabout

I looked beyond Mrs. Prushark's pleading gaze and focused on the fact that she'd bought her way into my hotel room with a lie.

Questions flooded my mind. Had she come to help me or delay us for her daughter's arrival? As for the name of her husband's killer, I only wish I knew. "Tell me where you were the night your husband was killed. Did you see or hear anything?"

The old woman paled. She covered her heart with a trembling hand and took a second to compose herself. "I was returning from my office, when I heard a scuffle. There were several thuds as something tumbled down the stairs. When I rounded the corner, Sheila was alone..."

Her lips moved soundlessly as she gestured toward a non-existent flight of steps.

Why had she asked if I knew the killer? Was she in denial? Feeling like a monster, I continued to probe. "Did you see her push her father?"

She pinched the bridge of her nose. "It couldn't have been anyone else."

"Did you tell this to the police?"

"I couldn't." Her whisper was so faint I barely heard the words. "Now she's after you."

"Was Todd around?" When she shook her head, I pressed on. "Did Sheila say anything at the time?"

"Her back was to me." She saw the surprise on my face. "She glanced at the security camera, then hurried off."

A nice, neat story. It covered all the basics except one. "Why would Sheila kill her father?"

"Power." She met my gaze with a straightforward one of her own. "My husband planned to resume control. Sheila's responsibilities would be curtailed."

As were yours and Todd's, I added silently.

Her steady tone and smooth delivery were hallmarks of a truthful statement. The explanation also dovetailed with the Prushark dynamics.

Why did her responses leave me unsatisfied? Why did my brain refuse to insert the answers into my crossword puzzle?

And where was Vandercoy? The man could have taken a crosstown bus and been here by now. "Was Todd involved in his father's murder?"

The pale blue eyes spat fire. The blaze died instantly. "How could he be? He was with Pete and Matt Monroe when I went to my office."

That wasn't true. Even I knew the Monroe meeting ended long before the murder. "Does he know Sheila's guilty?"

The look the old woman gave me was empty. Her shoulders slumped as if burdened by an unbearable weight. "I have no idea."

Her husband was dead.

Her daughter was a supposed murderer.

Mrs. Prushark had taken one body blow after another. However, for all the evidence of defeat, her glazed eyes and pursed lips put me on edge. An image lurked in the shadows of my mind. Finally, a form appeared out of the darkness.

A harpy. That's what she reminded me of, the mythical half-woman half-bird that hovers, waiting for a chance to strike at their victim.

Mrs. Prushark had lurked in the background for years. First, her husband had taken over her business. Later, she'd watched her daughter fight for recognition against less talented brothers. Then, her husband's stroke gave the matriarch an opening to try her wings again. The past seventy-two hours had been a whirlwind, leaving me no time to investigate what she'd been involved in during the last two years.

My brain slammed on the brakes. I'd caught the older woman in one lie. How could I trust anything she said? How did I know her daughter was actually on the way to confront me?

Sheila must have been furious.

My gaze flashed to Kevin as his comment flashed in my mind. I had a vague impression of Rabi, Marcus, and Mrs. C waiting silently in the background.

If Sheila had reason to be angry, didn't the same hold true for Mrs. Prushark?

"*Sheila* believed him." Though I uttered the words in a soft tone, Mrs. Prushark's expression froze. The cornflower in her eyes hardened to the sheen of blue diamonds. She exuded the aura of a cobra about to strike.

My spine stiffened. Rabi and Kevin would protect my son

and Mrs. C. Certain of that fact, I focused my attention on uncovering the truth.

"*Sheila* believed him," I repeated. "You never did. You knew all along he wouldn't give anyone else real power. Not his sons. Certainly not his wife or daughter."

Mrs. Prushark's narrowed eyes met mine with a hint of a challenge, as if daring me to continue. Which I did.

"You saw Sheila do the work, while her younger brother, Paul received the accolades. It was a replay of how your husband benefited when he absorbed your company and you lost your independence."

Mrs. Prushark's face could have been carved from marble.

Though both dramas had taken place in the past, Quinlan's words were barely twenty-four hours old. Henry Prushark's murder was a crime of passion and fury, committed in the family citadel. What had prompted the fury to burst forth two nights ago? What had changed?

Henry stroked out. Todd took charge.

Fraud. Adultery. Pictures.

I rearranged my crossword questions with frantic haste, but the answers weren't coming together. That's when the answer slammed into me with the force of a freight train.

I re-grouped for another onslaught. "When did your husband discover that Sheila gave birth to Ben?"

All hint of softness vanished from the other woman's expression.

"You're not as talented as Mr. Rickson, but you're intuitive." Mrs. Prushark arched a brow. "I didn't expect it of you."

She avoided my question with a deft parry. Her silence confirmed I was on the right track.

I ignored the snide comment. It wasn't the first back-handed compliment I'd received. I doubted it wouldn't be the last. "I've been asking myself why those pictures and that box resurfaced five years after the fact. Why weren't they used at the time?"

No one answered my rhetorical question. Mrs. Prushark gave me a flat stare, seemingly convinced I had no answer. But I did.

"The answer has been right in front of me. You just alluded to it. So did Rickson when he mentioned that Ferguson stole the box from the client." I paused, partly for effect, partly to give the still absent Vandercoy another nanosecond to arrive. "For Todd to complete the takeover, he needed his father's papers. In some forgotten file or safe, he discovered the pictures."

A sneer marred the older woman's elegant features. "Henry sent spies to watch Paul and Sheila. He intended to hold their mistakes over their head when they returned."

"Instead," I said, taking up the thread, "he got the surprise of his life. He kept the photos. No doubt to throw Sheila's deceit in her face if the moment arose, but it was Todd who found the packet years later. Did he seal the pictures in the toolbox?"

The older woman's jaw tightened. "One of his typically impulsive gestures. He should have burned them."

"When did you find out the truth?" How did she find out? The woman obviously kept herself well informed. My mind whirled as if caught in a loop. She wouldn't have openly spied on her family. She would have used a trusted network of informants.

"You took care of the household." Clues and answers came together. "After your husband's stroke, Todd took over security, but I'll bet you found a way to wedge yourself into the process."

The matriarch of this shattered clan gave a regal nod. "When you're denied real power, you manufacture your own.

When security was put under my son's control, I inserted myself into the workings. It was so easy."

She was awfully open with her secrets. The realization made me nervous. I resisted the impulse glance at the window for Vandercoy. He should have been here by now... if he was coming.

How far did the woman's tentacles extend? Could she have bought off the detective? The sobering thought cast a pall over my hope of getting out of here without further violence.

Mrs. Prushark's eyes narrowed to slits, a sly gleam escaped. "Money can hide any number of questionable records. Erase a shady past. Help families. Line pockets. Before long, I had my own staff of loyal soldiers."

How many? Would they burst through the door before the police? Were they waiting for us to leave? Since Vandercoy appeared to have lost his way, I steeled myself to save my friends and family, not to mention me. Time to go on the attack.

"One of your guards fudged the security tape the night of the murder." I reclaimed control of the conversation. "But you, you were the one who screwed up."

Mrs. Prushark stiffened as my bolt shot home.

"You were the only one who didn't know the truth of Ben's birth." I aimed my derogatory tone at her like a dagger. "When the blackmailer claimed to have proof the boy wasn't Paul's son, you panicked. You were determined to protect the family name from Linda's supposed affair. Your husband knew the boy was a Prushark and he didn't' tell you."

As much as I disliked what I'd heard of Henry Prushark's condescending attitude, I had to get my hooks into this woman.

"Rickson recorded your husband's words in his notes. He didn't refer to Ben as Paul's son, only as 'My grandson.'"

Finally, the disjointed words made sense. "Your husband would never have dealt with the blackmailer."

"He cared only for himself and his power." Mrs. Prushark's clenched jaw muffled her words. A touch of venom edged her words. "I don't care whose child Ben is, no one is going to drag my family into a public scandal."

Her expression chilled me. I swallowed my heart out of my throat. I didn't like my odds against this woman, but I was determined to win. "The blackmailer is still out there. He can still cause problems."

Her expression faltered. Her barely controlled fury vanished before a frown. She turned abruptly toward the window. "Where *is* that detective?"

The change of topic, coupled with her indignation threw me completely off my game. After all, only *one* of us expected Vandercoy to show up.

I followed her gaze. I didn't have to fake *my* annoyance. "He should be here by now."

Mrs. Prushark swiveled to face me, uncertainty shown in her gaze. "You don't suppose…"

Despite myself, I moved closer. "What?"

"Maybe he's been bought off." Mrs. Prushark lowered her voice to a confidential whisper. "That could be how Sheila learned of your location."

For a millisecond, I almost believed her. Then I pulled back. What kind of a fool was I to trust anything this woman said? I took a deep breath. This case was making me crazy.

"It's not a long trip." I could almost hear Kevin's comeback. I glanced at him, standing by the door. His encouraging nod reassured me.

A grip on my arm brought me instantly alert.

Mrs. Prushark surged to her feet, pulling me with her. "You and your friends are not safe here."

At least, we agreed on something.

She leaned close, enveloping me with her cloying perfume. "We should leave together. Then I'll know you're safe."

Now I know how a fly feels as a spider reels it in. "What about Vandercoy?"

Her worry-laced eyes met mine. "I'll get you out of here."

Not without a police escort.

Now I knew her plan - to get us away from the hotel. What then? Take us to Sheila? Was her daughter even involved in this scheme? Or would her soldiers drive us into the desert and kill us?

Fear coursed through me. Stalling was no longer good enough. I had to get us out of this. But how?

"One step at a time." My father's motto for training horses ran through my mind.

Mrs. Prushark's narrowed gaze focused on the door.

I stared at the older woman's calculating profile.

Mrs. Prushark jerked my arm. Her tone took on a note of urgency. "We must leave. Now."

A hard pounding shook the door.

My heart seized in my chest.

"Mrs. Prushark?" Girard's voice sounded through the door. "Is everything all right?"

No, everything's not all right. If my heart hadn't been blocking my throat, I might have said the words aloud.

I grabbed her bony arm, pulling her to face me. "You never spoke to Vandercoy."

She drew away.

I fueled my fear into anger. "I called his office. He and his team are in the mountains, following a lead in Quinlan's shooting. Signals can't get through."

I congratulated myself. The old lady wasn't the only one who could string together a good story. "You couldn't have spoken to him in the past hour."

A subtle change rolled across her face. Like a wave returning to the sea leaves the sand hardened and set, her features turned glacial. "I underestimated you."

"It happens. A lot actually." Must be something about me.

"People underestimate my daughter." Mrs. Prushark reached into the pocket of her Chanel jacket. Her hand toyed with an object.

Everything came back to Sheila... or did it? I kept my gaze locked on hers. I had to keep her attention on me. Ignoring the urge to check her hand for what might be a gun, I decided to follow my gut.

"Her father's attitude must have frustrated Sheila." My heart rate slowed as I focused on the puzzle. "But she's young. He could hardly dismantle *her* accomplishments."

Mrs. Prushark eyed me with the unblinking stare an eagle reserves for a mouse.

"Word had leaked that your husband planned to re-take control." I'd have to send Nancy and Josh chocolates for feeding me the local gossip. "It wasn't Sheila's legacy your husband planned to destroy. He was taking away your power. Again. This was your last chance."

Mrs. Prushark and I locked gazes. Her hand crept slowly out of her pocket. Her bony fingers gripped a small pistol.

Tense muscles forced the air out of my lungs. I didn't waste time analyzing the gun. Any bullet would kill at this range.

Another knock sounded on the door.

"Mrs. Prushark." Girard's voice rang clear and strong. "It's time to go."

"You think you're so clever." The older woman shook her head. "You know nothing."

Like me, she ignored the goon hammering at the door. I had the added struggle of blocking out the nagging voice that suggested perhaps Vandercoy *had* been bribed.

"You of all people knew how much your husband had recovered from his stroke." My lungs felt tight. "You also knew he'd never leave you in a role of responsibility."

Mrs. Prushark readjusted her grip on the weapon. "I've done as much as anyone to build that company. It was my cash reserves that gave him the money to expand originally. I worked for years building and protecting our brand. That night, he said none of that mattered, things would be the same as they were before. Matters would be taken out of my hands. As if *I* had failed."

The knob rattled. The door shook. The deadbolt held.

With fierce concentration I kept my attention focused on her, rather than the pounding, the yelling, or the weapon. "But you'd had a taste of freedom. You couldn't let him take that away from you again. You argued."

"He told me the truth about Ben." The whispered words slipped out. Surprise flickered across her face. She put a hand over her lips. "He laughed at me, said I was incapable of running the family's affairs. He planned to face the blackmailer. He didn't care if the if the family's private lives would be paraded in public."

Her bony fingers caressed the gun.

In the tense silence, I inched closer. "I'm sure you didn't realize how fragile the stroke had left your husband."

The pounding on the door renewed. "Open the door."

As if the voice was a catalyst for action, her hand snapped up with the speed of a striking cobra.

With the handgun pointed at my face, I could see it was a twenty-two. From this vantage point, it looked plenty big.

Her eyes narrowed. "You think you have me all figured out."

Not really or I wouldn't be on the wrong end of a gun.
Again.

"You didn't know when to shut up and walk away."

There she had me.

"Now, you've endangered your friends."

With Mrs. C at hand and Marcus stuck in the corner, the admonishment struck home. Guilt threatened to choke me.

"Don't worry about me, luv." Mrs. C's piping British accent would have been right at home in an English country garden. "These cases of yours are a bright spot in my life."

From anyone else, I would have written the comment off as an attempt to assuage my guilt. Not Mrs. C. I had no doubt she meant every word. Truth be told, I'm sure Marcus agreed with her.

The puzzled expression on Mrs. Prushark's face was priceless. However, her gun hand didn't waver.

I seized the moment and buried my guilt beneath an avalanche of outrage.

"You're in no position to lecture me." I gathered my wits, such as they were, and stopped my retreat. I was running out of room anyway. "Your family's history of secrets, betrayals, and power struggles are enough for reality TV. You topped it off with murder."

So, what if I didn't have the evidence to back up my rant? I might as well get it off my chest.

She drew herself up to her full height. "I don't know what you're talking about."

More knocking rattled the door.

"Mrs. Prushark." Girard's voice rang clear and strong. "It's time. We have to leave."

The old woman's lips curled up in a humorless smile. "You underestimated me."

"There's a lot of that going around," I muttered, determined not to follow her husband to his fate. "It's time to end this, Mrs. Prushark. Your husband can't stand in your way anymore."

A sly look filled her eyes. She shook her head. "It's not

over."

"Yes. It. Is." I clipped off each word, adding a touch of steel to my tone. I only hoped I hadn't pushed too far, too fast. I was willing to fence with this woman until dawn, before I'd let her take my son or my friends anywhere. "This case has spun out of control since I hit town. Now, it's out of your control. You were desperate because I said I knew the killer."

She pressed her mouth to a thin line.

With my heart hammering against my ribs, I inched forward. "You came here and gambled on one more, bold move. But I don't care who's outside that door. I'm not going anywhere with you."

I'd closed the distance between us to half an arm's length.

Mrs. Prushark's lips turned up in a cold smile. "Do you intend to wrestle me to the ground?"

"I intend to wait you out." I spoke with more confidence than I felt, but one thing I've learned is how far attitude can take me if I play it right. "You're as trapped as I am. Someone has called the police by now. How will you explain being here?"

"I'll tell the truth." Mrs. Prushark slipped the gun into her pocket. Her hard expression melted into one of fear. "You called and begged me to come. When I arrived, you threatened to spin this wild tale that I was a killer unless I awarded your pathetic little company the contract."

I caught my breath. She was good. She had the bases covered.

A gleam of triumph showed in her eyes. "Say whatever you want. Who do you think the public will believe? You and your ragtag group of losers? Or me? Let's find out."

The final threat rolled off Mrs. Prushark's tongue like shards of glittering glass.

No one spoke. No one moved.

The knob rattled. The door shook.

Dread filled me as I privately admitted the truth of her words. Fairy tales are fun, but good people don't always win. That isn't how the world works.

"Should I call the police?" A distant voice from outside the room sounded honestly concerned.

Yes. I wanted to scream. What do you need? A grenade to go off? For pity's sake, someone had to have called the cops by now.

"We are the police." A familiar, impatient voice called out. "Get in your room."

Why hadn't Vandercoy identified himself to begin with? Then, I remembered the gun and her goons. Okay, maybe he had to take care of business first.

Out of the corner of my eye, I saw Kevin move to the door.

A clink of metal sounded.

The door swung open. A waft of air stroked my cheek.

Vandercoy filled the doorway. Several uniformed police officers stood in the hall behind him.

Shock rooted me to the floor. Relief quickly followed. But with this woman free, a darkness hung over the future.

Mrs. Prushark put a hand over her heart. Her lower lip started to quiver. "Thank goodness you've arrived, Detective. This woman asked me here--"

"Can it, lady." Marcus burst forth from behind Rabi. He held his phone up for all to see. A blinking red circle with the letters REC lit up the corner. "I recorded everything. Don't you call my family losers. Not when you come from a bunch of crazies."

As relief washed over me, I caught Mrs. Prushark's look of fury. I clapped my hand over my mouth to keep from laughing, but inside I was dancing.

My pint-sized hero had saved us.

24

14 Across; 7 Letters;
Clue: To come to a decision, wrap up
Answer: Resolve

The world turned without me Tuesday morning. After sleeping in—in our new room, since the previous one was taken over by the cops—I had a leisurely breakfast, swam in the hotel pool, and relaxed in the hot tub. I didn't care who had to wait. I deserved some downtime with my family and friends.

After lunch, Kevin and I settled in Vandercoy's now familiar office. I gripped my mug as if it were a life preserver on storm-tossed seas. It wasn't flavored but it was coffee, or at least a distant relative, and I needed all the caffeine I could get. I still had a few empty squares in my puzzle.

Rabi and Marcus were on a tour of the station. The promise of being locked in a cell sent my son bolting for the door. Now, a semblance of peace filled the room.

Mrs. C beamed from a chair in the corner, a vision in pink slippers. The steady tick of knitting needles once again sounded in our world. "I do appreciate you stopping at the store so I could start me coverlet again. I've lost a great deal of time, you know. Not that I regret the sacrifice, of course."

"Crawford would want you to have the best." Kevin smiled at her from the chair next to mine as he flipped a pencil in and out of his fingers. "You saved Quinlan's life."

"She looked pretty bad the last time I saw her." I don't know if I'd ever forget all that blood.

"She's going to make it." Vandercoy's voice sounded from the doorway without warning. He was resplendent in a three-piece charcoal gray pinstripe with a red and gold tie. His Italian leather shoes were polished to a mirror shine. He walked in and eased his bulk into his chair, smoothing his hair. "She gave her statement late last night."

"Sure, now she wakes up." Though I could've used her input yesterday, I was relieved to hear the good news. "How did Ulesh know she was looking into the fraud? What tipped her hand?"

Vandercoy pulled a small notebook out of his pocket, only to toss it on the desk unopened. As the detective sat in his chair, the light reflected off his slicked-back hair. "Our analysts found a program Ulesh inserted in the files. It alerted him if anyone reviewed his work orders. Quinlan's investigation for Ferguson sent up a red flag. So, Ulesh tapped her phone and followed her. She saw the tail, got away once. But she was scared. When Henry Prushark got murdered, Quinlan didn't know who to trust."

I took a sip of coffee, relishing the heat if not the taste. "No wonder she was panicky when she called me."

"Ulesh was losing containment." Vandercoy added the judgment with a frown. "He wanted to take out Quinlan before she found solid evidence. If she hadn't dropped her car keys, he'd have had a clean headshot."

Kevin shot me a sideways glance. The ghost of a smile crossed his face. "So, Belden turned a simple adultery case into extortion, fraud, and murder."

"A five-year-old adultery case is not simple." If I'd known what was coming when Rickson crawled through my window, I'd have hidden in the closet. "In my defense, the extortion and fraud happened on Rickson's watch, not mine."

"We have Ulesh and his partners in custody for the fraud. Mrs. Prushark for the murder. Pete and Matt Monroe are guilty of nothing and Linda was a faithful wife." Vandercoy planted his elbows on the desk. His words were matter-of-fact but a challenge gleamed in his eyes. "The only crime left, is the extortion. Got anyone in mind?"

I saluted the detective with my coffee cup. "I do have a suspect. Rickson had the puzzle pieces in his crazy notes. 'Loyalty betrayed' doesn't refer to Linda Prushark's non-existent adultery. It refers to the perceived disloyalty of Henry Prushark's family in the eyes of one longtime staff member who was loyal to the old man."

A frown creased Kevin's brow. He tapped the pencil on the arm of his chair. "You complain about my drama. It's nothing compared to your buildup. Spill."

I looked from him to Vandercoy, who watched me with a lazy expression. "Girard sent the threatening letters."

Mrs. C's knitting froze in mid-stitch.

The detective's double chin dropped in an infinitesimal nod.

Kevin's pencil went still. "How do you figure?"

Once you knew the answer, the clues all flowed together. "He knew the old man had Sheila and Paul followed in Europe. He probably arranged it. The security chief agreed with his boss's hardnosed, old-fashioned attitude about business and family. Over the years, Henry Prushark couldn't have resisted making comments to his longtime security chief about having two of his children behind the eight-ball."

"Girard admitted as much when we picked him up last night." Vandercoy's chair creaked as he shifted to plant his elbows on his desk. "Factoring in the timing of the birth and knowing Sheila was involved, it didn't take him long to guess the secret."

"The boy's Prushark looks came from Sheila, not Paul." Kevin resumed toying with the pencil. "Quinlan mentioned Ben and Linda are both blond. But his straight, sandy colored hair is nothing like her silver curls. Gramma Feilen always said, people see what they want to see."

Mrs. C frowned over her knitting. "Why did he wait two years to start this trouble?"

"The stroke wasn't the catalyst for Girard." I grimaced after sipping my lukewarm coffee. I'd have to ask Kevin to stop at a specialty shop before we headed home. "With Henry out of commission, Girard did what he could to help the family stabilize the company. It was Henry's unexpected recovery that deepened the family schism. Mrs. Prushark and her children were only concerned with holding onto power. What could Girard do? Cause trouble."

Vandercoy tapped an unlit cigar on his desk. "Everyone had settled into their new roles, especially Mrs. Prushark. She made it clear she was not going to let her husband's recovery interfere with her new plan to secure more power. That was the knife that cut Girard's loyalty to her."

Kevin balanced the pencil on his finger. "Girard preyed on her well-known phobia of scandal. That's why there was no demand for a payoff. He didn't want money. He wanted her to suffer."

"He knew his accusation that the boy wasn't Paul's son would lead Mrs. Prushark to assume Linda had an affair." I swirled the remaining coffee into a small whirlpool. "He couldn't have imagined the turmoil he set in motion."

"That's why he agreed to talk to Mrs. Prushark at the hotel last night." Vandercoy shrugged, his shoulders rolling like a wave. "Those letters led to the old man's death."

Kevin spun the pen around to use as a pointer. "Why did Rickson ask for Linda's medical records?"

"Give it to the big guy." The detective chuckled. "His note about covering the basics said it all. Somehow, he got a lead on Linda Prushark's background. Turns out, she can't have children. Some accident when she was in college. Paul never told his family. Henry Prushark wanted grandchildren of his own bloodline."

With Marcus's smiling face in my mind's eye, I could only shake my head. "So much for keeping the family name out of the papers. Diana Prushark has caused a greater scandal than those pictures ever could have. Sheila and Todd, the ones who benefit the most, are innocent of all the crimes."

Kevin flipped the pencil into a holder on the desk. "That ties up the loose threads."

I stared at my coffee and decided I'd had enough for one morning. All the squares in my crossword puzzle were filled in, and I had more important things to worry about, like going home and finding a way to paying the rent.

The door burst open and slammed against the wall.

Marcus stood on the threshold. He held up a piece of paper. "They fingerprinted me and put me in a cell."

Rabi hovered in the hall, a pleased expression on his face.

Vandercoy scowled at the intruder. "Why did they let you out?"

I set my mug on the desk. "That's our cue to leave."

Kevin held out his hand to Mrs. C. "Ready?"

She stuffed the latest creation into her flowered knitting

bag and took his hand. "Oh, yes, luv. I can't wait to tell the bridge club about me weekend."

Vandercoy slowly shook his head and closed his eyes.

Marcus pointed at him. "If you ever need help, our gang will be here like a shot."

The detective opened one eye and studied him. "I'm not sure Lake Tahoe could survive that."

Marcus spun on his heel and led the way to the elevator. A moment later, we walked out of the Lake Tahoe police station toward the Great White Beast.

"What about that nice Mr. Rickson?" Mrs. Colchester asked, shuffling along in her muffs.

"We'll visit him on our way out of town." Kevin spun his key-ring on his finger. "He has to stay in the hospital a few more days. Crawford will swing by on his return from Canada and drive him home."

"I like the way he checks in after we've done all the work." I intended to point that out the next time I saw my boss.

Marcus smiled at me over his shoulder. "We didn't need him. I told you we'd solve the case."

"I'll just be happy to go home and get to work." Seeing the inside of wealth and privilege made scraping by look good. Even if I did have to find a way to make ends meet now that my biggest account had dumped me. I stopped and turned to Kevin. "Speaking of which--"

Kevin held up his phone. "Godert sent me an e-mail. I've been reduced to twenty hours a week. No benefits for part-time employees. This is a good time to make a big push for B & T Inc."

"Thanks to Rickson and Quinlan we have a leg up on publicity." I smiled at him. "It seems a shame to have it be for nothing."

Kevin shook his head. "You just like having top billing."

I gave a satisfied sigh. "There is that."

"Now we can concentrate on getting ready for Halloween." Marcus sauntered ahead with a skip to his step. "I have the five-mile route all mapped out."

I held up my hand. "I told you once; you are not walking five miles."

"*We're* walking." My son continued. "And I decided on our costumes."

I had a bad feeling about this. "Who said I was dressing up?"

"You, me, and Kevin." Marcus spun around and walked backward. He met my suspicious look with a cheeky grin. "We're going to be the Three Stooges. I'm Moe. With my black hair, I'm a natural."

Kevin tossed a teasing my way. "I'm going as Larry. I just need a wig and some old clothes."

"That won't be so bad. I can do that." After all, my son wouldn't want to go trick-or-treating with me much longer. "So, I'm Curly? Wait a minute. Is he the bald one? I don't want to be bald. I don't have to wear one of those skin caps, do I?"

Marcus and Kevin just laughed and kept on going.

"Guys? Talk to me." I had a bad feeling about this. I don't care what they thought, my Curly was going to have hair.

Either way, I loved my men, and I was headed home.

TWO DOWN IN TAHOE CROSSWORD

The crossword puzzle related to this book (with the solution) can be solved online at: http://crossword.info/Paws42/mystery_puzzle_2

ADVENTURES IN VEGAS

CROSSWORD PUZZLE COZY MYSTERY, BOOK THREE

CHAPTER ONE

1 Across; 7 Letters;
Clue: An event causing sudden damage or distress
Answer: Calamity

"Go away. You're a potential boyfriend, not a hired gun."

Though nerves added an edge to my tone, Kevin Tanner's sapphire eyes held no acrimony. "At least I finally have potential."

After ten years as besties, he and I have been a couple for a few months. I couldn't be happier. I returned his smile with one of my own as I fought to hide my impatience.

Twenty minutes after the appointed time, my contact, a whistleblower with files to share, was a no-show.

Not good.

Not only was I worried for him, the man's tardiness was

eating into my getaway weekend. Okay, so this trip was supposed to be strictly business. I can multi-task. Once I got the stolen files, I'd overnight them to Crawford, my boss; then, the weekend was mine. Well, mine and Kevin's.

A man matching the client's description started toward me. I perked up. Then the tide carried him away like an eddy of sand caught in the current. I sighed in disappointment.

So far, Kevin was the only male interested in me. At twenty-eight, he's seven years my junior, part of the reason I'd resisted his advances for so long. He also resembles a six-foot-two-inch black-haired Greek god with a body honed by construction work.

This would be our first weekend away as a couple, but it couldn't start until I collected the documents and got them to safety. The lucrative exchange would pay December's rent and, if I were frugal, buy a few Christmas presents.

The client would be here. He'd been delayed, that's all. I didn't want to think about the alternative, that he might have been caught in the act.

"You sure you'll be okay?"

"I'm thirty-five, not thirteen. I got this." Tracy Rae Belden on this side of the conversation. Short brown hair. Run-of-the-mill gray eyes. Able to blend into a crowd without trying. "Las Vegas is your hometown. Go cheat the casino."

I buried a pang of regret at his ten years of honesty. He could have paid for the entire trip if he'd chosen to use his talents.

"Did that. Broke even." Born to a family of con-artists, Kevin had been cursed with a conscience. A defect that made him useless to his grifting relatives. "I thought you'd be done by now."

"So did I." Pleased at the impatience underlying his words, I couldn't ignore a growing worry. The client had already wired a big retaining fee to my boss, Crawford. He had no excuse for not showing. "Harrison said no one suspected him. I'm beginning to wonder if the guy got caught."

Kevin froze like a panther who'd sighted prey.

I followed his line of sight. Touching his arm for balance, I stood on my toes. At six-two, he topped me by five inches. "Is it--"

"Not your guy." His narrowed eyes tracked his quarry through the crowd. Curiosity glinted in his gaze. "Someone I once knew."

I craned my neck at a fast-moving female with short brown hair. "You mean that girl in the cute boot-cut jeans?"

He took two steps, then stopped. His hand reached toward me as his eyes remained on the target. "Belden, you're okay if I – ?"

"I'm fine." I gave him a shove. "Go."

The crowd swallowed his muscular form in a heartbeat, leaving me wondering who had struck a nerve. Could it be a family member? The acrimonious break with his relatives had cost the Feilen family big money. From what I knew, they weren't the forgiving type.

With a new worry on my list, I leaned against a pillar disguised as a palm tree, crossed my arms, and studied the crowd. Harrison, the lawyer client, had my description as I had his. His pink tie was the one standout detail. Otherwise, I was trying to find an attorney at a legal convention. Forty-three. Caucasian. Brown hair.

Seriously? The convention at the Aquarius Hotel this week was Legal Aspects of International Business or some such ilk. Dozens of men matching that description had hurried by in the past half-hour. Not one had made a move toward the Blue Nile meeting room, our rendezvous spot.

Crawford, my boss and a former police detective of

twenty-five years, hadn't heard from Reginald Harrison this morning. I'd gotten no answer on the guy's cell number.

Fifteen minutes after Kevin left, I resorted to making bets with myself to pass the time. I lost half-a-mil, which summed up my luck with gambling. Even worse, I'd lost Kevin, which

Frustration ate at me. I glared at the convention goers, wondering if the PI manual had a rule on how long I had to wait. I'd memorized a nearby display. A net full of tiny starfish, a small book with a conch shell on the cover, and a miniature beach bucket, all promoting the benefits of working in Latin America.

"Who are they kidding?" I muttered.

The shifting waves of people gave a glimpse of a dress with a bright Hawaiian print. The woman wearing it walked next to the slim form. A child? Who would bring a child to a Vegas conference?

I basked in a glow of self-righteousness. I'd left Marcus, my eleven-year-old, Korean, foster son in the care of my friend and apartment manager.

The tide of humanity ebbed again. The gaudy muumuu was wearing pink, fuzzy slippers.

My self-righteous glow wavered. My heart sank. She couldn't. She wouldn't. I didn't want to know, but could there be two old ladies in the world who'd wear those slippers in public?

The crowd parted like the Red Sea. My son's black eyes glittered in excitement as he put a hand on Mrs. Colchester's arm. His straight black hair and golden coloring contrasted with her pale, parchment-like skin. The seventy-plus, white-haired woman shuffled forward doing a slow but determined two-step. Not even her firm grip on my son mollified me.

They were supposed to be in Langsdale, a pricey resort town of twenty-five-thousand souls a fast two-and-a-half-hour drive north of Vegas.

Silly me, I'd expected one of them would act like an adult. If the client showed up now, followed by villains, my son and Mrs. C would be caught in the line of fire.

A glance showed a few forty-ish men around. None headed my way. Instead, a crowd gathered at the mouth of the corridor directly behind Marcus and Mrs. C. My gaze returned to the boy and the old woman. Her ever-present, gardenia scent wafted into my nostrils.

"Thank, heavens, we found you." Mrs. C's shrill British accent rose above the background noise. She leaned in close enough to whisper. "Your contact is dead."

The scolding died on my lips.

"He's been murdered." The older woman's tone underscored the final word as if personally offended. She jerked her head in the direction of the growing excitement behind her. "Far hall. Body in a side alcove."

I sucked in air as my mind refocused on business. "What makes you think it's my guy?"

"You're in Vegas, luv. Play the odds." Mrs. C's voice held a thread of disdain. The same tone she'd adopted when she'd insisted this case wouldn't be as simple as it sounded. "Middle-aged white male. Brown hair. Pink tie. Brown leather briefcase handcuffed to his wrist."

She sniffed and looked down her nose. "Bit amateurish that."

Though she denied any history with cops or criminals, her terse report had the earmarks of a professional.

My hope withered. "Sounds like Harrison."

Had he been meeting someone else? Had he been caught by his pursuers?

"What are you doing in Vegas? What are you doing in this hotel?" Questioning Mrs. C gave me time to think. Besides, no way was I letting her off the hook. "How did you just *happen* to walk by the body?"

"Kevin's with the dead guy." Marcus grabbed my arm. His brow furrowed. "We saw him through the crowd, but we couldn't keep up with him. He went into the hall marked 'Employees Only'."

The floor dipped beneath my feet.

"By the time we peeked into the alcove, hotel security was on the scene." Marcus's grip tightened. "His hand is covered with blood."

Fear burned through my stomach like a hot coal. "Whose hand?"

"Kevin's." My son jerked my arm. "He's in trouble."

The older woman folded her hands beneath her sagging breasts. She cocked her head toward the far hall. "A bobby is on the scene. Plainclothes."

I did *not* like the way this was shaping up. Kevin just happens to follow an old acquaintance into a murder scene with a cop nearby? A setup seemed an easy guess, except no one could have known Kevin was in town. "I'll talk to them. Crawford's time as a Vegas cop should buy some goodwill."

Marcus stepped forward. "I'll come, too."

"You. Two. Stay. Here." I set him firmly on his heels, then reinforced the words with a steady stare at my erstwhile sitter. "We can't afford any mistakes if this is murder."

"Absolutely right." Sounding like Churchill during the blitz, the old woman settled a firm hand on my son's shoulder. "We have to stand together. Give the authorities an inch, and they're bound to get the wrong man."

"Right." Marcus's early years as a street urchin had left him with a strong penchant to blame authorities or run from them. Sometimes both.

Though I usually try to dissuade his mistrust of those in power, I grabbed any excuse to keep these two from interfering. I bent to meet his eyes. "I'm counting on you."

"Don't worry." He leaned close enough to whisper. "I'll keep an eye on her."

Sad fact was, I couldn't say which of them I trusted less. My smile felt forced, but he seemed satisfied. I turned and walked away. After two steps, I glanced behind me. They were still in place. No telling how long that would last, but I had little choice.

Cutting across the current wasn't as difficult as it would have been moments before. Though the ringing of slots could still be heard, the crime scene was drawing a crowd worthy of a chorus line. A security officer was visible at the mouth of the hall. A dozen feet behind him, Kevin faced a man in a dark suit. To the right was an opening to another hall.

Casino security was stretched thin by the growing crowd. I marched up to a gap on the left side, shouldering aside a woman with a camera.

A chunky security guard thrust an arm in my direction.

Without slowing, I flashed my private investigator license. "Crawford sent me."

My certainty gave him pause. I strode by before he realized he didn't know Crawford. Moving at a steady clip, I approached Kevin and the detective. Only a few steps into the hall, and I had a clear view of the alcove.

The corpse of a man was slumped against the wall. He looked to be a very old forty-three, the brown hair was heavy with gray but otherwise Mrs. C's description was spot on. The only details lacking were the blood on Harrison's crisp, white shirt and the knife sticking in his chest.

Once past the body, I eyed Kevin. He flashed me a warning look over the head of the man facing him. The guy finished snapping pictures of Kevin's right hand, covered with blood. Then the detective pocketed his phone and clasped his hands behind his back.

Mrs. C's plainclothes cop was five-ten with a squat, square build. Feet set wide to balance his broad shoulders. Head thrown back, so the light reflected off the bald spot in the middle of his light brown hair.

Recognition washed over me. Fred Pierce. The one detective in Vegas who hated me. Okay, maybe not the only one. Pierce had no use for Kevin either.

I'd hoped Mrs. C might be wrong and the guy would be casino security, but my bad luck was running hot.

Pierce had to have been in the building to get here so quickly. The suspicion of a setup flared again. I raised my chin.

Sucking in a deep breath, I looked for an angle worth playing and came up empty. Pierce was too young to have known Crawford and too old to be impressed by my boss's reputation. Then, there was the guy's animosity. I clenched my jaw and warned my tongue to play nice.

"Belden." Pierce spat out my name without turning around. "I should have known. Where there's one of you, the other follows, especially with a corpse on the floor."

"Too bad it's not yours." And there went my resolve.

Humor flashed through Kevin's sapphire eyes then he zeroed in on Pierce. "I told you. When I tried to help the man, he grabbed my hand. Then he died."

I walked to Kevin's side, then swiveled to face the detective. With a firm hold on my self-control, I tried again. "Kevin has nothing to do with this man. We're in town on vacation."

Pierce leveled a hard stare at me. "It's never that simple with you two. You attract trouble. Tell me the truth, and I'll see what I can do."

"I'd sooner cut cards with the devil." My mouth can't help itself. "If you'd take one minute to check your facts, you'd know Kevin and I have been in town less than an hour. You'd also know he has no motive to kill your victim."

Pierce's sneer was too common to cause concern. However, the triumph in his eyes was worrisome. The guy swung back to Kevin. "Once a criminal, always a criminal."

Kevin's blue eyes flashed with the right amount of indignation. "I've never been convicted of a crime."

The disclaimer set off a purple flush in Pierce's neck that rose like molten lava to his face. Steam would pour out of his ears any second. "You've never been caught because your family is too slippery. You're all guilty."

Looking down from his six-foot-two-inch height, Kevin remained impassive. "I haven't been in contact with my family in almost a decade. I'm a partner in sub-contracting business."

He was telling the truth, but he could have lied as convincingly. He'd been raised by the trickiest con artists to hit Vegas in decades.

Pierce's lips stretched wide. His bared white teeth reminded me of a lion ready to gut an antelope. He rocked on his heels. "Is it a coincidence I was staked out in this hotel?"

Kevin said nothing.

The seconds stretched out as I waited for the lion to quit toying with his prey and go for the kill.

The heavy-boned man leaned into Kevin's face. "A *coincidence* that the woman who entered this hall on the heels of the victim was your twin sister?"

Coming Summer 2021

Dear Readers,

Welcome to the adventures of Tracy Belden and her son, Marcus, along w/ their adopted family: Kevin Tanner, Mrs. Colchester, and Jack Rabi as they are drawn into Tracy's cases as a PI. While Tracy would prefer to drink her flavored coffee and create crossword puzzles, like most of us, she has to pay the bills and keep food on the table. So, she puts her puzzle solving talents to good use as she dives into her cases.

While most of her cases are simple, the ones involving murder are often so complicated she despairs of solving them. However, Marcus, with the confidence of youth and his pride in the detecting heritage of the Belden family, never wavers in his belief that the Belden Agency can solve any case as long as they work together.

Among the many books I read while growing up weas the YA mystery series involving Trixie Belden and her group of young friends. While no part of this book is based on those stories, Tracy did tell Marcus that she was a distant cousin of Trixie's. Her good intentions were based solely on her efforts to get him off the streets, but her alleged relationship with Trixie is a claim Tracy is never allowed to forget.

I hope you enjoy your time in Langsdale, Nevada, and the adventures of Tracy and her adopted family. If you enjoyed the book and have the time, please leave a review at your favorite bookseller or at Goodreads.

Find me on Facebook: Louise Foster, Author

https://www.facebook.com/Louise-Foster-Author-107517717508196/?modal=admin_todo_tour

I love to hear from readers:
Louise.louisefoster@gmail.com

Thank you for giving me your time to read this book and your support by buying it. I don't take either for granted.
I hope you enjoy Tracy's next case as well,
Louise Foster

MEET THE AUTHOR

I didn't pursue a writing career until I was well out of college. However, a lifelong love of reading and working on crossword and jigsaw puzzles proved to be good training when the writing bug bit. While I enjoy reading many different types of books, from thrillers to fantasy to science fiction, mysteries have always called to me.

Working on jigsaw puzzles as well as crossword puzzles with my family has also been a constant part of my life. A habit that carries through to today.

In the Crossword Puzzle Mystery Series, my love of writing and solving puzzles came together. I hope you love the quirky characters and their high-spirited adventures as much I enjoy writing them.

To learn more about the Crossword Puzzle Cozy Mystery series, visit my website www.louisefoster.com and sign up for my newsletter. An on-line crossword puzzle related to each of the books will be available on my website as each book is released.

Find me on Facebook: Louise Foster, Author

https://www.facebook.com/Louise-Foster-Author-107517717508196/?modal=admin_todo_tour

I love to hear from readers: Louise.louisefoster@gmail.com

ACKNOWLEDGMENTS

I'd like to acknowledge a few of the many people who helped make this book a reality:

My editor, Mary-Theresa Hussey, for her awesome input.

Lee Hyat, who created my beautiful book covers.

Debbie Manber Kupfer, who used her skill and talent to create the crossword puzzles in this book and on my website.

Keith Jones for setting up my wonderful web-site.

ALSO BY LOUISE FOSTER

CROSSWORD PUZZLE COZY MYSTERY SERIES

An Ex in the Puzzle

Tracy Belden's first solo case in the field lands her in the middle of a murder when her ex-husband's second wife disappears and Tracy becomes a suspect.

Two Down in Tahoe

When a PI friend asks for help, Tracy and her trusty gang head to Tahoe, but things go from bad to worse when her friend goes missing and the client dies with Tracy on the scene.

Adventures in Vegas

A getaway weekend in Vegas turns dangerous when Tracy's whistleblowing client is murdered and both the secret files and a priceless golden artifact go missing.

A Question of Murder

Tracy is drawn into the world of fine art and a possible forged masterpiece when a friend's involvement in a present-day murder uncovers a hidden past and a connection to a 50-year-old murder.

Made in the USA
Monee, IL
11 May 2023